Deadly Date

The Boyfriend

The Girlfriend

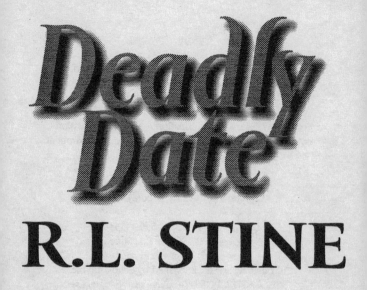

R.L. STINE

POINT

SCHOLASTIC INC.

New York Toronto London Auckland Sydney
Mexico City New Delhi Hong Kong Buenos Aires

The Boyfriend, ISBN 0-590-43279-6,
Copyright © 1990 by Robert L. Stine.

The Girlfriend, ISBN 0-590-44333-X,
Copyright © 1991 by R.L. Stine.

12 11 10 9 8 7 6 5 4 3 2 1   5 6 7 8 9/0

Printed in the U.S.A.   01

This edition created exclusively for Barnes & Noble, Inc.
2005 Barnes & Noble Books

ISBN 0-7607-9509-6

First compilation printing, April 2005

The Boyfriend

The Girlfriend

Contents

The
Boyfriend

Chapter 1

Am I going to do it? Joanna asked herself.

She looked down the brightly lit mall at the blur of faces, shoppers balancing packages, pulling young children, peering into colorful display windows, teenagers walking in twos and threes, beginning their Friday night prowl.

Of course I am, Joanna decided, a smile spreading slowly across her face. Once I get something in my mind, I always go through with it.

"Daddy's little go-getter." That's what Sherman Collier, Joanna's father, always called her. His highest compliment: "Daddy's little go-getter. She'll never take no for an answer."

There were lots of compliments from Dad, Joanna thought bitterly, walking quickly away from the meeting place by the bookstore, crossing the wide aisleway, then stopping. I was Daddy's girl, "a *real* Collier."

Of course, thought Joanna, her smile now completely gone, that didn't stop him from leaving. That didn't stop him from running off with that cheap-looking redhead, off to Tucson or some crazy place. Her mother refused to tell her where.

She hadn't heard from her father since, not even on her sixteenth birthday.

Mom had done all right, though, thought Joanna. Tiny, meek little Mom. Well, she wasn't so meek when divorce time came around. She must have taken Daddy for every penny he had, which was considerable. The two of them had lived really well ever since. Mom and Joanna. They enjoyed being rich and not having Daddy around.

At least Joanna did.

Daddy's little go-getter didn't miss Daddy at all.

So why was she standing on the edge of this mall now, watching the Friday night crowd pour in, thinking about him?

Breakups.

That was why.

Family breakups. Boyfriend breakups.

Breakups weren't so sad. In fact, they could lead to better things.

She thought of Shep. His wavy blond hair. The dimple in his left cheek when he smiled that funny, lopsided smile. She wondered what Shep was doing tonight while she was supposed to be meeting Dex.

What was that song on the loudspeaker? Some ancient Elvis song from the fifties. "Don't Be Cruel."

Joanna nearly laughed out loud. Don't be cruel? Why not?

It was a cruel world.

She was about to do something really cruel. And, she had to admit, she was enjoying it already.

She turned and caught her reflection in the candle store window. Not bad, she thought.

She knew she was beautiful. Why should she force herself to have false modesty and pretend she didn't know, like some simpering young thing in one of those embarrassing Elvis movies Dex had forced her to watch on TV?

She had the Collier good looks. That's what her father always told her — usually as a dig at her mother. She had the high cheekbones, the perfect, straight nose, the clear blue eyes that always seemed to be opened wide, the proud, high forehead, and the sunlight-blonde hair, so smooth and straight that it looked beautiful even cut so stylishly short.

The Collier good looks.

Maybe that's why she and her mother could never be that close, as close as other girls and their mothers. Or was that something from a dumb fifties movie, too?

Her mousy little mother. She always looked so small and funny inside the glamorous fur coat she wore everywhere with the collar pulled up almost over her head. It always made Joanna laugh — to herself, of course.

She couldn't blame her father for wanting a little more.

Yes she could.

Breakups.

Well, of course breakups were on her mind tonight.

Two wiry twelve-year-old boys on skateboards came whirring down the aisle. One of them nearly barreled into her. Joanna jumped out of the way just in time. "Hey, you — " She stopped herself.

The mall police would catch them sooner or later.

And she didn't want to call attention to herself. She was hiding, after all. Hiding from Dex.

Hiding from her boyfriend.

She thought of how Dex smelled. Sort of fresh. Almost flowery. Soapy.

It almost made her sad.

Almost.

Was that him across the hall at their usual meeting place?

No. It was some other guy in jeans and a rock T-shirt.

She leaned against the concrete column, the back of her head resting against a sign announcing some kind of mall band concert.

What kind of jerks would go out of their way to listen to a band playing in a mall? It was no wonder people turned their noses up at the suburbs. Everything here in Middlewood was so . . . tacky. Joanna knew she would move to New York as soon as she graduated. Enroll in a few modeling programs. And with her fabulous looks and drive, well . . . who knew how far she could go?

Which was one reason why Dex had to go.

There he was now. Hurrying to the bookstore entrance where they always met. Late again.

He'll be late his whole life, she thought, surprised by her bitterness. He'll never catch up.

He stopped in front of the open entranceway, looking from side to side. He seemed to relax. From across the crowded aisle, she could see that he looked relieved.

He thinks I'm late, too. What a hoot.

Look at him, she thought disapprovingly, pressing herself flat against the column so he couldn't see her. That's how he dresses for a date. Those faded jeans, torn at the knee. That stupid T-shirt. Probably not even a clean one.

He did have that wonderful, soapy smell, though. And when they were all alone late at night in the front seat of her car, he . . . Well, why get into that?

She was standing him up, after all.

And watching him while she did it.

She shifted her down vest to her other hand. Across the wide aisle, Dex started to pace back and forth in front of the bookstore. He looked at his watch. He jammed his hands into his jeans pockets and continued to pace.

He's short, she thought. Why hadn't she ever noticed how short he was? And his jeans are baggy in back.

Look how nervous he's getting. He knows I'm never late.

And he knows I've been losing interest in him.

I haven't been too subtle about that, have I!

You're cruel, Joanna, she told herself. Actually, it's one of your most admirable qualities.

How else to survive in a cruel world?

Dex would have to find it out sooner or later. Why not sooner? This was good for him.

He stopped pacing. He ran his hand back nervously through his thick, black hair.

She had loved to pull on Dex's hair, tug at the back, tease him, pulling until it hurt. Now it just looked greasy to her.

Get a haircut, she thought.

No. Don't go overboard, Joanna. You love his hair. Don't deny it. You love the way it tickles your cheek when he puts his head on your shoulder and pulls you close.

I'm not giving in, she thought, shifting her weight against the column. She straightened her blue sweater, the one her father had bought because it matched her eyes so perfectly. It was getting a bit tight now. Why did she insist on wearing it?

I'm not running over to him. I'm just going to stand here and watch him squirm. I'm enjoying this too much.

He looked angry now. He stopped pacing and stood with his hands in his pockets, looking down the aisle toward the movie theater at the end.

"Breaking Up Is Hard To Do," Joanna thought. What was that? An old song title? Well, she knew it wasn't going to be easy with Dex. He was so dramatic, so moody, so theatrical.

Dex wanted to be an actor. And he had the dark good looks for it. He looked a lot like the actor Matt Dillon. Sounded like him, too.

The previous spring, he had invited Joanna to come see him in the lead role in *Julius Caesar* at his school across town. Joanna obligingly came, worrying if her BMW would be safe parked on the street across from the three-story brick school. The neighborhood didn't look very appealing. She had locked the car and hurried into the building, surprised by how tacky and run-down everything looked. It had been so long since Joanna had been inside a public school.

Dex had been good. He had a clear, expressive voice, and he looked very handsome on the stage. But everyone else was terrible, the scenery was practically nonexistent, and the lights kept flickering.

Afterwards, Dex was so excited. He was positively high! Joanna told him how good he was. But all the while she was feeling sorry for him. If only his aunt could afford to send him to a private school, like Landover, where Joanna went. Then maybe he'd have a chance to get somewhere with his acting ambitions.

But his old aunt had no money at all. And she hadn't wanted to become Dex's guardian in the first place. She didn't care if he went to school or not. She lived in her own gray world.

A world I don't ever want to be pulled into, Joanna thought, watching Dex across the mall. Two guys she had never seen before had stopped to talk to him. She could hear them laughing about something, but Dex didn't join in, and he kept looking past them, looking for her.

This anxiety will help Dex's acting career, Joanna thought. Heartbreak. An actor needs some heartbreak in his life to draw on during his performances, right?

"Heartbreak Hotel." Wasn't that an Elvis song, too?

Why do I have Elvis on the brain? she wondered. I guess Dex looks a little like the young Elvis, the Elvis in all those movies. Was that why Dex liked watching those old films so much?

Time to go home, she decided suddenly.

The two guys had headed on to the movie theater. Dex was alone again, pacing back and forth in front of the bookstore entrance.

This is so mean, she thought, turning her back on him and heading to the doors that led to the parking lot.

So why do I feel like laughing?

Chapter 2

"So you just stood there and watched him?"

Mary's voice rose several octaves as she asked the question. Joanna pulled the phone away from her ear before the high-pitched voice did any damage. She could just picture Mary, lying on her stomach on her bed, a shocked look on her angelic little face.

"Yeah. It was kind of . . . interesting," Joanna said. She knew that would get a reaction from her friend — and it did.

"Interesting? Joanna — that's so cold!" Mary cried.

Mary was always so sweet, so nice to everyone. So angelic. Joanna loved shocking her, making her voice rise.

Across town, Mary, lying on her stomach on the bed, in the oversized man's shirt she used for a nightshirt, looked at the phone as if to ask, "Am I really hearing right?" Her brown hair, falling in tight curls down her neck and shoulders, was still wet from the shower. She shivered.

But she knew that it was Joanna who was making her feel cold.

How can this person be my friend? The question flashed through her mind. And then: Why has Joanna changed so much?

They had been friends since grade school. When Mary's family moved out of Middlewood to the less fashionable area known as Westside, the friendship had continued, mostly over the phone.

Joanna had always been a little snobbish, Mary realized. And that snooty private school she went to had done a lot to make her even more so. But she was so smart and funny, and so pretty, and such a good friend, someone you could always talk to, confide in, tell just about everything.

So when had she turned so cold, so mean?

Had she been that way all along, and Mary simply hadn't noticed?

No, Mary thought, as Joanna's voice continued to murmur in her ear. No. Joanna has changed. Since the divorce, I guess. . . .

"You'll have to meet Shep," Joanna was saying. "I think you'll really like him. He's very good-looking, and — "

"He goes to Landover?" Mary asked.

"Yeah. He's a senior this year. He's already been accepted at Yale. Everyone in his family goes to Yale."

"Nice," Mary said. She didn't really know what to say. "I — I'm just so surprised. I mean, totally.

I thought you and Dex were really serious."

"We were," Joanna said. "Too serious. It wasn't good for either of us."

"What do you mean, Joanna?"

"I mean Dex has no money and never will have," Joanna replied, talking very quickly, the way she always did when she got excited. "Sure, I care about him. But a person has to be practical, too."

"Practical?" Mary truly was shocked, more by Joanna's voice than anything else. She sounded so hard, so removed, as if she were talking about a stranger.

"I'm thinking of both of us," Joanna said, not meaning to sound as defensive as she did. "I mean, how do you think Dex feels being driven around in my BMW all the time?"

"I don't think it bothers him," Mary said drily. Then she added, "You know, Dex wouldn't mind taking the bus once in a while."

Joanna laughed. "Get real. I'm really going to take the bus with a $40,000 BMW sitting in the garage!"

This isn't the first time she's told me how much her car cost, Mary thought, brushing back her wet hair uncomfortably. "What kind of car does Shep drive?" she asked, unable to keep the sarcasm from her voice.

"He has one of those cute Cabriolet convertibles," Joanna said. "A red one with a white top."

Which did she check out first — Shep or his car? Mary wondered. Then she scolded herself for starting to sound as cold as Joanna. This is just an act Joanna is putting on, Mary thought. She doesn't want to let on to me how bad she feels about breaking up with Dex. She probably doesn't even want to admit it to herself. So she's putting on this cruel act, pretending to be tough.

"Are you sure you know what you're doing?" Mary asked her old friend. "Dex is crazy about you."

"He's just plain crazy," Joanna said, sighing. "Know what he's been doing lately? He takes the crosstown bus over here in the middle of the night and climbs in my bedroom window. Just to talk."

"Sounds very romantic," Mary said, trying not to sound jealous.

"Are you kidding?! If my mother ever found out, she'd — she'd ground me for a month!"

And that $40,000 BMW would just sit in the garage, Mary thought.

"Dex is too melodramatic," Joanna continued. "He's too theatrical for me. He's — " There was a series of clicks on the line. "Hold on, Mary — I've got another call coming in."

The phone went silent on Mary's end. Frowning, she sat up. She placed the receiver down on the bedspread and went to get a bath towel to dry her hair.

"Hello?" Joanna asked brightly. She had a good idea who was calling. "Oh, hi, Dex." Keep it casual, she told herself.

"Hey — I'm still at the mall," he said. He sounded very upset. She could just picture the look on his face, his dark eyebrows low over his eyes.

He was probably biting the skin off his lower lip the way he always did.

"What? *Where* are you?" That's good. That sounds really innocent.

"I thought we had a date, Joanna. You were supposed to meet me — remember?"

"Huh?" She laughed. She knew the laugh would really infuriate him. "Oh, good lord! I completely forgot!"

Silence on his end.

More silence.

A click. And then the dial tone returned. She listened to the steady hum for a few seconds, then remembered that Mary was waiting on the other line. "Hello, Mary? Hi. I'm back. That was guess who."

"What did he say?" Mary asked, sitting back on the bed, the towel wrapped around her hair.

"Not much. I told him I just forgot." Joanna giggled.

"I can't believe you're being so mean. Why are you playing these games with him, Joanna? Why don't you just tell him you don't want to see him anymore?"

"Come on, Mary," Joanna chided. "It's much more fun to make him squirm for a while."

"You — you're not serious, are you?"

"No. I'm not. *Really*." Joanna couldn't decide if she was serious or not. She surprised herself at how aloof she felt about what she was doing, about how little feeling she had for Dex.

She had thought she was in love with him, after

all. But now she didn't feel much of anything at all. And deep down inside, she had to admit she did enjoy watching him squirm.

"I'd tell him straight out," she told Mary, "but you know how theatrical he is. He'd pull a big scene. Probably do the third act of *Macbeth* in my living room, have us all in tears." She laughed.

That's so cold, Mary couldn't help thinking again. I thought she cared about him. She really had me fooled. Had all of us fooled.

"I just think it'll be easier if I let him down slowly. You know, a few subtle hints. Then maybe let him see me out with Shep. That way he'll start to catch on."

"Joanna — really. You can't do that to Dex."

"Just watch me," Joanna said, admiring her dark red nail polish as she talked.

"Maybe we should change the subject," Mary said. "We've always been honest with each other, Joanna. But this time I — "

"You're right. Maybe we should change the subject." Joanna laughed, trying to keep it light, but it sounded phony even to her.

Silence for a few moments.

Finally Mary said, "Did you buy that winter coat you were looking at? The down one with the fur hood?"

"Oh, there were two I really liked," Joanna told her. "I couldn't decide which one I liked better. So I bought them both."

There was silence at the other end. Joanna

thought she heard a short gasp. She loved shocking Mary. But it wasn't much of a challenge. Mary was so simple and nice, and she shocked so easily.

"I'm so spoiled. It's disgusting, isn't it?" Joanna said.

"Yes," Mary answered quickly. "It sure is!"

"Hey, I think I hear my mother roaming the halls again — for a change. She never can sleep. I'd better get off."

"Okay. See you," Mary said.

"I'll call you tomorrow." Joanna hung up the cellular phone and returned it to its holder on her desk. She took a deep breath and stretched. She was feeling pretty good.

She listened to her mother's muffled footsteps retreat down the carpeted hallway. Poor Mom. She's always so nervous, so restless these days.

On an impulse, Joanna picked up the phone again. She looked through her directory for Shep's number.

Should I call him?

Why not?

It rang four times before someone picked it up. Silence. "Hello, Shep?"

Someone yawned loudly on the other end.

"Shep, is that you?"

"Yeah. Who is it?"

"It's me. Joanna. Did I wake you?"

Another yawn. "No. I mean, yes. I guess you did. What time is it? Hi."

They talked awkwardly for a few minutes. It didn't take Shep long to wake up.

"I'm surprised you're not out on a Friday night," Joanna said coyly.

"No. I stayed home in case you called," he cracked.

He has a good sense of humor, she thought. I like that. She decided to go ahead and ask him out. "Are you busy Saturday night?"

He seemed a little surprised by her directness. "No. I don't think so. I mean, no."

"Want to go to the movies or something?"

"I'll pick *something*," he joked. And then he added, "Hey, aren't you going with that guy from across town?"

"Well, no," she said quickly. "Not exactly."

"Great!" he said, suddenly very enthusiastic. She could picture his blond, wavy hair, his round cheeks, which made him look like such a little boy. He was probably blushing. He seemed to blush all the time, getting all rosy for no reason at all. "See you Saturday," he said.

"See you Saturday."

She was still replaying the conversation half an hour later, lying under the covers, watching the shadows of the trees outside her window shift and dip across the wall.

She couldn't have been asleep more than an hour when she was awakened by a loud clambering at the window.

She pulled herself up with a startled gasp.

Framed by pale yellow moonlight, Dex was climbing into the room.

The moonlight made his skin look green. And he had the strangest look on his face.

Joanna's breath caught in her throat.

"Dex — what do you want?" she cried.

Chapter 3

He stood by the window, eerily framed in the pale moonlight, catching his breath, staring at her across the dark room.

She pulled the satin sheet up to her chin protectively. "Dex, what are you doing here?" This is the end, she thought angrily. These middle-of-the-night visits have *got* to stop.

"It's a beautiful night," he said, still staring at her as he wiped off his hands. Climbing the tree to her second-story window was not an easy feat.

"So?"

"So come on." He flashed her his famous smile. Even in the near-darkness it was a fabulous, winning grin. "Get your car. We'll go for a ride."

"Huh? Are you crazy?"

"Yeah." He laughed. He took a few steps toward her.

"Dex, how did you get here?"

"Flew."

"Have you been drinking?"

"Yeah. I had a coupla root beers while I waited

for you at the mall. Come on — get dressed." She had left her jeans on the chair beside the bed. He picked them up and tossed them to her.

She ignored them. "You took the bus here? Doesn't your aunt know that you sneak out at night?"

"I don't know what she knows," he said. "We don't talk much."

"Well, I really don't think — "

"Stop wasting time," he said, pacing impatiently.

She suddenly saw him pacing at the mall again, looking so unhappy.

"Get dressed. Let's go for a ride. You know. Do something exciting, something no one else we know is doing. Dare to live, know what I mean?"

"Is that from a play?"

"Pete's with me," he said, ignoring her sarcasm. "He's waiting outside."

Joanna didn't really care for Dex's friend Pete. With his short, spiky hair, the diamond stud in his ear, and the heavy metal music rattling in his Walkman all the time, he was such an adolescent. What was he trying to prove — that he was cool or something?

She looked at Dex, his face half in shadow, half out.

What was I trying to prove by going with Dex? she wondered. That I was cool? That I wasn't who I am? Sure, he's handsome. Sure, he's exciting to be with in a crazy sort of way. But he's so . . . low-class. He isn't my kind at all.

Dex was my teenage rebellion phase, she decided

with sudden certainty. That's it. He was a phase I went through. Every teenager has to go through a rebellion phase, right?

"Come on, Joanna. Let's get moving! We're wasting time. What are you thinking about?"

"Nothing," she said.

"Well, all right. Get dressed. Pete's waiting. We'll drive to the Promontory. It'll be beautiful." He saw that she wasn't making a move to get up. "Just for a few minutes. Just so we can say we did it." She never could resist him when he pleaded like that, like a lost little boy.

"Well. . . ."

"And I promise I won't come here in the middle of the night anymore. Okay?"

"You promise?"

"Well . . . I won't come very often." He laughed, expecting her to laugh, too, then stopped abruptly, surprised by her hard expression. "What's wrong?"

"Nothing. Everything," she said, realizing that she was going to give in one last time, that she was going to go along on this wild escapade out to the cliffs in the middle of the night.

"I waited at the mall two hours for you," he said. "Come on. You owe me."

Now she laughed. "I owe you? Well, I guess I have no choice then." She turned and lowered her feet to the thick, shag carpet. "Do you mind turning around while I get dressed?"

"Hey, Jo — since when are you so modest?" He leered at her.

Ugh, she thought. He's so immature.

What did I ever see in him?

This is the last time I'm going anywhere with him, she thought, pulling on the jeans, then searching her dresser drawer in the darkness for a sweatshirt.

"It's so warm for October," he said.

"Spare me the weather reports," she said drily.

She didn't realize he had stepped up behind her. He put his arms around her and, turning her around, kissed her, tentatively at first, then harder.

He *does* have his good qualities, Joanna thought, returning the kiss. Then she shoved him gently away. "Pete's waiting, remember?"

"He likes to wait," Dex said, reaching for her again.

He smelled so sweet, so soapy sweet. She kissed him again.

No. This was crazy.

"Come on. I'll get the car." She pulled away from him and headed to the hallway. She grabbed her down vest, and they sneaked down the front stairs and out the front door.

Pete was waiting in the driveway, his Walkman headphones over his ears, as usual. The moonlight seemed to emphasize his bad skin. He was wearing a lightweight zippered jacket with the collar turned up. He grinned at Joanna.

She gave him a short wave and headed to the garage, pulling on the down vest. Climbing behind the wheel of the BMW, she took a deep breath. The leather smelled so good. She put the car into neutral and Dex and Pete pushed it backwards down the drive. If she started it in the garage, Joanna knew, it was certain to awaken her mother. This wasn't the first late-night drive the three of them had taken.

But it's the last, she thought, as Dex climbed in beside her, grinning excitedly, and Pete folded his long legs into the backseat. She started the car and headed toward the high cliffs at the edge of town that everyone called the Promontory.

The houses on both sides of the street were dark. There were no other cars on the road. "Turn on the radio," Pete said, leaning over the seatback. "Put on Z-190. It's Metal Maniacs Hour."

"No way, man," Dex said, lowering his window, letting in a blast of cold air. "We're listening to the quiet. Just listen to that. Beautiful, huh?"

He looked over at Joanna, who kept her eyes straight ahead on the curving white line in the middle of the road. She was more tired than she had thought, and driving was taking all of her concentration.

The houses gave way to woods, then open fields as they headed out of town. The Promontory was a popular makeout spot for Middlewood teenagers. But of course it would be deserted this time of night.

A large moving truck honked its horn as it headed past, startling Joanna. She gripped the wheel tighter as she turned onto Cliff Road, more of a gravel path than a road. The moon had disappeared behind clouds. Trees whispered and shook in the darkness.

"I feel *good*!" Dex shouted exuberantly out of the open window as the car sped over the gravel.

"Can't you close that window? It's freezing," Joanna complained.

He turned to look at her, surprised that she wasn't getting into the spirit of things. "Hey, lighten up," he said. "This is great! This is awesome!"

She didn't reply. She skidded to a stop as the gravel road abruptly ended at a low fence made of logs. A few yards beyond the fence, the high granite cliffs jutted out, overlooking the town.

Dex leaped out of the car, shouting up at the sky.

"Hey — you forgot to close your door!" Joanna called angrily after him. But he didn't hear her. He was already half running, half skipping to the cliff edge.

Pete climbed out of the back, tinny drum rhythms escaping from his headphones. Joanna held the car key in her hand, thinking about locking the car, then decided it was silly. No one else would be foolish enough to be up here at three o'clock in the morning.

She walked around to the other side of the car, the ground soft and wet beneath her sneakers, and closed Dex's door. Then, dropping the car keys in her vest pocket, she started walking slowly toward Dex on the cliff edge.

"Hey, it's a lot colder up here," she complained,

snapping her vest as the cold wind gusted about her.

"It's great!" Dex called, a dark shadow against a darker sky. "Come here! Take a look!"

She shivered. Was it the cold? Or the cliff edge? She had always had a problem with heights.

He took her hand and pulled her close to him. "Look — the whole town." He pointed.

"It's all dark," she said without enthusiasm. "All of the smart people are asleep."

His arm tightened around her waist. "Hey, you're a lot of laughs tonight," he said softly, bringing his face close to hers.

"It's too cold. I thought it was warmer out," she said.

"I'll warm you up." He squeezed her waist again.

She looked for Pete. He was off by himself several yards down, sitting on a large rock, staring down into the dark valley that held the town, his foot tapping to the music that pounded in his ears.

Why am I here with them? Joanna asked herself, as a strong blast of wind pushed her toward the jagged cliff edge. Why aren't I home asleep, safe in my bed, like every sane person in town?

She thought of her mother padding around the halls at all hours, unable to sleep. What if her mother happened to look into Joanna's bedroom and see that Joanna was gone? I'd be history, Joanna thought with a shudder. I'd be dead meat. She wouldn't let me out of her sight for the next decade!

And then I couldn't go out with Shep on Saturday night. . . .

"Hey, Dex — what are you doing?" Her voice caught in her throat. She looked up to see him standing ostrichlike on one leg at the very edge of the cliff.

"Just trying to get your attention," he said, laughing. "You seem to be somewhere else tonight."

"Dex — stop it! You're frightening me!"

"All right!" he cried. "I think I finally *do* have your attention! Now, for my next trick. . . ." He started hopping up and down on the one foot, his other foot stretched up in the air behind him.

"No, please! Stop! You'll fall!"

And as Joanna said the word, Dex slipped and fell over the edge.

Chapter 4

The sky seemed to blacken. The ground started to spin.

"Dex?"

She blinked her eyes, then opened them wide, thinking that when she opened them, he'd be back where he had been, standing on one foot, hopping up and down on the cliff edge.

But there was only darkness.

"Dex?"

Her heart felt as if it had stopped beating. She wasn't sure she could breathe.

She took a step to the edge. But she was too dizzy.

"Dex?"

He poked his head up from below the surface, a wide, delighted grin on his face. "Gotcha!"

She just stared at him open-mouthed. She couldn't speak.

He laughed. "Aren't you going to help me up?"

"You — you — "

"It was a gag." He reached his arms over the rock surface and started to pull himself up. "There's a little ledge here. Fooled you, huh?" He looked up at her expectantly.

"You creep," she muttered angrily, her heart beginning to beat again.

"See? You really do care!" he said, laughing.

"That wasn't funny, Dex."

"It wasn't really supposed to be funny," he said, pulling himself all the way up, standing up with a groan, and dusting off his jeans. "I guess it was like . . . performance art."

She made a disgusted face and turned away.

"Hey — what's wrong?" he asked, coming toward her. "You always used to enjoy my little performances."

"Well, I didn't enjoy this one!"

"Hey — what's going on?" Pete called from across the darkness. He had lit a cigarette, and all she could see was the glow of it.

"Huh? You missed it?" Dex called, disappointed.

"Missed what?"

"Never mind," Joanna said quickly. She no longer felt upset or frightened. Her anger had forced away those feelings. What a stupid, mean trick to pull!

"Hey, watch! I'll show you!" Dex yelled.

Pete stood up to get a better view.

A gust of wind battered all three of them. "Stop it, Dex!" Joanna cried. She turned and started going toward the car. "I'm leaving. Are you two coming with me?"

"One second," Dex said, holding up one finger. "I just have to do my little performance for Pete. Now watch carefully — "

"No — don't!" Joanna screamed. "I mean it, Dex! It wasn't funny the first time. It was horrible! I'll never speak to you again if — "

"You'll like it better the second time," Dex said, looking to see if Pete was watching.

"Dex — I'm warning you!" Joanna took another few steps toward the car. Her sneakers were soaked through from the wet ground. She felt cold and uncomfortable. "Are you coming?"

She turned back to see Dex back on the cliff edge, balancing again on one foot. "Ta-daa!" he cried, a gleeful smile on his face.

The smile suddenly faded as Dex's eyes opened wide in horror.

Joanna saw his expression change. Then she looked down and saw why.

A large chunk of stone was crumbling beneath Dex. The cliff edge was breaking away.

"No! No!"

He threw his arms up as he began to drop and frantically grabbed for the edge. But it crumbled in his hands.

"No — Dex!"

His head disappeared, and then his flailing hands.

She heard his body hit hard against the side.

"No — Dex!"

She heard him scream all the way down.

Then from down below she heard a cracking sound, the sound of eggs breaking.

This wasn't a joke.

This wasn't a performance.

This was real.

This was a death.

Joanna didn't even realize she was running until she reached the car.

She could hear Pete calling to her, his voice high-pitched and frightened, but she couldn't make out the words over the siren of her panic. The siren was drowning out everything. It seemed to echo between her ears, so loud, so unbearably loud.

She couldn't think.

She couldn't hear.

Was Pete calling to her? Was she running away? Was she climbing into the car, fumbling in her vest pocket for the car key?

"Joanna — come back!"

She couldn't hear anything. The siren had taken over her brain.

"We've got to help him! Joanna! Come back!"

What was he saying?

Come back?

But how could she?

If she stayed, her mother would find out she had sneaked out. Her mother would find out everything. Everyone in town would know what she had done.

How could she stay?

Her mother would take away her car. Take away her charge cards. Take away . . . everything.

For Dex?

Stay and have her life ruined for Dex?

She'd stay — if it weren't already too late.

But she heard him fall. She heard the horrifying sound when he hit the bottom.

She'd probably be hearing it for the rest of her life.

No. No way. No way, Dex.

Poor, dead Dex.

"Joanna — come back! We've got to help him! We've got to save him!"

Help him?

Is that what Pete was yelling?

The siren was just so loud, so overwhelmingly loud. Maybe if I drive real fast, the siren will go away.

The car was already in reverse. She was already backing away from the low fence.

No way. No way, Dex.

I can't ruin my life for you. I was going to break up with you, anyway. Don't you see? You're just not right for me. You're just not my kind. You understand, don't you?

Don't you?

The tires squealed as she floored the gas pedal, and the car began to race over the gravel road, slipping from side to side, noisily spitting a tidal wave of gravel behind it.

Lose my car? Lose my . . . reputation?

Shep's face flashed into her mind. He looked so good to her. So safe.

Sorry, Dex.

I'll get help.

Don't worry. I'm not abandoning you. I'll get help.

That's what she'd do. As soon as she got home, she'd dial 911. She'd tell them to hurry to the Promontory.

She'd save Dex after all.

She wasn't running away. She was running for help.

She started to feel better. The siren faded to a low, insistent wail.

I'm getting help. Pete will understand.

I'm getting help.

The tires squealed as she turned onto the Town Road. She realized she was going too fast.

But I have to go fast. I'm getting help for Dex. As soon as I get home.

As soon as I can.

She didn't see the truck until it was too late.

She saw the lights first. She wondered why she was suddenly bathed in light.

She thought it might not be real. It might be part of her panic, like the siren.

But the lights grew brighter.

They were truck headlights. The truck swerved to avoid her, but the road was too narrow.

By the time Joanna realized she was about to be hit head-on, it was too late to react.

The lights grew brighter, brighter, seemed to surround her.

Everything was glowing.

And then the siren was drowned out by the sound of breaking glass and bending steel.

And the lights gave way to darkness.

Chapter 5

The blackness lightened to a murky gray. Shadows in a dark fog. Clouds. Heavy, gray clouds. Then nothing at all.

She opened her eyes.

The room was a blur. A dark, warm blur. It was very still. Unearthly still.

The quiet is deafening, she thought.

And then she realized she was awake. And the room, coming quickly into focus, was her bedroom. She happily recognized the light through the open window, the shadows from the trees on the familiar flowered wallpaper. The two framed Picasso prints over the bookshelf next to the desk.

Home. She was home.

She raised her head, testing it. She raised her left arm, then her right. She stretched.

I don't hurt. I'm okay.

She sat up quickly.

I feel fine.

I must be dreaming. She yawned. No. The truck

was a dream. The headlights, those blinding, yellow headlights weren't real. The accident wasn't real. It never happened.

I'm fine.

She pushed down the bedspread and the satin sheet and started to climb out of bed. But a sudden fluttering at the window made her stop.

Just the curtains?

No. She heard a scrabbling against the side of the house, a soft thud.

That's odd, she thought, pulling the sheet back up. Why is the window wide open in October?

There were other things that puzzled her. The quiet was one of them. Except for the soft thuds outside, it was so eerily quiet.

Where was her mother? Why wasn't she waiting at her bedside for her to awaken?

Because there was no accident, she told herself. Because it was all a dream.

A dark form filled the window. It moved quickly, struggling, pulling itself into the room, one leg, one arm, then another leg. It stepped into the square of moonlight.

"Dex!" she cried.

"Ssshhh." He raised his finger to his lips, his eyes glowing like dark jewels.

"Dex — you're okay!" We're both okay, she thought.

His smile seemed to warm the room. "It's a beautiful night," he whispered. "Come on, get dressed. Let's go for a walk."

34

"A walk?"

She wondered what time it was, what day. How had she gotten back to bed?

She had to remind herself that she had been in bed all along. In bed dreaming a terrible dream.

"Okay." She rose quickly, feeling light as air, and floated across the room to pull a designer running suit from her dresser drawer.

"Hurry," he whispered, sounding very excited and happy.

She was dressed in an instant, headed for the door, then hesitated. She walked over to Dex, grabbed his arm, squeezed it hard.

He was real.

He was really there.

He laughed. "What's the matter with you?"

"Nothing," she said. Why go into it?

She remembered that she had decided to break up with him, not to see him anymore. I'll have to tell him, she thought. It won't be easy, but I'll have to tell him. Maybe I'll tell him during our walk.

They were outside now, and starting to jog. It felt so good to be moving, to feel the cool wind on her face.

She jogged a little faster, leaving Dex behind.

"Hey, wait up!"

He'll always be a little behind me, she thought. He'll never really be able to catch up.

It was still so silent. The silence was almost *thick*.

It must have been very late. No cars moved. The houses were dark. The wind blew but the trees didn't move. The fallen brown leaves, scattered all over the ground, stayed in place as if nailed down.

Strange.

Joanna jogged a little faster.

"Hey — " Dex called from several yards behind.

She didn't turn around. It felt so good to run, to move, to be okay.

"Hey — "

She looked back without slowing her pace. She was running really fast now, and not the least bit out of breath.

"Hey — "

Dex, she realized, looked angry. What was his problem?

She turned again. A streetlight cast a cone of white light down on him. His eyes were narrowed, his mouth pulled back in an angry frown.

He looks frightening, Joanna thought.

And her next thought frightened her even more: He's not running with me anymore. He's chasing me.

"Hey!"

She knew she was right. She picked up speed. She glanced quickly back. Dex picked up speed, too.

He was gaining on her.

Why was he doing this? Why did he look so frightening, so angry? She wanted to stop. But she was afraid.

Where were they?

The houses were gone. The woods gave way to flat fields. She could see low, black hills against the purple night sky.

How far have we run? It doesn't seem as if we've been running that long.

"Hey — you — "

His voice sounded so angry, so filled with hatred.

He's going to catch me, she thought, feeling her legs begin to ache, feeling her chest begin to heave for breath. He's going to catch me, and then —

And then?

A cold shudder ran down her body.

She forced herself to run harder. Every step hurt now, every thrust of her legs sent a flash of pain up her back. But she knew she had to keep running.

"Joanna — stop!"

She ignored his angry call, gulped in a mouthful of air, and ran, her sneakers sinking into the wet ground.

Ground?

Where were they?

The ground seemed to dip, then rise again. The soft ground gave way to granite.

The Promontory.

They had run to the Promontory. He had chased her to the Promontory. Had this been his destination all along?

She was only a few dozen yards from the cliff edge. She stopped, gasping for breath, her entire body throbbing, pulsing with pain. She spun around.

"Dex — stop!"

He came running right at her, his expression fixed in hatred.

"Dex — why are you doing this?"

He seemed to pick up speed rather than slow down. He was only a few yards away now. His dark eyes burned into hers. His mouth opened wide, and he tossed his head back in a silent scream.

"Dex — stop! *Please!*"

He ran past her, ran right over the cliff edge. His legs scissored in midair. His hands flailed wildly above his head. He spun, turned to face her, an accusing look on his face. Then he started to drop.

It was Joanna's turn to scream. She closed her eyes tight and tossed back her head, and screamed and screamed.

No sound came out.

When she opened her eyes, she was in a very bright, white room.

Her mother's face loomed over her.

Joanna could see the crisscross of lines at the corners of her mother's eyes, the small pores of her made-up cheeks, the crumbs of orange lipstick on her lips. She could see her mother's face so clearly. There was a damp path down the makeup on her cheeks where tears must have recently trickled.

Her mother's smile was broad. Too broad.

"She's coming out of it now," a woman's voice said from somewhere behind her mother.

"It's starting to wear off," another woman said.

Her mother's smile grew even wider. She leaned down over Joanna until they almost touched noses.

"What?" Joanna asked.

"She'll be fully awake soon," one of the unseen women said.

"She did very well," the other added in a hushed tone.

Her mother's face didn't move. It hovered above Joanna like a pink balloon.

I'm still dreaming, Joanna thought.

"You're going to be fine," her mother said, her smile still fixed. The face retreated a little. Tears formed near the tangled crisscross of age lines.

Yes, I'm going to be fine because I'm still dreaming.

She tried to sit up.

Everything hurt.

I'm paralyzed, she thought, and the sweet calmness of the dream sensation gave way to panic.

"Hey — "

"You're going to be fine," her mother said softly. The tears ran down the already defined tracks on her cheeks.

I don't believe you, Joanna thought.

She struggled to sit up. When that didn't prove possible, she struggled to move her arms. That wasn't possible, either.

"Help — Mom — "

"She's fully awake now," a voice said.

"That's a good sign," the other voice added.

Who *are* those women? Joanna wondered angrily.

"Don't try to move," her mother said.

"I can't," Joanna told her, her voice tiny, like a baby's voice.

I'm a baby again, she thought. I was just born again.

Crazy thought.

I've been drugged or something.

A crazy thought that was probably true.

She looked past her mother with her frozen, tear-stained smile to the white tile walls, the bright fluorescent lights, the white-uniformed nurses standing side by side in the doorway.

I'm in a hospital.

And I'm not dreaming now.

It all seemed too much to gather in. It was taking all of her strength, all of her concentration to *see*.

"You're going to be fine," her mother repeated, like a song chorus.

You always were a bad liar, Joanna thought.

She hated the smell of her mother's makeup. So orangey. So ugly.

She drifted back to sleep with the smell clinging to her nostrils.

"She needs to sleep," a nearby voice said.

"You really were lucky," her mother said, a few days later. She sat stiffly in a folding chair beside the hospital bed, her fur coat on her lap. "Your beautiful face wasn't touched."

"Just about everything else was," Joanna groaned.

"Joanna, really. Don't complain. A truck like that. You could have been — you could have been. . . ." She bit her trembling lower lip. "A few broken bones. Really, dear. You should be so grateful."

"Yeah. Grateful," Joanna repeated.

Whatever painkillers they were feeding into her arm made her feel as if she were not completely in the room. She felt as if she had traded places with her shadow. Her shadow lay braced and bandaged on this hard hospital bed. Her real body — and her mind — were off somewhere else.

She was continually drifting off to sleep, sometimes in the middle of conversations. She wasn't allowed visitors yet, only her mother. The visits tired her out. She wished her mother would stop staring at her so intensely. She wished they would stop pumping stuff into her, so that she could think straight.

"In another few weeks, you'll be strong enough to begin therapy for your leg," Mrs. Collier said matter-of-factly.

"Yeah. Well, I'm so grateful for that, too," Joanna said sarcastically.

"Just stop it, Joanna. Let's take this one day at a time."

"Don't you mean one *cliché* at a time?" Joanna cracked, knowing she was giving her mother a hard time and not caring.

"This has all been such a terrible shock for all of us," Mrs. Collier said, deciding to ignore her daughter's sarcasm. "When I got that call from the police at three in the morning that you — that you were in an accident and — "

Joanna realized she hadn't explained a thing to her mother.

"What were you doing out, Joanna? Why did you sneak out of the house?"

She just didn't have the strength to get into it now. Drifting halfway between the real world and the shadowy world induced by the painkillers, she hadn't even thought about that horrible night.

Hadn't even thought about Dex.

She drifted off to sleep, wondering how she would ever explain.

"Pete?"

Joanna tried to sit up, then remembered that she couldn't. She looked for her mother, but she wasn't there. It was Pete sitting awkwardly in the folding chair now.

His face was flushed. His eyes darted nervously from her face to the floor. His hands were clasped tightly in his lap.

"Pete?"

"Hi, Joanna. Are you awake? I mean — "

"No. I'm talking in my sleep. Pete, are you okay?"

"Yeah. Fine." His face turned a little brighter red. "Your mom says you're going to be fine."

"She says it four hundred times a day," Joanna said bitterly, rolling her eyes. They were the only part of her she could move without any pain. "So it's got to be a lie."

Pete just stared at her. "You're pretty beat-up, huh?"

She laughed a dry laugh. It made her broken ribs hurt. "Good question, Pete. Got any others?"

He pulled at the diamond stud in his ear.

They sat in silence for a while. He stared at her. She had the feeling that he was waiting for something.

Finally he broke the silence. "Aren't you going to ask me about Dex?" He asked it angrily, accusingly.

What's wrong with me? Joanna wondered. Why *didn't* I ask about Dex? Is it just these awful drugs? Am I losing my mind? Am I trying to shut out all memories of that night?

"Well, Dex died," Pete said, shouting now. He jumped to his feet, his face filled with disgust. "Dex died, Joanna. He didn't make it. He died that night. And you couldn't even bother to ask me about him."

Chapter 6

Mary came to visit a few days later. Or was it the same day? Joanna couldn't keep track of time, didn't even try.

"Sssh. I brought you something," Mary said, whispering, acting very secretive as she dug in the big, floppy embroidered bag she always carried.

"I like your hair," Joanna said.

"My hair? I didn't even brush it." She continued to rummage in the bag. "Here it is." She looked behind her to the door to make sure no one was coming in.

Joanna laughed at the secrecy. "Mary — what on earth — ?"

Mary handed her a Snickers bar. "Quick — hide it."

"A Snickers bar? Mary — I'm touched!"

"Just hide it," Mary insisted, "before they take it away from you. I figured this is probably the one time you won't be watching your weight."

"What a thoughtful present," Joanna said, slipping the candy bar under the sheet.

The girls talked, animatedly at first, then awkwardly in fits and starts. They both realized that they had less to talk about now that they didn't go to the same school or have the same friends.

They talked about Joanna's broken bones, and about how her mother was taking it all. And they talked about Mary's classes and a boy she had met at the mall.

Then, as if she had been leading up to it all along, Mary said, "Pete told me about . . . Dex."

"Yeah," Joanna said, reaching over to adjust the tube that still was stuck to her wrist.

"It — it must be so hard for you," Mary said, staring hard into Joanna's eyes, searching for something there.

"Yeah. Well . . ." Joanna didn't know what Mary expected her to say. And why was she staring at her so intensely?

The silence grew really awkward. "I wish I felt more," Joanna said, mainly to fill the silence.

"Huh? What do you mean?" Mary looked very surprised.

"I mean, it's so awful. When Pete told me that Dex was dead, my first reaction was, Now I don't have to break up with him."

Mary's mouth dropped open. "Really? That's really the first thing you thought?"

Uh-oh. I've gone too far, Joanna thought. I've been too honest. I should have known better. I should have known that would shock Mary.

It shocks me, too, in a way.

"You really didn't feel *anything*?" Mary asked, shifting uncomfortably on the small folding chair, her hands playing with the folds of her bag.

"I guess it just hasn't sunk in," Joanna said, beginning to feel tired again, wishing Mary would just leave.

"Oh."

"I mean, I'm just numb, I guess. You know. From the painkillers and stuff. I'll feel it later. I'm sure."

Mary just stared at her, much the way Pete had.

"Well, I know it sounds a little cold — " Joanna started to say, and then decided she had nothing to be defensive about.

My feelings are my own business, she told herself. I don't have to explain how I feel to Mary, or Pete, or anyone else. I'm the one who saw Dex die, after all. I'm the one who saw him fall off the cliff. I'm the one who saw the look on his face when he knew he was falling.

That's horrible enough for one lifetime.

You ran away, a voice inside her said. You didn't help him. You ran away.

I hurried to get help, was Joanna's reply to herself. I would've gotten help for him if that truck hadn't . . .

Who cares? Dex is dead, and I'm lying here wrecked.

Who cares?

Stop staring at me like I'm some disgusting kind of cold fish.

As if reading Joanna's thoughts, Mary jumped to her feet. "I've got to get going. I didn't realize how late it was."

She didn't even look at her watch, thought Joanna. She has no idea how late it is. "Thanks for coming," she said.

"Feel better," Mary said. "Get some rest."

"What else can I do?"

Mary laughed, a nervous giggle. "I'll come back sometime. I mean, when I can. 'Bye." She hurried out of the room without looking back.

"What was it — something I said?" Joanna asked aloud.

She settled her head back on the pillow.

"So what? So what? So *what*? Sorry, Dex. But so what?"

"You're not going to study tonight, are you, Joanna?"

"No, Mom. I was just carrying these books up to my room. I have a date tonight."

"Oh, I'm glad." Her mother collapsed wearily into the oversized living room armchair and raised her feet onto the ottoman. "You've been working so hard, I've been a little worried about you."

"Well, I missed six weeks of school, you know."

"I'm very pleased by how well you're doing, Joanna," Mrs. Collier said, raising her feet to examine her ankles, which were swollen. "The therapist says your leg is coming along so nicely, you can probably quit by Christmas time."

"Maybe people will stop thinking of me as 'The Gimp,' " Joanna said, and started out of the living room, forcing herself to walk without a limp, even though her leg really throbbed with pain.

"I haven't seen Mary around in quite a while," Mrs. Collier said, not noticing that Joanna was trying to leave. "Did she come visit you in the hospital?"

"Yeah. Once," Joanna said, allowing more bitterness to escape than she had intended. She quickly added, "I guess she's just real busy. It's hard, you know, to keep up with kids from other schools."

She started to leave the room again, but again her mother refused to let the conversation end. "And what about Dex?" she asked. "Did you say you were meeting him tonight? I haven't seen him once the whole time you . . ."

Joanna uttered a silent gasp. Her mother kept talking, but her voice seemed to fade as if someone had turned down the volume control.

I never told her, Joanna realized.

She never asked anything about Dex, and I never told her. She doesn't know a thing. She doesn't know that Dex is dead. Doesn't know why I was out in the middle of the night. Doesn't know anything.

And doesn't really *want* to know.

Any other mother would have demanded an explanation, Joanna told herself. Any other mother would have wanted to know every detail.

Maybe I'm lucky.

Lucky that she doesn't care enough to ask.

I don't care, either.

So, we're both lucky.

"I'm not seeing Dex anymore," she said, finding it easy to keep her voice flat and emotionless.

"Really?"

Mrs. Collier was trying to play it cool. But Joanna knew how much that news would thrill her. Her mother never could stand Dex, mainly for the same reasons that had Joanna planning to break up with him.

"I have a date with Shep tonight," Joanna said.

"Shephard Forrest?"

Joanna nodded.

"Hilda Forrest's son? How nice." A pleased smile formed on Mrs. Collier's face.

"I'm glad you approve," Joanna snapped. It bothered her to see her mother so happy.

"I didn't mean — Well . . . it's just that Shephard is much more appropriate."

"Appropriate?" Joanna laughed, a scornful laugh. "What a word!"

Why am I giving my mother such a hard time? she wondered. I *agree* with her that Shep is more appropriate.

It's just not her place to say it.

I should tell her that Dex fell off a cliff and died. Just to see her squirm. Just to see her come up with an *appropriate* response.

But instead, she shifted the books she'd been

carrying to her other arm, and walked quickly up to her room to get ready for her date with Shep.

"I love that sweater, Shep," Joanna said. "Is it cashmere?"

"I guess. I'll let you touch it if you wash your hands first." He gave her that adorable lopsided grin, the one that made the dimple appear in his left cheek.

She laughed and rubbed the sleeve of the pale blue sweater. "Yep. It's cashmere."

"My grandmother gave it to me," Shep said, blushing a little as Joanna kept her hand on his arm.

He had insisted on taking her to the winter dance at Garland High, the public high school he had attended before switching to Landover. "It'll be a goof," he said.

Joanna didn't know any of the kids there, and the whole idea of going to a dance at a public high school seemed like a real downer to her, but she didn't want Shep to think she was a bad sport, so she agreed with a smile.

"Maybe I should dress down a bit," she had said when he told her his plans for the evening after arriving at her house. She was wearing a maroon silk blouse and a dark suede miniskirt over black tights.

"I think you look okay," he said, a little uncomfortably.

She liked his shyness. He was so incredibly good-looking, she thought, a little shyness made him more human.

"Shall we take my car?" she asked. She was so accustomed to driving Dex around, the question came automatically.

"No way," he said. "Look." He led her to her front door and pointed to the drive. Basking in the light from the porch was a brand-new silver Jaguar.

Joanna's mouth dropped open. "It's yours?"

"My grandmother gave it to me." He was grinning now. He ran a hand back quickly through his wavy, blond hair.

"*Nice* grandmother!" Joanna exclaimed.

"Well, she's very old and very rich," Shep said seriously. "And very lonely. And I'm her only grandson."

"Lucky you," Joanna said, resting her hand on his arm again. "I guess we'll be going in style to the Garland High hop!"

When they got to the Garland High gym, everyone seemed so glad to see Shep. A steady stream of kids kept coming up to greet him and ask him how he was doing at Landover, and if he missed all of his friends at Garland.

Shep seemed right at home with these kids. I thought this was supposed to be a goof, Joanna thought, a little resentfully, seeing how excited and pleased Shep was to be back here. "Good lord — look at that girl's outfit," she said, pointing to a girl in a brown, fringed skirt and white plastic boots. "How tacky."

"I think it's kind of sexy," Shep said, almost defensively.

"They could have spent a few dollars to decorate

the place a little better," Joanna griped. "I mean balloons and crepe paper streamers? Get real!"

But to her surprise, Shep didn't join in her laughter. "It doesn't look so bad. You know, they can't afford to have their dances at a hotel ballroom, the way we do at Landover. Everyone seems to be having a good time, anyway, don't you think?"

Joanna quickly agreed. "Yeah, it's great," she said, trying not to sound as unenthusiastic as she felt. "Oh, no! Look at that girl's hair! Unbelievable!"

Shep looked at her, an odd smile on his face. "Joanna, you're such a snob." He said it jokingly, but there was definitely a tone of disapproval in it.

I'd better be careful, Joanna thought. Shep doesn't seem to appreciate my sense of humor.

She danced with him to the blaring music over the terrible loudspeakers and tried to join in shouted conversations with his friends, who seemed pretty nice. It was about eleven o'clock when she asked to leave for the first time. And by eleven-thirty, he had said good-bye to everyone, and they were walking across the street to the car.

"I told you it would be a goof," he said, his arm casually around her shoulders. His coat smelled like the gym.

Mine probably does, too, Joanna thought unhappily. "Yeah. I like your friends," she said, working hard to sound genuine and enthusiastic.

She sat very close to him as he drove her home. A heavy frost had settled over the lawns. As they drove past, the ground looked silvery white, as if it had snowed. She nestled her head against his shoulder, looking up to see if he seemed pleased by it.

"You want to go to a movie or something next weekend?" he asked, his eyes straight ahead on the road.

"Yeah. I would," she said softly, secretly feeling as if she had scored a victory. Shep was hooked, definitely hooked.

She inhaled deeply. "I just love the smell of a new car," she said happily.

He kissed her good night at her door. He started to end the kiss, but she grabbed the back of his head with both hands and pulled him back, pressing her lips against his in a long, lingering kiss. Finally he headed back to his car, a goofy grin on his handsome face.

She stood and watched him get into the car. He pressed down on the gas, making the engine roar, the blast of exhaust white against the darkness of the night. Then he backed silently away.

Score one for Joanna, she thought, as she turned the lock and entered the house. He's just right for me. A little lacking in the sense-of-humor area, maybe. But he can be shaped up.

She hurried up to her room and was getting undressed when her cellular phone rang. She glanced at the clock. It was a few minutes after midnight.

Who could it be?

She picked it up after the second ring, her arm tangled in the sleeve of her blouse. "Hello?"

She heard crackling at the other end. It was either a bad connection or someone was calling long distance.

"Hello?" she repeated, a little louder.

"Hi, Joanna." A boy's voice, sounding very far away. "It's me."

"What?"

"Joanna — it's me. Dex. How you doin'?"

Chapter 7

Joanna didn't reply.

She dropped the phone back into its holder.

The voice. It *was* Dex's voice, she thought.

But that's impossible. Of course, that's impossible.

Someone was playing a cruel trick on her. But who could it be?

Who could sound so much like Dex? Who would want to scare Joanna, to make her feel bad?

Pete?

Was it Pete? She hadn't seen Pete since that day in the hospital. Since the day Pete had come to tell her that Dex was dead.

Pete was so angry at her, Joanna remembered, so shocked that she hadn't asked about Dex immediately. So outraged when Joanna didn't cry at the horrible news.

Outraged. That was the only word to describe it.

Pete was the only one who knew that she had

run away from the Promontory that night, that she hadn't stayed to try to rescue Dex.

But I didn't run away, she insisted to herself.

I drove away as quickly as I could to get help.

She wished she had had a chance to explain that to Pete.

That creep. She never had liked him. He was so ugly with that pockmarked face, and that awful spiky hair.

He was just stupid enough to make that phone call and pretend to be Dex.

But she knew it couldn't be Pete. Pete had such a high-pitched, scratchy voice. There was no way he could sound so much like Dex.

So exactly like Dex.

She shivered, and realized she was still undressed. She hurried over to her closet, stepping over her clothes, which she had tossed on the floor, and pulled out her warmest flannel nightshirt.

What is going on? Who would play such a stupid, mean joke?

The question repeated in her mind. She just couldn't answer it.

It took hours to fall asleep. And then she slept fitfully, waking up every few hours, thinking the phone was ringing.

Sunday was spent doing homework and watching endless, boring old movies full of stupid romance on TV.

She thought maybe Shep would call, but he didn't. So she called him after dinner, and they had a nice, short chat.

He's never asked me about Dex, she realized. Of course, he never knew Dex. But he did know that I'd been going with someone for a long time.

And he's never really asked about my accident, either.

That's strange.

Maybe he just doesn't like to bring up unpleasant subjects, she thought. A lot of people are like that.

The next day was a blustery, cold day that showed winter was getting serious. Low, gray clouds hovered overhead as she headed home in the late afternoon after her French tutorial. Even though it was still afternoon, it was as dark as night, an eerie, heavy darkness that made it feel as if it might start to snow at any minute.

I wish I had the car, she thought, even though her French tutor lived only a couple of blocks from her house. She pulled the fur hood of her coat up, and picked up her pace. The cold made her foot throb, but she forced herself not to limp. Any change in the weather made her foot and ribs and shoulders ache. It was just something she was going to have to live with, she realized.

As she approached Trafalgar Avenue, the street-lights flickered and came on. The sudden light startled her. It made everything suddenly look different. New shadows shifted and played across the sidewalk.

It took Joanna a few seconds to realize what had happened. She stared up at the street lamp above her head, and for a split second, the yellow light reminded her of the truck headlights, the truck headlights that had seemed to grow and grow, widen and widen until they were all around her.

With a silent gasp, she looked away quickly, turning her gaze across Trafalgar, one of the busiest avenues in Middlewood.

Leaning against a bus-stop post across the street, illuminated by a circle of yellow light from a street lamp behind him, she saw a young man staring at her.

"Dex?"

He didn't move.

She froze.

She recognized the red windbreaker. He had worn it a million times.

"Dex?"

The traffic light was against her. A steady stream of cars poured down Trafalgar, people on their way home from work.

Except for the windbreaker, he seemed all yellow and black, bathed in the light from the street lamp.

He stared at her, unmoving. And she stared back.

It can't be.

It's impossible.

Dex, you're dead.

She knew her eyes were playing tricks on her. It had to be another boy, another boy with black hair, bold, black eyes, and a red windbreaker. Another boy who leaned just like Dex.

Who looked just like Dex.

She heard his voice again, the voice on the phone

Saturday night. "Hi, it's me. How you doin'?"

The voice from so far away.

The light changed.

He didn't move. He leaned against the narrow yellow post, staring straight ahead at her. She shivered. Not from the cold.

She had to know the truth.

"Dex?"

She started across the street. But a city bus ran the red light, roaring through the intersection.

Joanna leaped back to the curb, startled.

When the bus had passed, she looked across the street.

Dex was gone.

Chapter 8

Joanna rolled over with a weary groan and tugged hard at the covers. The bottom of the sheet pulled out from under the mattress. She sat up. Now I'll have to remake the bed, she thought. She couldn't stand to have her feet sticking out from under the covers.

She stood up in the darkness and glanced at the clock on her desk. Twelve-fifteen.

Why can't I get to sleep?

It was chilly in the room, even in her flannel nightshirt. Maybe I should close the window, she thought. She pulled the sheet down and tucked it in. Out on the street a car drove by, its radio blaring country music.

I'll never get to sleep, Joanna thought, climbing back under the covers. I'm not even sleepy. Maybe I should get up and work on my book report.

The scrabbling sounds outside the window made her sit up with a start. She heard scraping noises. Sneakers against the tree trunk.

No.

It wasn't possible.

She had to be imagining it. The way she had imagined seeing Dex standing on that street corner.

She uttered a soft cry as a hand grabbed the window ledge from outside. A head popped up, hidden in shadow.

No.

Joanna gripped the edge of the bedspread, pulling it up to her chin as if to shield herself.

She leaned over and, her hand trembling, struggled to turn on the bed-table lamp. She nearly knocked it over, finally managing to click it on just as Dex pulled himself into the room.

He grinned at her, that warm, familiar grin, and walked stiffly away from the window into the yellow light. He was wearing black, straight-legged jeans and a worn, leather bomber jacket. "Hi, Joanna." His voice was a whisper, almost ghostly.

"Dex?"

"Yeah. It's me."

Don't scream, don't scream, don't scream.

She realized that she'd been holding her breath. The bedspread was still pulled up to her chin.

"But — "

"How are you?" Still a whisper.

He looked pale in the yellow light, and thin. He took a few steps toward her, limping slightly, holding his left leg stiffly.

"But — Dex — you're dead!"

Joanna didn't recognize her own voice. Her

throat felt so tight, it was hard to breathe. She suddenly felt cold all over.

Don't scream, don't scream, don't scream.

"Huh?" His mouth dropped open. His face filled with surprise. He shook his long, wavy hair as if shaking off her words.

Joanna gripped the bedspread, staring into his bewildered face. He looks different, she thought. So thin, almost wasted away.

"What did you say?"

She coughed. Her throat felt tight and dry. "Dead," she said, the word sounding odd, not sounding like a real word. "Pete said you were dead, Dex."

"Huh? Really?"

He looked stunned. He pulled out the desk chair, turned it around, and sat down on it backwards, leaning his chin against the chairback. "He said I was dead?"

"Yeah. He told me. He said you didn't make it. That you — "

"But why would Pete say that?" He gripped the back of the chair and made it rock back and forth.

He's alive, she thought, starting to calm down, starting to get over the shock of seeing him climb into her room again. He's alive. He's really sitting there.

To her surprise, she realized she had mixed feelings about seeing him, sitting there, rocking the desk chair up and down. She had gotten used to the idea of him being dead.

Am I glad to see him? she asked herself.

Not really.

Mainly, she realized, seeing him made her feel less guilty.

"Yeah," she said, loosening her grip on the bedspread. "Why *did* Pete tell me that?" Her shock was beginning to turn to anger. "Was that some sort of stupid joke he was trying to pull?"

"Poor guy," Dex said softly, staring down at the plush carpet, not picking up on Joanna's anger. "He must've been in shock. He was so upset about — about what happened that night."

"He was so upset, he *thought* you were dead?" Joanna pulled herself up and leaned against the headboard. Why did she feel so cold? The room seemed to grow even colder after Dex entered.

"I guess," Dex said. A sad expression crossed his face, an expression she had never seen before.

It's not just sad, she thought. It's mournful.

"Well, where were you for the past two months?" she asked. The question came out more angry than concerned.

Her tone seemed to surprise him. "I was banged up really bad," he said, looking into her eyes. She noticed that he was holding his left leg stiff, straight out in front of him. "I had a lot of broken bones, some internal bleeding and stuff. They took me to a hospital upstate. I've been there the whole time."

"I'm sorry," she said.

You're supposed to be dead, she thought.

I felt so bad. I felt so guilty. Why did I have to go through all that for nothing?

Why did Pete do that? Out of spite? Out of anger? Did he do it for revenge, because I left him there that night?

"I wanted to call you," Dex said. "But my hands were bandaged. I looked like a mummy. My aunt tried to call, but there was never an answer at your house. Maybe she was trying the wrong number. She isn't too swift these days."

He shifted uncomfortably on the small chair. "It was so terrible, so unbearable," he said in a low, flat voice. "All the time in the hospital. All those weeks. Know what I did? I pretended I was in a play, that I was just playing a role, that it wasn't really happening to me. Pretty pathetic, huh?"

"You look good," she said, ignoring his question, looking him up and down.

You look like a skeleton, she thought.

"So you really thought I was dead?" He scratched his head. A grin crossed his face for some reason. "That explains it, I guess."

"Explains what?"

"Why I never heard from you. Why you never visited. Why you hung up on me the other night."

"I was in a hospital, too," Joanna said, sounding defensive.

"You were?" He stood up. Joanna noticed that it wasn't easy for him. He had always been so agile, so athletic. But now his legs seemed stiff. He seemed to move with real pain. "What happened to you?"

"When you fell, I — I ran for help."

It's the truth, Joanna thought. Why do I feel as if I'm lying?

"Yeah?"

"Yeah. I started driving to town to get the police, or an ambulance or something. But I — I was so upset, I got into an accident. I was unconscious for a day. But I guess I was lucky."

"We both were," Dex said with real emotion. "I've missed you a lot."

He hurried to her, leaned down, put his arms around her shoulders, and kissed her. Joanna kissed him back, suddenly feeling emotional, too.

He's real, all right, she thought. He's not a ghost.

The kiss lasted a long time. She grabbed the back of his head and held him to her.

What am I doing? she thought.

Shep's face flashed into her mind.

Pressing her lips against Dex's, holding his head, gripping his long hair, she felt terribly confused.

I *do* feel something for him, she thought.

Don't I?

Or am I just relieved that he's okay?

This isn't right. This isn't what I want.

So why am I doing it?

Again, Shep's face flashed into her mind.

She pulled back suddenly and dropped her hands to her side. He stayed there, leaning down over her, his dark eyes burning into hers.

"I really thought you were dead," she said.

"I'm not. I'll prove it," he said, and kissed her again.

Something's wrong, she thought. Something's different.

This kiss was much shorter. She heard noises, footsteps in the hall.

"My mom — she's up."

"Okay. I'd better go. I'll pick you up Friday night," he whispered. "I'll prove to you I'm not dead."

"Friday night?"

"Yeah." He kissed her again.

"But, Dex — "

She had to tell him about Shep. She didn't really want to go out with Dex.

But she did.

She was terribly confused.

He disappeared out the window. She listened to him slide down the tree.

Something is different about him, Joanna thought. His kiss. It felt different. Just not the same.

Trying to figure out what it was that was different, she fell into a troubled sleep.

Chapter 9

"Well, I'm sorry, Shep. I'm disappointed, too." Joanna blew on her nail polish, cradling the phone on her shoulder.

Shep whined on the other end.

She didn't mind the whining. She was pleased that her breaking their date had gotten him so upset.

"Well, what about tomorrow night? I'm sure the same movie will be playing tomorrow night."

Shep had to go somewhere with his parents tomorrow night.

"Well, maybe next week," Joanna said, glancing at the clock. She was supposed to meet Dex at the mall in five minutes.

Oh, well. Let Dex wait a while, she thought. It wouldn't be the first time. She thought of that night back in October when she had hidden behind a post and watched him wait. What a hoot!

Why won't these nails dry?

Now Shep was asking if he could stop by later. No way, dude.

"No, that's not a good idea, Shep. My mom is really sick. It's the flu. That's why I promised I'd stay home."

He wanted to talk more, but she hung up, careful not to smudge her nails. What a good liar I am, she thought. Even I believed that story. Dex thinks he's such a good actor. But I can act circles around him!

Dex.

Was she really going out with Dex?

More to the point: *Why* was she going out with Dex?

She really didn't feel anything for him anymore. She didn't like admitting it — even to herself — but she had felt that tiny little bit of disappointment upon learning that he was alive.

She tried to force that thought from her mind. It was an unspeakable thought, after all. But somehow it kept drifting to the surface of her thoughts.

So why *was* she standing up Shep so she could go to the movies with Dex tonight?

Frankly, she admitted, she didn't know. She felt very confused.

She was sure that after spending the evening with Dex, she'd be able to start sorting things out in her mind.

Shep was so sweet, so boyish, so charming. So right.

It had to be guilt. That was the only reason she was pulling on her best blue Ralph Lauren sweater over her designer jeans, giving her hair one more quick brush, and hurrying downstairs to get the car.

"Night, Mom," she called. "Don't wait up!"

What a laugh. Her mother had never cared enough to wait up, not once.

"You and Shep have a good time!" her mother called from the study.

"Right!" Joanna called back.

What she doesn't know won't hurt her. She doesn't even know that I thought Dex was dead. She doesn't have to know that I'm seeing him again.

She grabbed her big, expensive, fur-lined coat. She always felt so safe and protected inside it. She stepped into the garage from the house entrance. The light went on automatically. She slid behind the steering wheel of her mother's new BMW. The leather seat felt cold against her hand. The car started with a gentle hum, and she backed down the drive and headed to the mall.

Dex was pacing back and forth in front of the bookstore. *This is where I came in,* Joanna thought drily.

He looked so pale.

That was the first thing she noticed about him.

The high fluorescent lights made everyone else look yellow. But Dex's skin, Joanna immediately noticed, was white, nearly as white as cake flour.

He was wearing the same black jeans and leather bomber jacket. His black hair was brushed straight back and tied in a short ponytail. He was limping slightly as he paced, favoring his left leg.

She had the sudden urge to turn around and drive to Shep's house. She hadn't been looking forward to this date. In fact, she'd been dreading it, in a way. Dreading what they might talk about. Dreading what they couldn't talk about.

"Hi, Joanna!"

Too late. Dex had spotted her. A crooked smile crossed his face.

That's not his smile, she thought. His smile was always so straight, so open. That's not his smile at all. It's a stranger's smile.

Oh, just knock it off, she scolded herself. Stop looking for differences.

Of *course* Dex is different. He fell off a cliff, remember? He broke nearly every bone in his body. He was in a hospital for two months.

That could make you seem a little bit different.

"Hi, Dex. Sorry I'm late." She took his hand. It was ice cold.

"Cold hands," she said, startled. His hands were always so warm. He was always so warm. He'd walk around in his shirtsleeves in the coldest winter weather and never seemed to notice that everyone else was freezing.

"Oh. Sorry." He pulled his hand away with an apologetic smile. He seemed really nervous. "The movie just started. I'm sure we didn't miss much," he said, leading the way across the mall to the theater, limping as he walked.

The movie was some kind of action comedy with Robert DeNiro grinning and shooting a lot of people, and then driving a pickup truck the wrong way on a freeway with a dozen police cars chasing him.

Joanna couldn't concentrate on the movie. It seemed so strange to be sitting next to Dex, sitting so close to him in the dark again.

A few minutes into the film, he slid his arm around her shoulder. She leaned against him, her eyes on the screen.

What was that odor?

She sniffed once, twice, then stopped because Dex was beginning to notice.

It was a slightly musty smell, sour like old fruit. Or meat that had gone bad.

She turned her head away, but the stale odor followed her.

Dex had always smelled so sweet.

What was causing that sickening smell?

Chapter 10

"Dex is alive," Joanna said, unable to suppress a grin.

Mary's mouth dropped open. She turned positively pale. "No!" she cried when she could finally speak.

"Yes. He's alive. I went out with him last night."

Mary put her hands over her ears and shook her head, her tight, brown curls seeming to vibrate around her. "I don't think I'm hearing right, Joanna. Dex — ?"

"He's alive," Joanna repeated, enjoying her friend's shocked reaction.

It was Sunday afternoon. Mrs. Collier had gone out shopping again. Mary had dropped by unannounced, the first time Joanna had seen her since the hospital visit.

"But — but — Pete told me — "

"Me, too," Joanna interrupted. "What's Pete's problem, anyway?"

"I don't know. I haven't seen him," Mary replied,

still stunned. She flung herself back onto the crushed velvet sofa, rested her head against the back, and stared up at the elaborate crystal light fixture suspended from the ceiling. "Whew. Joanna. Really. Just let me catch my breath. What a shock."

"Tell me about it," Joanna said drily, tucking her legs beneath her on the big, overstuffed armchair. "He climbed in my bedroom window last week. Can you imagine?"

"At night?"

"At night. I was terrified. I thought I was seeing a ghost."

"But Dex is okay? Really?" The color still hadn't returned to her face.

"Yeah. Pretty much. He limps a little. I guess he was beat up pretty bad by the fall. He was in a hospital upstate for the past two months. But he seems perfectly okay now."

Except for the cold hands and the weird smell, Joanna added to herself. But what was the point of mentioning that to Mary?

"Wow," Mary said. She closed her eyes tightly. "Wow."

"I should call Pete and tell him that was a really rotten joke he pulled," Joanna said, more to herself than to Mary. "It's really the sickest thing I've ever heard. And I believed him."

"Of course. Me, too," Mary said, opening her eyes. "Why would he tell a stupid lie like that? It's so cruel. Pete's a pretty strange guy, but I never thought he was cruel."

"I never liked him," Joanna confessed. "I only put up with him because of Dex."

"And you really went out with Dex?"

"Yeah. Last night. I had to break a date with Shep to do it."

"Shep?"

"Yeah. You remember Shep. Blond hair. Really tall. Has a great smile. And a Jaguar." Joanna laughed.

Mary was thinking too hard to laugh. "Dex is really alive? How come he never called you?"

Joanna shrugged. "He was beat up too bad. He asked his aunt to try, but you know how flipped-out she is. She probably doesn't remember how to use a phone. Besides, I was in the hospital for over a month, too. Dex didn't know that."

"And you're going with Shep now?"

Joanna nodded.

"Well, are you going to tell him about Dex?"

"No. What for? I think I can string them both along for a while."

"Won't Shep get suspicious when — "

"Shep is so crazy about me, he'll put up with anything I do," Joanna said. She realized it sounded a bit boastful, but it was the truth.

Mary made a disapproving face.

"Don't look at me like that," Joanna said, only half teasing.

"You're awful," Mary muttered. She was only half teasing, too.

The two girls stared at each other without any

real warmth. Joanna realized that she couldn't be as close to Mary as she had been. They had obviously grown apart.

It's not my fault, Joanna told herself. Mary's just changed. What right does she have to sit on my couch like that and judge me?

"Well, how do you feel about it?" Mary asked, still struggling to understand. "Do you still like Dex?"

Joanna yawned. The conversation was becoming tiresome to her. She had enjoyed shocking Mary with the news and watching the stunned expression on her face. But now she wished Mary would go home.

"I don't really know if I like Dex or not," she said flatly. It was kind of fun trying to shock Mary with her coldness.

"Huh?"

"I don't think I like him anymore. I mean, as a boyfriend. I guess I just . . . feel guilty."

"Guilty? What do you mean? Because you thought he was dead, and he wasn't?" Mary pulled herself up straight and leaned forward, her hands on the knees of her faded jeans.

Joanna realized that Mary didn't really know the details of that night. She didn't know that Joanna hadn't stayed to help rescue Dex. That Joanna had driven off without seeing if Dex was dead or alive.

"I mean, I feel guilty because I'm the one who drove him to the Promontory that night. He wouldn't have fallen if he hadn't been showing off for me."

"Oh. I see." Mary seemed disappointed by Joanna's answer.

What does she want from me? Joanna asked herself.

She decided to change the subject. "Let's talk about *you* for a while, Mary. What's new in your life?"

Mary sighed and flopped back against the couch. "Nothing compared to you," she said. "I'm sorry, Joanna, but I just can't believe that Dex is alive. It's like — like a miracle! And you're being so calm about it."

So cold, she means, Joanna thought. "So are you going out with anyone?" she asked, running her hands back through her short blonde hair.

Mary shook her head. "No. My life is as boring as ever. I had my hair highlighted last week. See?" She lowered her head so Joanna could see the blonde streaks among the dark curls. Joanna hadn't noticed the change. "That's about the most interesting thing that's happened to me."

Joanna laughed, but quickly cut it off, realizing it wasn't an appropriate response. Mary was really feeling sorry for herself. Joanna just wasn't in the mood to cluck sympathetically and say, "There, there."

She was grateful when the ringing telephone interrupted their conversation.

"Hello. Dex? Hi." She gave Mary a meaningful look.

"Let me talk to him," Mary said. She leaped off the couch and grabbed the phone from Joanna's hand. "Dex? Is it really you? It's me, Mary."

Mary's dark eyes were wide with excitement. She was breathing heavily.

"I — I can't hear you very well," she said, frowning. "You sound so faint. Like you're very far away."

Dex said something. Mary obviously had to struggle to hear him. Joanna wished she'd give back the phone.

"Dex — I'm so happy!" Mary gushed. "I'm just so glad you're okay. Pete told us — well . . . never mind. I'm just so glad! I can't wait to see you sometime. Here. I'll give you back to Joanna."

She handed the phone to Joanna. "He sounds weird," she said. "Very far away."

"It's just a bad connection," Joanna said, raising the receiver to her ear. "Hi, Dex. What? You'll have to speak up. There's a lot of static or something."

He continued to talk quietly. It was as if he couldn't raise his voice. He asked her out for Friday night. "Yeah. I guess," she said, thinking of Shep. They chatted a few minutes more, but she really couldn't hear him. It wasn't just the background static. It was also the fact that his voice sounded weak and thin. Tired.

When she hung up, Mary was pulling on her blue down jacket. "Guess I'd better be going."

"I'm so glad you stopped by," Joanna said, putting on a sincere smile, then adding, "stranger."

Mary stopped at the door, and turned back with

a concerned look on her face. "You know, Dex's been through so much. You should be fair with him, don't you think? You really should tell him about Shep."

Joanna shrugged. "It's too interesting this way," she said, holding the door open for her friend. "I think I'll just play it out and see what happens."

Chapter 11

Joanna swung easily and the ball sailed over the net.

"Perfect," Rod, her instructor, said, flashing all 320 zillion perfect, sparkling white teeth. "Placement. Placement."

What does *that* mean? Joanna asked herself, shaking her head.

I'm going to have to say bye-bye to you, Rod, if you keep up that "placement" nonsense. She had the sneaking suspicion that she could probably beat him in a real game.

"Pick a spot, then place it there," he said, wiping his tanned forehead with a white handkerchief.

I haven't worked up a sweat. What's *his* problem? Joanna thought. "Hey, can I work on my backhand a while?" she called. She was paying for it. Why couldn't she work on what she *wanted* to work on?

"Okay, sure." He stuffed the handkerchief back into the pocket of his tennis shorts. "I'll hit a few to your left. Let's see your backhand. Try to smooth it out today, okay?"

Smooth it out?

What did *that* mean?

Was she losing her mind, or was Rod just an inane idiot?

This was definitely the last day for Mr. Smile Face. He hadn't given her a single pointer she could use. At sixty-five dollars an hour — plus tip — she expected a little more than "smooth it out."

He tapped the ball to the left. She jogged easily and smacked it back, using her backhand. She loved the *ping* the ball made on contact with the racquet. It was her favorite part of tennis. That little *ping*. So satisfying, somehow. She could hear dozens of *pings* all around her, as people played or took lessons on the vast indoor courts of the private tennis club.

Look at that fatso over there, wearing a parachute for tennis shorts, she thought, snickering at the woman chasing a ball across the next court. If I looked like that, I wouldn't play tennis. I'd shoot myself instead.

Another high bouncer from Rod. She reached back and returned it easily.

"Smooth. Very smooth. Nice follow-through," he called.

"Thanks a bunch."

"Time out. I've got to collect some more balls," he said, running across the court to get the ball basket.

Joanna sighed and lowered her racquet. She looked down the row of courts. A guy down at the end court looked a little like Shep. Not quite as good-looking.

She thought about Shep. He had come over Sunday night and they had gone for a long drive in his Jag. It was a clear, cold night. He had wanted to park up at the Promontory. She had hesitated at first and started to make an excuse. That was a place she never wanted to visit again.

But then she decided, what the heck.

It was just a place, after all. Just a rock cliff.

Just a makeout spot.

Just a place to get close to Shep.

She could probably push what had happened there out of her mind. It had been months ago, anyway.

What the heck.

And to her surprise, being back on that high cliff overlooking the town, being back on the very spot where the rock had crumbled and Dex had fallen, wasn't disturbing to her at all.

Dex had lived, after all.

Dex was okay.

Everyone was okay. So why should she feel funny about being back there?

It was so warm and cozy in the Jaguar with Shep. The windows all fogged over, and they were in their own world, their own little cocoon. Not on the Promontory. Not in the boring, little town of Middlewood. But locked away in their own tiny space capsule, just the two of them, so close, so close.

When that carful of teenagers drove up behind them with their brights on and the radio blaring, laughing and honking the horn, Joanna just wanted to kill them.

What right did they have to bring her back down to earth?

Sighing, she looked back to the tennis club waiting area. Shep was supposed to pick her up after her tennis lesson. Maybe he was early.

When she saw Dex back there behind the mesh wall, she uttered a low cry of surprise.

Dex?

What on earth is *he* doing here?

He was pacing back and forth behind the wire-mesh wall that separated the courts from the spectator area. Why was he walking so stiffly? His limp seemed to have gotten much more pronounced. Both legs appeared stiff now.

She raised her racquet over her head, trying to get his attention. Then she quickly lowered it.

His skin.

What on earth was wrong with his skin?

He looked positively green.

Maybe it's just the lights, Joanna thought. But there were other people watching the matches from behind the mesh wall, and their skin looked perfectly normal.

With that stiff-legged walk and the greenish skin, he looks just like Frankenstein, Joanna thought.

"Hey, Joanna — "

She realized Rod was calling to her. But she couldn't take her eyes off Dex. Was he sick or something?

"Hey, Joanna — " How long had Rod been calling? "Don't lose your concentration. Come on!"

"I'm ready," she said, turning back to face the net. But she couldn't get the sight of Dex out of her mind, the green face, the pained, straight-legged walk.

"Remember your follow-through," Rod said, lobbing a ball over the net.

She had to run for this one. "Darn!" She was off-stride and the ball hit the edge of the racquet and bounced into the next court. "Sorry."

Rod sent one into the back court. This time she got there in time and, using her backhand, sent it sailing over his head.

"Out!" he cried.

Oh, who cares? she thought.

She turned back. Dex was gone.

Maybe it wasn't Dex, she thought. Why would Dex be here, anyway? He doesn't know I have a tennis lesson this afternoon. And why would he be all the way over on this side of town on a school day?

"Time's up," Rod said, smiling, twirling his racquet in his hand. He walked around the net and joined her on her side of the court. "Good workout?"

"Yeah. Fine," Joanna said without enthusiasm. She turned around again, searched the waiting area. No Dex.

"I like your racquet," Rod said. "I was going to buy that one, but I couldn't afford it."

"Yeah. It's good," Joanna said, looking down at the racquet. "See you next time." She started toward the locker room.

"Okay. Good backhand," Rod called after her. "We'll work on it more next time."

She didn't reply, just kept jogging off the courts. Maybe he isn't such a bad instructor, she thought. I mean, a tennis instructor doesn't exactly have to be a genius.

She showered quickly and changed back into her school clothes, carefully folding her tennis shorts and T-shirt into the canvas bag she had brought. Shep was waiting at the door. "How'd you do?" he asked, giving her a warm smile and carrying the bag for her.

It was a cold, sunny day. She zipped up her down jacket. "Fine. The instructor is a real jerk. But I got in some practice on my backhand." She followed him across the street to his car.

"I can't wait to get you on the court at the country club this spring," Shep said, tossing her bag in the back, then sliding into the driver's seat. "I'll give your backhand a workout."

"Are you any good?" Joanna asked.

"No," he replied. "Not very. Just good enough to be all-state my sophomore year."

"Big deal," she said. She started to make a joke, but her breath caught in her throat.

Dex.

It really was Dex. He was standing close enough to be seen clearly now.

He was leaning against the brick wall in the half-empty parking lot beside the tennis club, his hands shoved into his jeans pockets. Even in the sunlight, his skin looked green.

Almost reptilian, Joanna thought queasily.

Dex had been looking at the ground, but now he looked up and directed his stare at them.

Does he see us? Joanna wondered.

He must. He's looking right at me.

Shep reached into his pocket for the car keys, dropped them on the floor.

Joanna stared across the street at Dex.

Dex's eyes caught hers. They suddenly seemed to glow ruby-red, like the red eyes in a bad flash photo. Glowing red eyes like a dog's eyes at night.

Chapter 12

"So tell me again," Shep said, standing very close to her at the entrance to their school, making Joanna back up till she bumped into the coat closet door. "Why can't you go out with me both Friday and Saturday night?"

She gave him a playful little shove to give herself breathing room. A couple of girls she knew giggled as they passed by in the fast-emptying corridor. "I have to get home," she said, trying to avoid the question. "Why are you pushing me into the coat room?"

He grinned and took a big step forward, forcing her further back. "Just answer the question."

"Really, Shep. You're being a pig."

"Oink. Oink."

Joanna hated it when he tried to be playful. It just wasn't the right style for him, she thought. She liked him much better when he was serious and quiet and played it straight.

"I already explained it to you," she said wearily, shoving him again, a little harder this time, then dashing out into the middle of the hall so he couldn't back her up again.

"Hello, Mr. Munroe," they both said, as their French teacher passed by, probably on his way to the teachers' lounge. The paunchy, middle-aged teacher nodded and smiled and kept walking.

"I have to study Friday night," Joanna lied. "I missed so much school because of the accident, Mom insists that I spend one weekend night studying. That's the whole reason, Shep. So stop being insulted."

Was he buying that story?

Yes. He seemed to be.

"Well, fine," he said, kicking at the wall plaster down by the linoleum floor with the toe of his brown Frye boot. "So why don't I come over Friday night, and we'll study together?"

"No way," she said, her grin mirroring the devilish grin on his face. "If you came over, we wouldn't study, and you know it."

"We could study," he said. "Really."

"No. Really," she insisted. "No way. At least not this weekend, okay?"

"Well. . . ."

She loved how disappointed he looked.

"I'm really serious," she said. "I want to graduate on time. I don't want to have to do an extra semester because of that stupid car accident. I *have* to catch up with the work. Understand?"

"Of course I do," he said, brightening a little. "Of course."

She looked both ways to make sure no one was

in the corridor, then kissed him quickly on the cheek. "Thanks," she whispered.

I love the fact that he's so gullible, so trusting, Joanna thought, pulling on her jacket. I'm also glad that Dex lives way on the other side of town. It makes it so much easier to keep Shep and Dex from knowing about each other.

She realized she'd have to break up with Dex soon. She didn't really care about him at all. But he was useful. It was kind of fun to keep Shep guessing, to make him uncomfortable. And the idea of having two boyfriends at once really appealed to Joanna. It was a lot like having two winter coats, she told herself. It was nice to be able to trade them off.

Friday night she drove across town to meet Dex. He slid into the car, holding something carefully out of sight. Suddenly he reached for her, and something silver glinted in his hand. "Dex!" gasped Joanne, jumping. The car swerved.

"Surprise," said Dex, pinning a corsage to the shoulder of her coat. "Oh," said Joanne. "How nice."

They went to a small dance club in his neighborhood. "Why is it called Barks?" Joanna asked, carefully locking the BMW.

"You'll see," Dex said, climbing stiffly out of the car.

Once inside, the reason for the club's name became obvious. There were giant dogs painted on all the walls. "This place is really tacky," Joanna said, shaking her head as she surveyed the awful dog paintings and then the small dance floor with its flashing strobe light.

"And what is that awful moose head doing on the wall?" she asked. "Mooses don't bark!"

"I knew you'd like this place," Dex said, laughing.

His cheeks seemed to sag when he laughed, Joanna noticed.

He looks so different, she thought.

"The sound system is good," he said, leading her onto the dance floor. "And it doesn't get too crowded."

There were six or seven couples on the floor, dancing to a slow, rhythmic Gloria Estefan record. Joanna looked across the dance floor at a particularly ugly wall painting of a German shepherd rearing up on its hind legs with its head tilted back in a howl.

"Come on, let's dance," she said, shouting over the music. "It's better than staring at these paintings."

He took her hand. Again, his hand was ice cold. He smiled at her, his old, familiar smile. But it seemed somehow lifeless, as if it were a real struggle for him to smile.

He seems so different, she thought, as they started to dance, bumping into other couples until they found a space for themselves on the small rectangular floor. He was always so lively, so theatrical, so excited about everything all the time.

Now he was dancing half-heartedly with her, almost moving in slow motion, hardly moving his feet at all.

The rhythm slowed. It became a tuneful song with a slow salsa beat.

He moved closer to her, holding her with his cold hands.

That smell again.

That musty odor.

The odor of decay.

"Dex — are you wearing cologne or something?"

"What?" He struggled to hear her over the deafening sound system.

"Are you wearing cologne?" she repeated, shouting right by his ear.

He made a face. "Of course not."

He laughed, an unpleasant laugh.

I've never heard that laugh before, Joanna thought, staring into his face.

He's like a stranger, she thought. He's just so different.

Then suddenly he stopped dancing and held his hand up to his mouth.

"Dex — what's the matter?"

He didn't reply. Maybe he didn't hear her over the blaring music.

He seemed to flicker on and off under the flashing strobe light. One second he was bright and colorful in the maroon shirt he wore over his faded jeans. The next second he was shrouded in darkness, a dark figure holding his mouth, walking stiffly off the dance floor.

"Dex?"

She followed him. "Hey — wait up. What's the matter?"

He bumped into a girl in a woolly white sweater

and short red skirt and just kept going. The girl turned around angrily, surprised by his rudeness.

Joanna wasn't sure whether Dex wanted her to follow him or not. It was as if he'd forgotten about her.

He stopped in front of a floor-to-ceiling mirror against the back wall and peered into it as he fiddled with something in his mouth.

Reluctantly she came up behind him. "Dex — what's the matter?"

"Oh nothing," he said, removing his fingers from his mouth. He turned to face her, looking embarrassed.

"Nothing?"

"Loose teeth. That's all."

She laughed, then realized it wasn't funny. "Aren't you a little old to still be losing your teeth?"

He stared at her coldly. "It's just loose," he said. "It'll be okay."

She suddenly realized that it must have been caused by his fall off the cliff. He'd never wanted to talk about the injuries he had gotten from the fall. And, of course, neither did she.

She assumed that he was beat up pretty badly, but that he was basically okay now. But the fact that he suddenly had a loose tooth made her wonder.

"Dex — your legs. You've been limping. Is it because — "

"They'll be okay," he said quickly, not letting her finish.

He suddenly looked very tired.

They stared at each other awkwardly. "My legs are all right," he said finally. "I guess I'm doing a lot better than I ever expected." He laughed for some reason, a bitter laugh.

"You've got to get some sun," she said, touching his shoulder. "You look positively green."

He shrugged. "Maybe I'll charter a private jet and fly to the Bahamas."

"Hey, Dex — that's not your kind of joke. That's *my* kind of joke."

"You and your mother take a winter vacation every year," he said thoughtfully, ignoring her remark. "Maybe you'd like to take me along this year." He reached up and played with his loose tooth, turning back to the mirror.

What a thought! Joanna nearly laughed out loud. She could just picture her mother's reaction if Joanna asked to bring Dex along to St. Croix.

What a thought!

She was sorry she had said anything about his looking so green. She was sorry she had brought up his appearance at all.

She was sorry she had gone out with him.

He used to be so exciting, she thought bitterly, watching him in the mirror as he fiddled with the loose tooth.

"Want to dance some more?" she asked, trying to get him away from the mirror and end their conversation at the same time. "That's why we came here, right?"

He turned around slowly. "Let's get a Coke or something first, okay?"

"Yeah. Sure. Why don't you do that? I'll wait over by that table for you."

He nodded agreement and, walking stiff-legged, practically dragging his left leg after him, he headed toward the bar on the other side of the dance floor.

He really does look green, she thought.

I think he was more badly injured in the fall than he's letting on to me.

I think his knees are really damaged.

And his face. . . .

Suddenly he stopped at the edge of the dance floor.

What's his problem? Joanna wondered, staring across the room at him. Why did he stop there?

"Oh good lord — no!"

She didn't realize she had screamed out loud.

Her breath caught in her throat. She suddenly felt sick.

She was sure she had just seen Dex reach up and pull a big chunk of skin off his face.

Chapter 13

"You look wonderful, Joanna. Stand up straight."

"Mom, I *am* standing up straight."

"Well, maybe it's the dress then."

"Mom — just stop it," Joanna cried. "You're just trying to make me feel self-conscious."

Mrs. Collier's mouth dropped open. "Me? Why on *earth* would I do that?"

Because you know you look like a frumpy little mouse in that dreadful evening dress you're wearing, and you want me to feel as bad as you look, Joanna thought. But she decided not to reply at all.

She walked side by side with her mother up the concrete steps of the old armory and into the brightly lit Main Hall. "Ugh! Those hideous portraits!" The walls were filled with gigantic, dark paintings of nineteenth-century town founders and other dignitaries.

"Joanna — please. Don't be so negative."

"What a place for a party," Joanna said, slipping

off her coat and handing it to the young man behind the coat check counter.

"You just have to be nice and charming for a few hours," her mother said, fussing with her enormous fur coat. She couldn't manage to unbutton the top button. Joanna finally did it for her. "That's all I'm asking. It isn't that hard, is it?"

Joanna looked glumly around the drafty old hall. "I'll do my best, Mom."

Every year the Ladies Club had their winter charity drive here in the armory. This year, her mother had volunteered to be chairwoman of the event.

Why not? Joanna had thought. She has nothing better to do.

But then Mrs. Collier roped Joanna into coming to the affair and helping serve at the punch table.

It was going to be an endless night, Joanna knew, even though it was supposed to end at eleven. She had done everything she could to get out of it, even faking the stomach flu. But her mother wasn't buying any excuse.

An entire Saturday night wasted, she moaned to herself, adjusting the straps of her green velvet dress and making her way over to the gigantic crystal punch bowl on the table by the wall.

I could be out with Shep. Or Dex.

She hadn't seen Dex for over a week, not since that unpleasant night at that dreadful dance club. He had called a couple of times during the week and had actually sounded very pleasant, a bit more like his old self.

She and Shep had gone to a movie the night before, a very funny Tom Hanks comedy. Shep had laughed like a lunatic. She had never seen him let go like that. He had a ridiculous laugh, she decided. She actually liked him a lot better when he was serious. But she was glad to see him loosen up like that. They had a really nice night.

And now here she was in the armory, of all places. Staring up at the dour, bewhiskered face of William Beathard Rogerson, 1849–1910. Why did he pose with his hand in his shirt like that? Joanna wondered. Did he have an itch?

The hall filled quickly, mostly with old and middle-aged people in furs and formal evening wear. Joanna sighed wistfully. Is this *me* in forty years? she asked herself.

No way, José.

She plastered a smile on her face and, thinking about Dex, wondering what he was doing tonight, she started to serve punch in the crystal cups stacked beside the punch bowl.

"Aren't you Dorothy's daughter?" asked a woman in a violet strapless gown.

"Yes, I am," Joanna said through her plastered-on smile. "Would you like some punch?"

The woman was wearing purple lipstick that matched her dress. Her face was heavily rouged. She had wavy, silver hair, very stylishly short. "Certainly, dear. Your mother tells me that you're dating Shephard Forrest."

Joanna, startled, spilled a little punch over the side of the cup. "Yes, I am." What was her mother doing — broadcasting it to the whole town?

"Well, I've known his family for years," the woman said, reaching out a violet-gloved hand to shake Joanna's free hand. "I'm Sylvia Norris."

"How do you do, Mrs. Norris." Joanna handed her the cup of punch.

"He's a fine young man, and you're a perfect couple."

"Thank you."

Luckily a white-haired gentleman in a satiny black tuxedo tapped Mrs. Norris on the shoulder. She turned to greet him and they strolled off together chattering enthusiastically.

She's actually very well preserved for her age, Joanna thought. I hope I can still wear purple lipstick when I'm a doddering old geezer.

And she's right about Shep and me. We *are* a perfect couple.

So why do I keep going out with Dex?

It's crazy.

It's just not like me.

She poured out two cups of punch and placed them in waiting hands.

It's obviously a character flaw, she told herself.

That's what it is. Dex is just a flaw in my character.

I'm going to say good-bye to him next weekend. Maybe I should just write him a letter.

No. He would never believe it in a letter. The next thing I'd know he'd be climbing into my bedroom in the middle of the night, saying let's go for a ride, or something crazy, pretending he never even received it.

No. I have to break up with him in person. Face to face.

She pictured Dex's face. He used to be so good-looking.

She pictured his green complexion.

Then she saw the chunk of skin drop off.

That didn't really happen — did it?

Of course, she had imagined it. But why was he so different? Why did he act and look so different?

It's all over between him and me, she thought, pouring more punch, smiling like a robot at two plump, well-dressed women who returned the robot-smile.

That's it. I'm breaking up with him next Saturday night.

I don't care if he did almost die that night on the Promontory. That was his own stupid idea. The whole thing was his fault. Going there in the first place. Showing off like a fool on the cliff edge. Falling.

I don't feel guilty anymore. I just don't.

I don't feel anything. And I can't keep seeing him week after week, pretending that I still care about him because of that one stupid night.

Having made the decision, she banished Dex from her mind. She concentrated on thinking about Shep for the rest of the evening. He was so good-looking. So nice. So right for her.

She decided she even liked his silly laugh.

At about eleven-fifteen, Joanna's mother, looking flushed and excited after the successful evening, told Joanna to take the car and go home. "I'm going out with the Waynes and the Sturbridges," she said, squeezing Joanna's arm. "They'll drop me home later. Thanks for helping out, dear."

"Thanks for forcing me," Joanna said, and laughed so her mother would know it was a joke.

A few minutes later, she had wrapped her coat around her and hurried down the armory stairs to the parking lot. She started to hand the parking ticket to the attendant, and then stopped in surprise.

"Pete!"

It took him a little while to recognize her, probably because he had never seen her so dressed up. "Joanna?"

"How are you? I mean, what are you doing here?" she sputtered. He looked exactly the same, same bad skin, same spiky hair.

"I'm . . . uh . . . parking cars," he said somewhat defensively. "The pay is really good. And I get overtime for Saturday nights."

"Hey, that's great," she said with false enthusiasm. They stared at each other. She still had the parking ticket in her hand.

"So how've you been? I haven't seen you in so long," she said, wishing she could get her car and get out of there without having to make small talk with Pete.

"Yeah. It's been a while," he said, slapping his hands together, probably to keep them warm. He frowned.

"Listen, I've been seeing Dex," Joanna said, fumbling for something to say. "I'm surprised he hasn't mentioned you. He — "

Pete's face filled with confusion. "You *what?*"

"I've been seeing Dex. Something's wrong with him, don't you think? He looks so — "

"Joanna — what are you talking about?" He shook his head, a strange grin on his face. "You're putting me on, right?"

"Putting you on?"

"Yeah. That's a real bad joke, you know." He kicked at the curb.

"Pete, I saw Dex last week and — "

"Have you totally flipped out? Dex is dead. He's dead, Joanna."

"Pete, stop. He isn't dead. Why do you keep telling me that? I saw him last week. I touched him. I danced with him. He's not dead. Why do you insist on — "

"I don't get what you're trying to pull. Are you crazy, or what?" Pete glared at her angrily, searching her eyes as if trying to discover whether or not she was serious. "I only know one thing, Joanna," he said in a low voice she had to struggle to hear. "Dex is dead."

"But — "

"I went to his funeral. I saw him in the box. He was dead. Stone-cold dead."

"Pete — "

"Maybe you *think* you see Dex," Pete continued heatedly. "Maybe you imagine it out of guilt or something. I mean, you *should* feel guilty, you know. You left him there to die."

"I did not! I — " Oh, what's the use of trying to explain? she thought.

"Maybe you need some kind of help or something. I'm no shrink. Like I said, I only know one thing. Dex is dead. He's dead, Joanna. I saw him die. And I saw him at his funeral. He's dead. Forever. And that's the truth."

Chapter 14

Joanna drove home slowly, carefully, her mind spinning from her conversation with Pete. She gripped the wheel to stop from shaking. Even though she turned the heater up full force, she couldn't get warm.

She was still trembling when she climbed out of the car and entered the house through the garage. She changed into warm, comfortable clothes, a heavy wool sweater and soft, blue running pants. Then she made herself a cup of tea. But she still couldn't get calm, couldn't stop hearing Pete's frightening words.

I believe Pete, she decided.

But how *could* she believe Pete?

What did that mean? If she believed Pete, that meant she'd been dating a *ghost*.

And Dex was no ghost. She was sure of that.

"It doesn't make sense!" she screamed aloud, immediately regretting it because she didn't want to wake the maid.

She carried her tea from the kitchen into the living room, and turned on all the lights. The tea warmed her a bit. The trembling stopped.

There has to be a logical explanation for this.

There's a logical explanation for everything, right?

She sat down on the big, overstuffed armchair, curled her feet under her, and placed the mug of tea in her lap.

Let's just think about this. . . .

But there was no way to think about it logically.

Dex was dead. Pete had told her that back in October in the hospital. Then in December, just a few weeks ago, Dex reappeared. He had been hurt, he said. And he looked and acted as if he'd been hurt. But he was alive. He was definitely alive.

Except for the fact that Pete insisted he was dead. And Pete had been at the funeral.

So that meant . . .

That meant . . .

What?

When Mrs. Collier returned home shortly after one, Joanna was still sitting in the armchair in the living room, still staring at the wallpaper, the now empty tea mug in her hand.

"Good heavens, Joanna. I thought you'd be asleep."

"Well, no, I — "

"What a night!" her mother gushed. "And what a smashing success. Do you know how much money we raised for the charity fund?"

"No." Joanna didn't pretend to be interested.

"It was a lot. Do you know what Mrs. Norris said to me? She said . . ."

Her mother rattled on. Joanna tuned her out. Her voice became a quiet hum in the background of Joanna's thoughts. She nodded occasionally and said "Uh-huh" to make her mother think she was listening. She could go on like this for half an hour without taking a breath, Joanna thought. Well, let her. This is the highlight of her year, after all. Poor thing.

Joanna thought about Dex, trying to arrange the puzzle pieces of this mystery together. But the pieces just wouldn't fit.

Dex, even though he seemed different, was definitely Dex.

She thought about how he had changed. The green tinge of his skin. The stiff, straight-legged walk, the musty, stale odor, the loose tooth, the skin that peeled off like . . . like a zombie.

Night of the Living Dead.

Yuck.

She scolded herself for getting carried away. Now think logically.

Zombies aren't logical.

"I don't think you've heard a word I said." Her mother stood up and headed to the front stairway.

"Of course I did. I heard every word," Joanna lied. "Listen, Mom, I've got to go out."

Mrs. Collier looked at her diamond-encrusted watch. "At this hour? Are you crazy?"

I *hope* I'm not crazy, Joanna thought.

"Uh . . . I'm just so wound up. From the party and all. You know. All the excitement. I can't seem to relax. I'm just going to take a short drive, just to get some fresh air."

"A drive? No, Joanna. Don't go driving late at night," her mother pleaded, wetting her finger and wiping something off the watch crystal. "Last time you went for a drive late at night, you — "

"I'll be careful, Mom." Thanks for pretending you care. "And I'll be back real soon. Promise."

Joanna hurried past her mother at the stairway, pulled her down coat from the coat closet, and headed to the garage. "Be careful!" her mother called after her. "I really don't approve of this!"

I don't approve, either, Joanna thought, backing the BMW down the drive. I'd much rather be tucked safely into my nice, warm bed.

But I've got to know the truth. I've got to know what's going on here.

As she turned onto Fairview, the street that would take her across town to Dex's house, a feeling of dread began to form in her stomach.

She suddenly had the feeling that knowing the truth might be even more frightening than *not* knowing.

Chapter 15

Dex's neighborhood was so much more squalid than she'd remembered. The houses were so claptrap, so small. They huddled together like little tents, one right after the other with hardly any front yard at all.

No wonder Dex always wants to meet on my side of town, Joanna thought, pushing the automatic lock button on the car door.

She slowed down as she neared his block. Across the narrow street, two scrawny dogs, looking like skeletons in her bright headlights, tipped over a garbage can. The lid clattered against the pavement and rolled into the center of the street. The mangy dogs began pulling at a large package wrapped in brown paper, each snarling at the other to let go.

Joanna swerved to miss the garbage can lid. The bony dogs were in her rearview mirror now. Even with the windows shut tight, she could hear their snarls and growls as they struggled to pull open the disgusting package.

Why do these people keep their garbage cans out on the street? Joanna wondered, holding her breath as if trying not to smell the garbage. And don't they ever feed their dogs?

Was that Dex's house up there? The small brick house with the newspaper stuffed in a broken window?

Yes, that was it. She'd been here once before.

Joanna slowed to a stop, but kept the car's engine running. The house was dark except for a single, low-watt bulb aglow over the narrow front stoop. An old tire sat in the middle of the small square patch that served as a front lawn. The yard seemed to be all weeds, weeds that hadn't been cut in months, bending first this way, then that in the shifting night wind.

Do I really know someone who lives *here*? Joanna thought.

How could I be going out with someone who has a tire in his front yard and newspaper stuffed in a window?

And what am I doing here now? The house is dark. He and his aunt are probably asleep.

This is crazy. Totally crazy.

She glanced down at the clock on the dashboard. One-thirty.

Dex usually stays up till all hours, she thought, staring up at the dark house. Maybe he isn't asleep. I drove all the way over here. I have to talk to him.

If I knock on the front door, his old aunt probably won't hear it anyway, and he'll come to the door.

Having made up her mind, she pulled the car to the curb. There was no driveway. She'd have to park on the street. She cut the headlights. The sudden darkness surprised her.

Can't they even afford streetlights? she asked herself.

Oh, well. When I break it off with Dex, I'll never have to come to this awful neighborhood again — unless it's part of some door-to-door charity drive.

Reluctantly she opened the car door and stepped out into the darkness. The wind was cold and strong. It seemed to push her away from the car. She pushed back, still clinging to the door handle.

This is a mistake. A stupid mistake.

No. I have to know the truth about Dex. I have to know — what?

If he's dead or alive?

The street was silent except for the wind. A narrow concrete walk, overgrown with weeds, led up to Dex's front stoop. Low shadows clustered against the front of the house like hunkering animals, caught in the dim yellow light of the bulb suspended over the door.

Joanna's footsteps sounded so loud as she walked quickly to the front door. Down the street another garbage can lid clattered against pavement, startling her. She gasped. The two dogs were barking in the distance, fighting over the garbage.

The smell of garbage floated around her, carried by the wind. She held her breath and stepped onto the front stoop.

For some reason she thought of the sweet smell, the smell Dex used to have whenever he held her close.

He didn't smell like that anymore. He smelled just like the garbage in the air.

She looked for a doorbell, but there wasn't one. The screen door, she saw, was torn at the top, one corner hanging down.

She took a deep breath and knocked gently on the door.

Dex — be awake.

Be awake, Dex.

Answer the door. And . . . be alive.

Tell me that Pete's a liar. Tell me that Pete has lost his mind. That Pete's been locked away in a looney bin. That he escaped and came to the armory just to scare me, just to make me as crazy as he is.

I always hated Pete.

With that stupid diamond stud in his ear and his hair standing straight up, moussed and sprayed so carefully. He's so disgusting and stupid.

I never understood why you liked him so much, Dex. I never understood what you two talked about, what you two were always laughing about.

Pete's such a stupid, typical jerk.

The wind gusted, pulling open the screen door.

Joanna, startled, uttered a low cry, and raised her hands to stop the door from swinging out and hitting her.

It was as if a ghost had pushed open the door, she thought.

Then she scolded herself for getting carried away.

Don't lose it totally, Joanna, she told herself. She knocked on the door, harder this time.

She listened. No sounds inside the house.

Maybe Dex isn't even home. It would be like him to be out till all hours.

Maybe I made this whole trip for nothing.

But what choice did I have? Pete got me so upset, I —

She knocked again, pounding the door with her fist.

Ouch. That hurt.

Still no sounds inside.

Okay. I tried.

She felt disappointed — and relieved.

She started to back off the stoop, still listening for signs of life inside — and bumped into someone.

Felt hot breath on the back of her neck.

Felt a hand on her shoulder.

Her scream seemed to be stifled by the wind. The sound caught in her throat.

She screamed again.

She couldn't help it.

And spun around to look into Dex's face.

"Dex?"

His dark eyes stared into hers, unblinking. His face revealed no emotion, no surprise at seeing her there, no excitement, no delight by her unexpected visit.

No emotion at all.

"Dex? Are you okay?"

He didn't reply.

"Sorry I screamed like that." She suddenly felt embarrassed. She had screamed like a little girl. That wasn't like her at all. "But you scared me. I wasn't expecting — "

He stepped into the dim light.

"Oh."

She couldn't hold in her cry of surprise.

He looked so terrible.

His skin was pea-soup green. His eyes, still not blinking, were red.

Joanna stared into his face, feeling the fear sweep through her, feeling the terror overwhelm her, freeze her there, hold her like the casts she had worn in the hospital.

His skin was peeling. His forehead was pocked and cratered, as if pieces of skin had fallen off.

His black hair, once so beautiful, so silky and beautiful, looked as if it had slipped to one side. The skin was missing from his scalp and a patch of gray showed through from underneath.

His *skull*?!

"Dex!" she cried, unable to stop staring even though she wanted to look away, to turn away — to run away. "Dex — are you all right?"

The smell. The horrible garbage smell.

It wasn't in the air.

It was coming from Dex.

It wasn't garbage, she thought, feeling sick. It was decay.

"Dex — why aren't you saying anything?"

He stared, unblinking.

"Dex — *please*! You're really *frightening* me!"

Finally he smiled.

The grin formed slowly, almost in slow motion.

I'm in a dream, Joanna suddenly thought. A slow motion dream.

Wake up, wake up, wake up.

As the grin formed, Dex's mouth opened.

"No!" Joanna screamed as she realized that his front teeth were gone.

He stepped forward, pressing her back against the torn screen door. He raised his hand. He was holding a corsage, a faded, tattered corsage, stabbed by a long, silver pin. Something dark dripped down the petals. He smelled like rotting meat. He grinned at her, his toothless grin.

"How about a kiss, Joanna?" he asked, his voice nothing but wind.

Chapter 16

"Joanna — what's wrong? Why aren't you getting dressed?"

"I — I can't." Joanna lifted her head from the pillow with a groan. "I think I'm sick."

Her mother, already dressed in a very stylish gray suit, shook her head, resting one hand on the doorway. "I knew you shouldn't have gone out driving around town at all hours," she said quietly.

She doesn't know how right she is, Joanna thought drily.

"Now you've caught that terrible flu that everyone is getting."

"No, I don't think so, Mom. I think I'm just exhausted. One day in bed, and I'll be okay."

I'll *never* be okay, she thought glumly.

I'll never get that hideous, decaying face out of my mind.

"Well, if you don't have the flu, I really think you should make an effort to come to church," her mother said, adjusting the string tie that hung down the front of her pleated silk blouse. "Everyone will be asking about you. I received such nice compliments about you at the fund-raiser last night."

Like I'm a prized pedigree dog, Joanna thought bitterly. My, what fine lines she has, Mrs. Collier. Could you put her through her paces for us? Make her heel or sit up and beg?

"I really can't go to church. I'm just going to sleep all day. I'm sorry."

Her mother looked more disappointed than concerned. "You know I won't be back till late tonight? There's a luncheon at the Wilkersons'. And then I have that cocktail party and dinner at the Smiths'."

Well, that's good news, Joanna thought. So go. Please — go, go, go, already.

"Is there anything I can get you, dear? You *do* look very washed out."

Thanks, Mom. Be sure to get that little dig in before you go.

"No, thanks. If there's anything I need, I'll call downstairs for Helen."

"Oh, no. I gave Helen the morning off. She went to visit her sister for a couple of hours. I guess I shouldn't have, but I didn't know. . . ."

That's even better, Joanna thought, burying her head deeper into the pillow. I'll have the whole house to myself. "Go, Mom. You'll be late for church. Please give my regrets to everyone." She rolled onto her side, her back to the door. Maybe her mother would take the hint and leave.

A few minutes later, she heard her mother going

down the carpeted stairs. A few minutes after that, she heard a car door slam and her mother's car start up and then drive off.

Now what?

Lie here all day and think about how my life has turned into a horror show?

Go back to sleep?

I can't sleep *forever* — can I?

What should I do? Pretend that last night didn't happen? Pretend that Dex hasn't become some kind of ghastly creature?

Joanna rolled over, unable to find a comfortable position. She suddenly realized that being all alone wasn't exactly the best idea in the world.

Because all alone there was nothing to take her mind off what had happened.

And she would lie there and see his distorted, leering face with its green, crumbling skin, its patches of protruding skull, its missing front teeth, again and again and again.

"No!"

She sat up and dropped her feet to the carpet.

She started to stand up, but her ankle still hurt from when she had fallen on it, running away from him. She stepped down on it gingerly, then applied more weight. It wasn't so bad, she decided.

Had she really run in terror from Dex? Someone she had once thought she cared about, someone she thought she knew better than she knew anyone else?

Yes. She had leaped off the stoop, dodging away

from his sickening embrace, and had run through the tall weeds of the front yard.

It didn't seem real now. It seemed like a scene she had seen in one of those disgusting horror movies on cable late at night.

But the faint, throbbing pain in her ankle told her it was real.

And the grinning green face she saw again and again in her mind told her it was real.

Last night, when she had run from him and tripped over the tire in the middle of his yard and fallen into the wet weeds, she looked back up to the stoop. Dex, she saw to her relief, wasn't coming after her. In fact, he hadn't moved. He stood stiff-legged, his back to the screen door, staring after her, the hideous grin frozen on his decaying face.

That smell.

Oh, that smell.

Her ankle throbbing with pain, Joanna had hobbled the rest of the way to the car. As soon as she got home, she tore off her clothes, tossed them down the laundry chute, then jumped into the shower.

She took the longest shower of her life, making the water hotter and hotter, trying to wash away that awful smell, trying to wash away the sight of Dex, trying to wash away her fear, her confusion.

But the shower wasn't the answer. Stepping out, she felt as chilled — and as scared — as she had standing on that dimly lit stoop, staring into his unblinking red eyes.

Now it was Sunday morning and the horror of

the scene clung to Joanna like a cold, damp fog.

I should've gone to church with my mother.

No. I've got to talk with someone.

I have to tell someone.

But who?

Mary.

Yes. Mary. Of course. Mary.

When it came right down to it, Mary was her only friend. The only one who knew Dex. Who knew all that happened. Or almost all.

Mary was the only one who would understand. The only one who would believe her.

If *anyone* would believe it.

Joanna wasn't sure she believed it herself.

She walked across the room, stretching, walking gingerly on her bad ankle, and picked up the cellular phone from its holder on her desk. She dialed Mary's number and carried the phone back to the bed, sitting on the edge, staring out the window at what appeared to be a gray, threatening morning.

Someone picked up on the sixth ring. "Hello, Mary?"

"Hi," said a sleep-clogged voice, sounding confused.

"Mary, it's me. Joanna. Did I wake you?"

"No, I had to get up to answer the phone."

"Funny line," Joanna said.

"I stole it from some TV show, I think. What time is it, anyway, Joanna? It's still the middle of the night, isn't it?"

"No. It's nearly nine. Can you come over?"

"What?"

"I really need to talk to you, Mary." Joanna was a little embarrassed by the neediness in her voice. She didn't like sounding like a helpless little girl, which she knew was how she sounded.

But for the first time in her life she really did feel helpless. For the first time in her life she really felt that things were out of control, that she was in a situation she couldn't handle.

It was a strange feeling. She hated it. She wished she sounded more together. She didn't like being so honest, so vulnerable, even with such a close friend. *Especially* with such a close friend.

"So can you come?"

"When? Now?" Mary still sounded half asleep.

"Yeah. Can you?"

"Can't we just talk over the phone, Joanna? I'd like to come, but I'm supposed to go over to my cousin's for lunch, and — "

"I really need you, Mary." This was so embarrassing! Why was Mary giving her a hard time, making it so much more difficult for her? "Something very scary happened last night."

"Okay. I'll be there. Give me an hour or so, okay?"

"Oh, good. Thanks."

"Joanna?"

"Yeah?"

"Are you okay?"

"I — I guess. Yeah. No. I don't know. I'm all mixed up." She could feel herself start to crumble.

She had the feeling she might cry, something she hadn't done in years and years.

So don't start now, she told herself, using all of her strength to hold herself together. Don't start now.

What is there to cry about, anyway?

Just because Dex has joined the Living Dead?

Just because your boyfriend smells like rotting meat and his face is falling off?

Well, he isn't your boyfriend. You don't even care about him. And that's the truth.

You don't care if he lives or . . .

. . . dies?

"See you soon," she said into the phone, then walked over to the desk to put it back.

The sound at the window made her nearly jump out of her skin.

That scrabbling sound.

Someone tapping at the window.

Dex!

No. No — please!

She grabbed the top of the desk for support. Her knees felt weak, about to collapse. The room began to spin.

She was afraid to turn around.

Why was he climbing into her window in daylight? What was he doing here?

"Go away! Please — go away!" she screamed.

Chapter 17

The tapping again.

It wasn't Dex.

Too light to be Dex. Dex would be pounding on the glass, demanding that she open up.

She saw his green face in her mind, that gruesome smile, the dark pit that was his mouth, the glowing red eyes.

Still holding onto the desk, she turned to face the window. A pigeon stood on the outer windowsill. It pecked at the glass. *Tap tap tap.*

Joanna, get a hold of yourself, she warned herself. You can't let yourself go mental because a stupid pigeon taps on the window.

Another shower maybe?

The hot water might make her feel better, help to cleanse away the memories, the pictures, the horrors of the night before that stuck to her skin like stale perspiration.

She took a long, hot shower and shampooed her hair.

Drying herself off, she felt refreshed. A little better.

She got dressed quickly, pulling on a pair of soft, green corduroy slacks and a long-sleeved yellow cotton T-shirt. Then she went downstairs and fixed a breakfast of orange juice, cornflakes, and buttered toast.

She was dropping the breakfast dishes into the dishwasher when Mary's little Toyota pulled into the drive. Joanna dried her hands hurriedly on a dish towel and ran through the front hall to let her friend in.

"Coffee!" Mary roared as soon as Joanna pulled open the door. "Make us coffee! I need a jump start this morning."

"You do look a little out of it," Joanna said, examining Mary's pale face. "Late night last night?"

"No. Nothing special," Mary sighed. She followed Joanna into the kitchen. "Are you feeling better? You sounded so awful over the phone."

"I guess," Joanna said, filling the Krups coffee maker with water.

"You — you sounded so scared, Joanna. Not like yourself at all." Mary pulled off her down vest and tossed it over one of the tall kitchen stools. She climbed up onto the stool next to it and leaned on the white Formica counter, watching Joanna measure out the coffee.

"I — I really don't know where to begin," Joanna said, hating this feeling of vulnerability that was so new to her, but eager to share everything with Mary. "It's about Dex."

"Are you still going out with him?" Mary stifled a yawn with her hand.

Joanna pushed the button on the coffee machine. "Yeah, I guess. I — "

"Him and that other guy. Shep."

"Yeah. Well, I'm going to break up with Dex. For good," Joanna said uncomfortably, sensing Mary's disapproval.

This wasn't the way Joanna wanted this to go. She wanted sympathy from Mary — not disapproval. She wanted some understanding. An explanation, maybe.

An explanation?

Who was she trying to kid?

How could there be an explanation?

"Listen, Mary, something weird is happening to Dex."

"Huh?" That seemed to wake Mary up. She sat up straight on the backless kitchen stool.

"I mean, I think Dex is sick or something."

"Oh. You mean like the flu?"

"No. Not like the flu. Some other kind of disease. Something really serious, I think."

"Joanna — how do you know? Did he tell you he's sick?"

"No. He didn't tell me. But — wait. Let me pour the coffee. Then I'll tell you everything." She reached in the cupboard for the coffee mugs. "It was really nice of you to drive all the way over here so fast. Sorry I woke you."

"That's okay," Mary said. "You sounded so . . . troubled."

Joanna poured the coffee. They added milk and sugar and carried the mugs into the den. Then, sitting beside Mary on the long, red leather couch, Joanna told her the whole story, starting with the date at the dance club, climaxing with the scene of horror on Dex's stoop the night before.

Mary listened in silence, taking long sips of her coffee. Her face remained expressionless. Joanna couldn't tell what she was thinking.

"And that's it," Joanna said. "Up to now, anyway. I just don't know what to think, Mary."

"I don't, either. I really don't," Mary said, staring down at her coffee mug thoughtfully. "You're right, I guess. Dex must have some kind of weird disease. Something that's making his body fall apart."

"But what could it be?" Joanna asked. "I've never seen anyone get a disease like that — not even on *General Hospital*."

It was meant as a joke, but Mary didn't laugh. She seemed to be thinking very hard about something. "The puzzling part is Pete," she said finally. "Pete says that Dex is dead."

"Yeah. When I told him Dex wasn't dead, he looked at me like I had totally lost it," Joanna said. "Pete says he went to his funeral. He still can't talk about the whole thing. He had tears in his eyes last night, Mary."

"This is all so weird," Mary said. "But there's a logical explanation for this. I know we'll figure it out if we keep at it." She held up her coffee mug. "Can I have another cup?"

"Sure. Help yourself," Joanna said. "I want to — "

The phone rang, interrupting her.

She reached over the hump of the couch arm and picked up the phone off the side table. "Hello?"

"Hello, Joanna. Man, I'm glad you're there." The boy's voice was frightened, breathless.

"Who is this?" Joanna cried.

"It's Pete. Joanna — you've got to listen to me."

"What? What's the matter, Pete? You sound so weird."

"Please — don't talk. Just listen. There isn't much time."

"Pete, please — what on earth are you talking about?" A feeling of dread was forming in her chest. She gripped the phone tightly, so tightly her hand started to ache.

"Joanna, I saw him, too."

"Dex?"

"Yes. I saw him." Pete's voice was trembling. It was hard to understand him.

"Pete, try to calm down," Joanna said. "I *told* you I've been seeing Dex. He — "

"Joanna — *please!*" He was shouting now. "You don't understand. Dex is back. Back from the dead!"

"What?!"

"It's true, Joanna. I'm so sorry, but it's true."

"Pete — you're not making any sense. Where are you?"

"Never mind. Just listen to me. He was dead. Dex was really dead. I did go to his funeral. I saw his corpse. But he's come back from the grave, Joanna. He told me."

"He told you?"

"He told me. Oh, lord, he looks so horrible. He's

124

falling apart. I mean, really. Pieces of him are just falling off. And he smells so bad. He's rotting. Just rotting."

Joanna smelled that ghastly odor once again. Two long showers and she couldn't get rid of that odor. She pictured Dex's grinning, toothless face.

"Pete, listen — "

"*You* listen. Just listen," Pete continued, sounding even more frantic. Joanna could hear traffic noise in the background, a horn honking. Pete was obviously outside in a phone booth somewhere.

"He's come back to punish you, Joanna," he said, his voice trembling. "He's come back from the grave because he wants to pay you back — pay you back for letting him die."

"But I — "

"He knows, Joanna. He knows you ran away and left him. And he's come back to get revenge."

"Pete, stop — I — " Joanna's words choked in her throat. She suddenly felt terribly sick.

"You've got to run!" Pete cried, shouting over a passing bus. "You've got to get out of there. Dex is on his way to your house — now! He's going to kill you, Joanna. He told me. He came back to kill you. He'll be there any moment!"

"Pete — "

She could hear the traffic in the background, but Pete didn't answer.

"Pete?"

The line went dead. The hum of the dial tone returned.

"What was *that* all about?" Mary asked, returning from the kitchen with a fresh cup of coffee.

"Dex. He — "

Joanna stopped and listened.

Yes. She had heard correctly.

There was a loud pounding on the front door.

Chapter 18

"Why do you look so frightened?" Mary asked, putting her coffee cup down on the counter. "It's only someone at the front door."

The knocking repeated, a little louder, a little longer. The doorbell chimed.

"Are you okay?" Mary asked. "I'll get the door."

"No — Mary — " Joanna tried to stop her, but the words caught in her throat. Her heart thudding, she followed Mary into the front hall. "No! Don't!"

But she was too late.

Mary had already opened the door.

Shep walked in, shivering from the cold under his oversized wool overcoat. "Hi, I'm Shep," he said, reaching out to shake Mary's hand.

Mary introduced herself. Shep looked beyond her to Joanna, who was leaning against the wall, breathing a sigh of relief.

"Thank goodness. It's only you," Joanna said breathlessly.

Shep laughed. "What's that supposed to mean? Is that a compliment?"

"We have to go," Joanna said, unable to keep the fear out of her voice.

"Where are you going?" Shep asked, unbuttoning the heavy coat. "I just got here."

"Joanna — what's wrong?" Mary asked. "You look so frightened. Was it that call?"

"Yes. I — " She looked at Shep. He didn't know anything about Dex. He only knew that she had broken up with someone after her car accident so that she could go with him.

How could she begin to tell him what was happening? Especially since she could barely believe it herself.

"You'll think I'm crazy," she said, her heart still pounding in her chest.

"I already think you're crazy," Shep joked, flashing her a warm, reassuring smile. "Hey — do I smell coffee?"

"Yes. I just made a fresh pot," Mary said.

"I'd kill for a cup," Shep said, rubbing his hands together to warm them. "It's freezing out there."

"We don't have time for coffee," Joanna said impatiently. "Dex — he's on his way here."

Shep's handsome face filled with confusion. "Dex?"

"He's coming here?" Mary asked, startled.

"That was Pete on the phone. He — he saw Dex. He knows Dex is back. He — "

"Who's Dex?" Shep asked, draping his coat over

the banister. "What do you mean he's back?"

"It's too long a story," Joanna said, closing her eyes, wishing she could just disappear. "And you wouldn't believe it, anyway."

"Try me," Shep said, walking past her into the kitchen. He sniffed the warm aroma from the coffee maker. "Where are the coffee mugs?"

"Shep — you're not taking me seriously!" Joanna screamed.

Mary and Shep both stared at her, alarmed.

"Joanna — " Mary started.

"He's coming to kill me!" Joanna screamed. "Pete said Dex is coming to kill me!" She knew she sounded hysterical, but she didn't care. Somehow she had to get it across to her two friends that this was an urgent situation, that all three of them were in danger.

"But, Joanna, why?" Mary asked, walking over and putting a hand gently on Joanna's shoulder. "Try to calm down. What did Pete say to make you so — so frightened?"

Joanna pulled angrily away from Mary. "Dex has come back from the grave!" she screamed, feeling her face grow hot. "He told Pete. He's come back from the grave — to kill me!"

Shep stepped back from the coffee maker. He looked over to Mary, as if to say, What's wrong with Joanna?

"I'm not crazy!" Joanna shrieked. "Dex was dead. Pete went to his funeral. But now he's back. Do you understand? He's back! He came back to kill me!"

"Maybe we should get a doctor," Shep said, talking to Mary. "Is Joanna's mother home? Is anyone else in the house?"

"No. No one's home," Mary said. She turned to Joanna. "Listen, why don't we all go over to my house?"

"You don't believe me — do you?" Joanna cried, squeezing her hands into tight fists, so tight her nails dug into her skin.

"We believe you're very upset about something," Shep said softly, slowly. "Why don't we go into the den and sit down? Maybe if we discussed it — "

"There's nothing to discuss," Joanna replied angrily. "Dex is dead. He's on his way. He's going to kill me. He could kill us all."

"Okay. Then let's get out of here," Mary said, looking at Shep. "Get your coat, Joanna. We'll go to my house. Dex will never find you there."

"I don't understand," Shep said. "Is Dex the guy you used to date?"

"Yes," Mary said, pushing Shep toward the front hall. "Joanna can explain it all in the car."

"Explain about a guy who's come back from the grave?"

"You don't believe me! Well, I don't care if you believe me or not!" Joanna cried. "I'm getting out of here." She started toward the front hall, but Shep grabbed her arm and pulled her back.

"I believe you," he said. But he didn't sound very convincing. "But I think we should sit down for a moment, have a cup of coffee, and discuss — "

Before he could finish his sentence, the front door burst open, banging loudly against the wall, making all three of them jump and cry out.

"Shep — you didn't close the door?" Joanna cried.

"I — I thought the maid would," Shep said, looking frightened.

The storm door slammed.

They heard footsteps in the hall.

Dex, walking fast, his eyes wide, stepped stiff-legged into the kitchen.

"Dex — stop!" Pete came running in behind him, his cheeks bright red, breathing hard, his face filled with terror. "Stop! Can you hear me?"

All three of them gasped as Dex staggered under the bright kitchen lights. It was hard to believe that it was Dex. He looked like a creature from a horror movie. A large patch of gray skull protruded through a square bald spot in his hair. All of his teeth were gone. Purple liquid dripped from his eyes. His skin was as green as grass and seemed to be peeling off his cheeks and forehead.

He glared at Joanna, his mouth opened wide in a toothless grin. He staggered forward. It seemed to take every ounce of his strength for him to move. One arm hung limp at his side.

"Dex — stop!" Pete screamed. He turned to Joanna. "I tried to stop him. Really — I tried. But he won't listen to me. I don't think he hears me!"

"Dex — " Joanna tried to cry out to him, but her words choked in her throat. She suddenly felt as if she couldn't breathe, couldn't move.

I'm paralyzed with fear, she thought. So this is what it feels like.

He's going to kill me. I know he's going to kill me. And I'm just going to stand here and let him.

"Joanna, I'm back," Dex said suddenly. His voice could barely be heard. It was a rasping whisper, like wind blowing through the crack in a window.

"Joanna, I'm back. I came back from the grave."

"No! Dex — no!" Joanna managed to find her voice and scream.

"You shouldn't have left me to die, Joanna."

Dex raised his good arm high in front of him. In his hand he held a large, black-handled kitchen knife.

Chapter 19

"Stop him! We've got to stop him!" Pete cried.

He leaped at Dex, reaching for Dex's broad shoulders.

With startling quickness, Dex spun away from Pete. Pete slammed hard into the kitchen counter, looking dazed.

Dex, his dripping eyes staring into Joanna's, staggered forward. "I'm back," he said in his raspy whisper. "Joanna, I'm back."

With one quick chop of his open hand, Shep knocked the big knife from Dex's hand.

"Hey!" Dex cried out in surprise.

He dived for the knife but Joanna got there first.

She didn't even think about it. She grabbed up the knife by the black handle, leaped at Dex, and plunged the blade deep into Dex's chest.

Bright red blood spurted out from Dex's sweat-shirt.

His eyes opened wide, first with surprise, then

with terror. He stared at the knife. Then his eyes slowly went up to Joanna.

"No. This isn't right," he said, grimacing in pain.

He slumped to the linoleum and lay in a puddle of his own bright blood.

"No!" Pete screamed, grabbing Joanna and pulling her back, pulling her hard, angrily.

Joanna stared down at Dex's unmoving body. She felt numb. No feeling at all. Then bewilderment as Pete jerked her away.

Mary stood back by the sink, her hands up to her face. Shep leaned against the kitchen counter, looking very frightened and confused.

"What have you done?" Pete cried. "You killed him, Joanna. You killed him!"

"I — what?"

What was Pete saying?

What did he mean?

How could she have killed someone who was already dead?

Pete dropped down to the floor and bent over the body. He put a hand on Dex's neck. Then he placed the back of his hand under Dex's nose.

"Dead," he said, after a long wait. "He's dead."

"Now, wait a minute — " Joanna started. "What's going on here? What do you mean — ?"

"It was just a joke," Pete said softly, looking up at her, still on his knees on the bloodstained floor.

"What?" Shep came up behind Joanna and put his hands on her shoulders.

Joanna leaned back against him, grateful for his support, for his caring.

"Pete — what are you saying?" Mary asked. She had tears running down her cheeks. She was shaking all over. Her eyes kept going down to the still body on the floor.

"It was just a joke," Pete repeated. He rubbed his fingers over Dex's face and held them up to Joanna. His fingers were green. "Just stage makeup," he said.

Joanna swallowed hard. "You mean — ?"

"It was all stage makeup. The green color, the blacked-out teeth, the stuff dripping from his eyes. Him staggering around like Frankenstein's monster. It was all a gag, Joanna."

"Pete — you said you went to his funeral," Joanna said, beginning to realize what really had happened, the horror of what she had just done starting to sink in.

"Just a joke," Pete repeated sadly. "Dex and I cooked it up. To pay you back. To teach you a little lesson. That's all."

"But — "

"But now you've killed him," Pete said, his expression hardening. "Now you've really killed him."

Chapter 20

"Call an ambulance," Shep said, still holding on tightly, comfortingly to Joanna's shoulders. "Maybe he — "

"He's dead," Pete said, sweeping a large hand back nervously through his spiky, blond hair. "It's too late for an ambulance."

"I — I'm going to be sick," Mary said, looking ashen. She ran out of the kitchen, holding her hand over her mouth.

"How could you just kill him like that?" Pete asked Joanna, sounding more accusing than questioning.

"But, Pete — " Joanna didn't know what to say.

"You saw the way Dex came at her with the knife," Shep said, coming to her defense. "She had to react — didn't she? She had to protect herself."

"That's right. It was self-defense," Joanna agreed quickly. Self-defense. Of course.

Self-defense.

Shep, you're a genius.

"I had to protect myself," she repeated. "He came at me . . . and I just reacted." She was starting to breathe normally, starting to feel a little more like herself.

"What a horrible joke," Shep said, looking down at Dex's body. "You know, Pete, you're as much to blame as Joanna."

"I didn't stab him with a knife," Pete said.

"But if you hadn't cooked up this whole thing, if the two of you hadn't planned for Dex to — to — "

"Why, Pete?" Joanna interrupted. "Why pull such a stupid joke?"

"I knew it was stupid," Pete said, sighing. He dropped onto one of the kitchen stools, his shoulders drooping, all of the energy seeming to drain from his body. "I told Dex it was really dumb. But it was that day in the hospital, Joanna. That day I came to tell you that Dex was dead. That's as far as we were going to take the joke. But then — "

"But then what?" Joanna demanded, anger replacing her fear.

"Then when you didn't even cry, when you didn't even look that upset, Dex decided to take the joke as far as he could."

"And you and he did the whole thing just to frighten me?" Joanna asked.

"You deserved it — the way you treated Dex. You used him." Pete's voice softened. "Dex loved acting. And he loved makeup. You should've seen him after he got out of the hospital. He was so turned on by the whole idea. He spent days just getting the right smell to make him smell like he was decaying."

"Ugh." Joanna made a face, remembering that sour smell.

"It was all just a stupid joke that went too far," Pete said sadly, shaking his head. "You're right, Joanna. I'm as much at fault as you are."

"But what are we going to *do*?" Joanna demanded. "We can't just stand around here talking about it."

"We've got to call the police," Shep said, squeezing Joanna's shoulder.

She stepped away from him and started to pace back and forth. "We can't," she said, thinking hard. "Do you really think the police would believe this story? They'll just think that I killed him."

"But we're all witnesses. We saw what happened," Shep said.

"They won't believe any of us. They'll think we made up the story after Dex was killed," Joanna said.

Mary came back into the kitchen, still looking pale and shaky. "Joanna's right," she said, sitting down on one of the tall stools, holding on to the counter edge. "The police will never believe the true story. We've got to get rid of the body. Drag it out to the woods or something."

"Yes!" Joanna cried. She felt like hugging Mary. What an excellent idea! "Mary's right. There's nothing we can do for Dex now. Why should our lives all be ruined because of a stupid joke?"

Joanna realized she was breathing normally again. Her heart had gone back to its normal beat. She was starting to feel a lot stronger, a lot more in control.

"Yes, we have to get rid of the body," she repeated.

Shep shook his head. "It's no good," he said. "They'll catch us. Dex's family will know where he was going. They'll — "

"He doesn't have a family," Joanna interrupted. "He only has an old aunt who never knows where he goes. There's no way the police can trace this to us. No way. Especially if we take the body some place far away."

"No. I'm sorry. We have to tell the police. They'll believe the truth if we all just — "

Joanna glared angrily at Shep. "Why are you being such a wimp?" she cried. "You know, *your* life will be ruined by this, too. Are you really willing to give up your entire future because of Dex's stupid joke?"

Shep didn't answer. He walked over to the back door and stared out the window at the long, sweeping backyard.

"Yeah. I guess you're right," Pete said reluctantly, staring hard at Joanna. "There's nothing we can do for Dex now."

Mary turned her head away. Her shoulders were shaking.

"Don't cry, Mary," Joanna said. "We'll be okay —
once we get rid of the body." She wanted to go over
and comfort her friend. But she was afraid she
might start crying, too.

She didn't want to cry. She wanted to keep herself in control.

She wanted to keep thinking clearly, to stay
alert.

They were going to get out of this mess.

She wasn't going to let Dex ruin her life.

She never should have gotten involved with him
in the first place.

Mary suddenly turned back. "Pete and I will take
the body," she said resolutely. She dabbed at her
wet cheeks with a tissue.

"I'm not helping," Shep said, still staring out into
the backyard. "I won't stop you from doing it. But
I don't think it's right. I won't help."

"That's okay," Pete said quickly, standing up and
walking over to Dex's body. "Mary and I can get
Dex into her trunk. We'll take him to the woods
near his house."

"Shep and I will clean up," Joanna said, looking
at Shep.

"Yeah. Okay," he agreed, looking very unhappy.

Joanna heard the front door open and close.

Everyone froze.

"Who's that?"

"Your mom?"

"It's Helen," she told them. "The maid. Mom

gave her the morning off. But now she's back. Quick — " She pointed to the body. "Out the back door. Hurry!"

Looking frightened, Pete bent down and grabbed Dex under the shoulders. He started to pull. The body slid across the linoleum. "I think I can drag him," he told Mary. "Just get the door, okay?"

Mary hurried to the kitchen door and held it open for Pete.

"I'll call you later," Joanna said, listening to the maid's footsteps in the hall. "Good luck. I know we're doing the right thing."

Just get it out of the house, she thought.

She breathed a sigh of relief as Pete and Mary disappeared out the door, and the door slammed behind them.

Shep stood, leaning against the kitchen counter, looking very upset.

Helen's footsteps grew louder, then fainter.

She's going to her room to change, Joanna thought. Then she'll come into the kitchen.

She looked down at the puddle of dark blood on the floor.

"Well, they're gone," Shep said quietly. "I hope the neighbors won't see what they're dragging to the car."

"The neighbors can't see. Their houses are too far away," Joanna said, thinking hard. "Besides, there're all the trees."

She went to the drawer and pulled out a small

steak knife. Then she advanced quickly on Shep.

Shep looked up, surprised.

He saw the knife in her hand and, as she strode toward him, a purposeful look on her face, his expression turned to fear.

"Joanna — stop!" Shep cried. "What are you going to do with that?"

Chapter 21

Joanna grabbed Shep's left hand, turned it up, and sliced a long line across the palm with the knife.

Bright red blood seeped to the surface along the line of the cut, then quickly dripped to the floor.

"Joanna — ?"

Shep pulled his hand out of her grip, staring at the flowing blood, then at her, horrified.

"Helen!" Joanna shouted, tossing the knife onto the counter. "Helen!"

"Yes?" the maid called from down the hall.

"Could you come here, please?" Joanna called. "My friend has cut himself. I'm afraid there's a lot of blood on the floor. Could you come clean it up?"

Helen came rushing in, buttoning the sleeves of her white uniform. She was a short, chubby woman, with a round face that frowned in surprise as she saw the large puddle of blood on the floor. She looked over to Shep, who was busily wrapping his bleeding hand in paper towels.

"You should go to a doctor. You've lost a lot of

blood," Helen said, hurrying to the mop closet.

"He'll be okay," Joanna said.

Shep glared at her. He strode past her and into the front hall, heading to the door, holding the towels tightly around his cut hand.

Joanna followed him to the door. "I'm sorry, Shep," she said, whispering so that Helen wouldn't hear. "I had to do something. I didn't want to hurt you. But it was the first thing I — "

"You're cold, Joanna," he said, his hand on the door handle. "You're not really human. I had no idea how cold you were."

He was out the door before she could reply.

She watched him get into his car, back down the drive, and roar away. Then she closed the front door, locked it, and hurried up the stairs to her room.

She sat down on the edge of the still unmade bed.

"I'm going to be okay," she said aloud.

I'm going to be okay.

This is all going to work out fine.

I'm going to be okay.

She repeated the word *okay* over and over until it didn't seem like a real word anymore.

Then she realized that she was trembling all over.

She saw Shep in school on Monday. His hand was bandaged. He walked right past, pretending he didn't see her.

She sighed, feeling sorry for herself.

Shep, I care about you, she thought.

We've got to get back together. We're so right for each other.

She thought of chasing after him, running up behind him, throwing her arms around his broad shoulders. I'll beg him to forgive me, she thought. I'll beg him. I'll apologize a thousand times, throw myself on his mercy.

She stood in the middle of the hall, watching the back of him until he turned a corner and disappeared.

She tried to concentrate on midterm exams, but it was nearly impossible.

Her mind kept wandering back to all that had happened.

Dex's face, his toothless, grinning, green face haunted her thoughts.

She couldn't study. She couldn't think straight.

Monday night she called Mary to find out what had happened with Dex's body. But Mary couldn't talk. Her parents were in the room.

Tuesday she drifted through two exams, struggling to concentrate. Afterwards, she was sure she messed up on both of them.

Wednesday and Thursday went by in a blur of studying and more exams. Thursday night she picked up the phone to call Shep.

But she put it back down.

What if he refused to talk to her? What if he refused to come to the phone?

After school on Friday, she thought of skipping her tennis lesson. But at the last minute, she decided to go ahead with it. A little exercise might do her good.

Maybe it would take her mind off Dex, off the blood-smeared kitchen floor, his body lying so still on the floor. Maybe it would take her mind off losing Shep.

I'll work up a good, honest sweat, she thought.

I've got to get my blood flowing again.

Blood.

She had to stop thinking about blood.

"I'm going to be okay," she said, juggling her bookbag and tennis racquet as she passed through the glass doors of the tennis club.

I'm going to be okay. It wasn't my fault. No one will ever know.

Gary was her new instructor. He looked more like a wrestler than a tennis player, with his long, curly black hair, his biceps bulging out of his T-shirt, his broad chest. "Let's warm up a little first," he said, dragging a basket of yellow tennis balls onto the court.

The club was crowded, mostly with kids having their after-school lessons. Voices echoed off the high rafters. Joanna had never noticed how noisy the club was before.

Gary hit some easy ones over the net. Joanna stood in place, hitting them back with her forehand, swinging casually, the racquet light in her hand.

After hitting five or six balls, something made her turn around. She looked back to the spectators' area behind the mesh screen.

That's where Dex had stood, she remembered.

That's where he had stood, looking so green, so weird.

She remembered seeing him in the parking lot afterwards, his eyes glowing red. It was so frightening.

And all so phony.

Just a fake.

She couldn't believe Dex had played such an elaborate prank. All that makeup. All that time and work.

And where had it gotten him?

Into a shallow grave in the woods.

Or maybe no grave at all. Maybe he had just been tossed into some thick bushes or high weeds.

She should've tried Mary again. Or called Pete. She should've found out what had happened with the body.

But somehow it was just as well not knowing.

The body was gone. Dex was gone.

So why was she looking for him now?

"Joanna? Joanna?"

She realized that Gary had been calling to her for some time.

"Are you looking for someone?" he asked.

"No," she said, still distracted.

"Shall we play a game?" He twirled his racquet in his hand.

"No," she said. "I — I've got to go."

She couldn't concentrate. She didn't want to be there.

I can't play on this court, she thought. I keep having the feeling that Dex is standing back there, watching me, staring at me with those frightening red eyes.

"Joanna — ?" Gary called after her.

But she turned and ran to the locker room without looking back.

I've got to get out of here. Out. Out. Out.

I've got to stop thinking about Dex.

What's wrong with me, anyway? I didn't even care that much about Dex. Why can't I get him out of my mind now?

She answered her own question: because you killed him.

She changed quickly into her street clothes. She drove around aimlessly for nearly an hour before heading home.

Maybe if I talk to Mary and hear the end of the story, I'll be able to put it out of my mind, she thought.

The end of the story. Would there *be* an end to the story?

She had read the morning newspaper every day, grabbing it up as soon as she came downstairs, much to her mother's surprise. But there had been no story about anyone finding Dex's body in the woods. She watched the local TV news at six each evening. They didn't have the story, either.

So, maybe the story had already ended.

She just had to talk to Mary. See how Mary was doing. Maybe Mary was doing better than Joanna. Maybe she wasn't thinking about Dex, thinking about the murder every minute of the day.

Maybe Mary can help me get it out of my mind.

But when Joanna got home, her mother was there. She had to talk to her mother, pretend to have a conversation. She talked about her midterms, how hard they were. She talked about her tennis lesson, making up some funny stories about the new instructor who looked like a wrestler.

That made her mother laugh.

Joanna, you're such a good liar, she told herself. If only you could lie to *yourself*.

She wanted to go upstairs and call Mary, but Mrs. Collier stopped her from leaving the room. "Helen's just about to serve dinner," she said. "She's made your favorite — leg of lamb. I have to go out tonight, but I thought for once we'd have a quiet dinner, just the two of us."

So Joanna had to make up more stories to tell her mother, stories about school, stories about Shep and what a great guy he was.

"You've barely touched your lamb," Mrs. Collier said after a while.

"I — I'm not all that hungry," Joanna said, which was certainly true.

"Are you feeling okay? You look kind of . . . tired." Joanna's mother was constantly accusing her of looking tired.

Joanna looked up from her practically untouched plate at her mother. For a brief moment, she felt as if she might tell her mother what was troubling her.

"You see, I killed Dex, Mom. He was playing a

joke on me, trying to make me think he had come back from the grave, and I stabbed him in the chest with a knife. Then Pete and Mary took his body and hid it in the woods. And that's why I'm having a little trouble digging into this lamb on my plate."

Wouldn't that go over big?

Joanna couldn't believe she had even *for a second* considered telling her mother what had happened.

I must be *really* losing it, she thought.

Helen served apple pie with cinnamon ice cream for dessert. Joanna managed to get a little of it down. Then she excused herself, and gave her mom a quick kiss on the forehead — which startled Mrs. Collier, who wasn't used to much affection from her daughter. "Joanna — ?" she started.

But Joanna was already running up to her room to call Mary.

She sat down at her desk, breathing heavily from running up the stairs. As she reached to pick up the phone, it rang.

Startled, she grabbed it up before the first ring had ended.

"Hello?"

"Hi, Joanna." A boy's voice cut through the static on the line.

"Shep? Is that you?"

Muffled laughter on the other end. "No, Joanna. It's me. Dex. I'm back, Joanna. This time I really *did* come back."

Chapter 22

"See you," Dex's voice said over the static.

"Dex?"

"See you."

Then the line went dead. Joanna uttered a little cry and sat staring at the phone.

She saw Dex's green face again, the skin peeling off. And she saw him lying on her kitchen floor in the puddle of blood.

Real blood.

Really dead.

It had all been real.

And now he was back.

It has to be a joke, she thought, feeling cold all over.

Someone is pretending to be Dex.

But it sounded so much like him. She even recognized the muffled laugh.

But Dex was dead. She'd killed him. Felt the knife go in. Seen the blood.

Oh, help me. Somebody — help me!

I can't think straight!

I've got to figure this out. I've got to know what is happening!

She dialed Mary's number. It rang four times. Finally Mary's mother picked it up.

"Mary can't come to the phone now. She's very busy."

"Oh, please. I've really got to talk to her." Joanna didn't recognize her own voice. It was so pinched with fear, so . . . desperate.

"I'll have her call you back."

Not good enough, Joanna thought. Not fast enough.

I've got to get out of this house, away from here.

"See you," Dex had said. Dead Dex.

"See you."

Did that mean he was on his way over to her house?

Dead Dex was on his way to . . . to do *what*??

Joanna dropped the cellular phone, jumped up, and ran down the stairs, taking them two at a time. "Mom? Mom?"

"She just left," Helen called from the kitchen. "Some club meeting or something."

I've got to get out of here, Joanna thought, her heart thudding.

I'll go to Mary's. She grabbed her coat from the closet and searched the front table for her car keys.

"I'm going over to a friend's," she called to Helen.

Helen called something back, but Joanna was already out the door.

Mary will know what to do, she told herself as the houses whirred by on both sides. It was a clear, cold night. Everything seemed to be in sharp focus, as if she were looking through a very expensive, fine camera lens.

Mary will know what to do.

But that was silly, wasn't it?

Why should Mary know what to do about someone who has come back from the grave?

Dead Dex.

Dead Dex . . . who wouldn't stay dead.

A few minutes later, she pulled the car into Mary's driveway and cut the headlights. The front of the house was dark. The porchlight wasn't on.

Joanna stepped out of the car and waited for her eyes to adjust to the total blackness. After a while, the black outline of the house loomed in front of her, against a somewhat lighter sky. Shrubs and a low, bent tree came into dark focus.

Joanna turned and looked back at the street. There were no streetlights.

She had a sudden chill.

Wrapping her unbuttoned coat around her, she started walking quickly up to the dark house. The ground felt hard and frozen beneath her sneakers. Her breath sent clouds of fog in front of her.

As she neared the front stoop, she could see lights on in the back of the house.

I'm almost there, she thought, nearly tripping over a smooth stone placed at the edge of the flag-stone walk that led to the front door.

Why does it have to be so dark?

She regained her balance and started to jog up to the front stoop.

Mary will know what to do.

I just need to talk with her, that's all.

She raised her hand to knock on the front door, then stopped.

She smelled him first.

That sour smell. That smell of rotting meat. But different from the phony garbage smell. Worse. Raw. Raw and rotting at the same time.

Then she felt the bony tap on her shoulder.

"Ohh."

She spun around, unable to breathe.

"Dex!"

In the darkness, she could see that one of his eyes was gone. There was nothing there but an empty socket.

"Joanna," he said, his voice a harsh whisper. "Why did you kill me?"

Chapter 23

It was so dark.

The smell was overpowering.

Joanna realized she'd been holding her breath. Now she let it out in a loud gasp.

"Why did you kill me, Joanna? Look — I'm still bleeding."

He held up his shirt. The wound was large and dark.

"Dex — I didn't mean — " She looked for an escape route, but he had backed her up against the front door.

She looked away. She couldn't bear to look at the empty eye socket, at his sagging, crumbling skin, at the gaping, dark wound in his chest.

Even in the blackness of the night he looked terrifying.

"Why did you kill me?" he repeated, his voice so weak she could barely hear him, the words floating out over his toothless gums.

"Help! Somebody help!" she screamed at the top

of her voice, and started to run, her sneakers slipping on the hard, wet ground.

"Don't run! It was so hard to come back!" Dex cried.

He was right behind her.

"No! Go away! Go away!"

"I went away, Joanna. But I came back."

He grabbed her shoulder. Then his hand slid down and he tackled her around the waist.

They both tumbled to the cold ground. He landed on top of her and pressed her into the dirt.

"No!" she screamed.

She was about to scream again, but stopped.

"Hey — " she said, pushing him hard, trying to shove him off her. "I can touch you." She grabbed his arm. "You're solid."

He was breathing hard from the short chase.

She reached up and touched his face. She pulled off a chunk of plastic makeup.

"You creep! You're not dead! This is still part of your ghastly joke!"

A broad, toothless smile formed on his face. "You're right," he said in his normal voice. "I'm alive." Then he added, "But the joke is over."

"Get off me! It's cold down here. You're ruining my coat!"

"The joke is over, Joanna."

"Did you hear me? Get off! What do you think you're doing? Ugh. You stink!"

She struggled to climb out from under him, but he was too strong.

"The joke is over," he repeated.

Reaching into his jacket pocket, he pulled out a switchblade knife and flicked open the blade.

"Dex — put that down!" she screamed.

The porch light came on. He looked even more gruesome in the shadowy yellow light.

And he looked angry.

"The knife is real," Dex said, staring down at her, holding the knife in front of her face. "It's real like me."

"Dex — "

"It's not a fake this time. It's not a retractable stage knife."

"Dex — *please!*" Joanna cried. "What do you *want?*"

"I want to show you that this knife is real," he said, bringing it down quickly.

Chapter 24

He plunged the knife blade into the dirt beside her head.

He was only trying to scare her.

"See?" he said, breathing hard. "It's real. A real knife."

With a burst of strength she shoved him off and struggled to her feet. He regained his balance quickly and stood beside her.

"Why, Dex?" she asked, watching the knife in his hand. "Why are you doing this?"

He turned away, and looked up to the front stoop. The porch light had come on, but the door was still closed. When he turned back to her, his face was filled with hatred.

"Why? Because you didn't care about me." He angrily pulled off the phony eye socket.

"But, Dex — "

"I loved you, Joanna." His voice broke on the word *love*. "You were the best thing that ever hap-

pened to me. I cared so much about you. And then
. . ." He looked down at the knife.

"I cared about you, too," Joanna said. But it
didn't sound convincing even to her.

"Then when I fell off that cliff, you didn't care
whether I lived or died."

"Is that what Pete told you?" Joanna asked
quickly. "Well, that's a lie, Dex. That isn't true.
I — "

"It *is* true!" he screamed, his dark eyes burning
into hers. "You can't lie to me anymore, Joanna.
You didn't care whether I lived or died that night.
And when Pete came to see you in the hospital — "

"I was totally drugged in the hospital!" Joanna
cried. "I was hurt, *too*, you know. When Pete came
to see me — "

"He told you I was dead, and you didn't even
react."

"I was drugged. I wasn't myself, Dex. I cried for
days."

He laughed, a bitter laugh. "It's no good, Joanna.
It's no good. When you stuck that knife in me last
Sunday, and I died a second time, you still didn't
care."

"I was so upset — "

"You just wanted my body out of the way. That's
all you cared about. I was just some mess to clear
away. So you and your rich boyfriend wouldn't have
your lives disturbed."

"Pete is behind all of this — isn't he?" Joanna
asked, looking over to her car.

It was so close, yet so far.

If she could just get into the car and lock the doors. . . .

"This is all Pete's idea, isn't it, Dex?"

He shook his head. He flicked the knife blade in and out nervously, staring hard at her all the while, his breath coming out in small, gray puffs.

"Pete helped me. That's all," he said softly. "Pete helped. But I don't need help now."

"What do you mean? What are you going to do?"

She looked to the house. Why didn't the door open? Why didn't someone come rushing out to save her?

Couldn't they hear all the yelling out here?

He took a step toward her. "I'm not going to die a *third* time," he said, his voice without expression, flat and calm now.

Insanely calm, she thought.

He's crazy. Dex is truly crazy.

"I'm not going to die again," he said. "It's your turn!"

She backed toward the drive.

He raised the knife and lunged at her.

"No!"

He stumbled over the smooth stone at the end of the walk, the same stone Joanna had stumbled over before.

The knife bounced out of his hand and stopped at Joanna's feet. She bent over quickly and picked it up.

"You're wrong, Dex," she said. "It's your turn *again*!"

160

Chapter 25

"Joanna — stop!"

Mary came running out of the house at full speed, wearing only jean cutoffs and a T-shirt.

Joanna turned toward her, startled, forgetting the knife in her hand. "Mary — what are you — ?"

She expected Mary to stop. But Mary ran right at her, pushing her hard, grabbing the knife out of her hand.

"Get away from him!" Mary screamed angrily.

Surprised by her friend's reaction, Joanna took a step back.

"Were you really going to kill him?" Mary screamed. "Haven't you done enough to him?"

She walked over to Dex and put her arm around him. He bent his head low, and she kissed him on the cheek.

"Mary — !" Joanna suddenly felt weak. The yellow porch light flickered. Shadows seemed to circle her on the dark ground.

This isn't real, she thought.

"Mary — you were in on this, too?" she asked, struggling to get the words out.

Still holding onto Dex, Mary smiled triumphantly. "It was all my idea," she said softly. "Right from the beginning."

"But why, Mary? I thought we were best friends. I thought — " Joanna just stared at them, waiting for the shadows to stop spinning, waiting for the darkness, the incredible heavy darkness to lift. "Why?"

"You had everything," Mary said bitterly, "and what did I have? Nothing. You had the big house, the expensive car — you had Dex. He was the one thing I wanted in the world." She looked up at Dex. He hugged her tight.

"But Mary — "

"It just broke my heart, Joanna. It broke my heart that you had Dex, and you didn't even care about him. You used him. Like you use everybody. It was all a game to you. You told me that yourself. He was a pet, a belonging, just one of the hundreds of things that belong to you."

"You're not being fair," Joanna said, staring hard at the knife, which was still clenched tightly in Mary's hand.

"Oh, yes, I am," Mary said heatedly. "Time and again you told me how Dex meant nothing to you. You were so *awful* to him. Standing him up and then bragging about it to me. Going out with Shep behind his back."

Mary was getting more and more worked up.

Joanna kept staring at the knife, wondering how over the edge Mary was, wondering if she was upset enough to use it.

"It was so ironic," Mary continued, her voice high and tight, her eyes wide with anger. "Because all the time you were telling me how little Dex meant to you, that's all I wanted — just Dex."

Before she realized it, Joanna found herself laughing. "Hey, listen, Mary — you're welcome to him. Really. Be my guest."

She started walking quickly to the car.

"Don't laugh at me, Joanna!"

In a fury, Mary leaped at her, holding the knife high.

"No! Stop!" Joanna turned just in time, and stumbled backwards onto the ground.

Mary raised the knife high, but Dex grabbed her arm.

"Let me kill her! Let me kill her!" Mary screamed.

But Dex gently pulled the knife from her hand and tossed it onto the ground. "Come on," he said softly, holding her close to him. "Easy. Take it easy." She was still breathing hard, but his words seemed to calm her. "Let's go inside. Let's forget all about Joanna. Let's forget this whole crazy time."

She glared at Joanna, then turned her face away.

They walked arm in arm up to the house.

They never looked back.

Joanna picked herself up and watched them until

the door closed behind them and the porch light went off.

Then she picked up the knife. The blade slid easily into the handle.

It was a phony stage prop.

At home in her room, Joanna sat at the desk, holding the knife in her hand, rolling it around between her fingers.

It's as phony as I am, she thought.

Mary was right. About everything.

And now here I am, all alone. I've lost everyone. No one is left.

I don't have a friend, a single friend. Maybe I never did.

Because I never really knew how to care about any of them.

Before she realized it, hot tears were running down her cheeks, and she was sobbing.

It felt so strange.

I haven't cried in years, she thought.

I haven't cried since . . .

She thought hard. When? When?

I haven't cried since the night Daddy left us.

For once, she didn't hold her true feelings back. She let herself cry, the tears flowing down her cheeks. She cried until she was all cried out.

To her surprise, she felt a little better.

She wiped her eyes, then tucked the knife away in a desk drawer.

Then she took a deep breath, picked up the phone, and dialed Shep.

He picked up on the third ring.

"Shep?"

"Hi . . . Joanna."

"Shep, I have to talk to you," she said. "I — I'm back from the grave."

He didn't understand what she meant.

She hoped he'd give her a chance to explain.

The
Girlfriend

Chapter 1

"I'd like to propose a toast to Scotty and Lora," Mr. DeMarco announced. He raised his fluted champagne glass above his head and held it there until the large, crowded room grew quiet.

Scotty tried to hide behind Lora, but she turned and pulled him beside her, her expression playfully scolding. "This is embarrassing," Scotty whispered.

"Get used to it," Lora told him, holding him in place with both hands so he couldn't escape. "My dad *loves* embarrassing people. It's his hobby."

"I know, I know," Scotty replied, shaking his head, his eyes on the front of the large rec room where Lora's dad was still holding his champagne glass in the air, waiting for all the guests to raise their glasses.

Scotty and Lora had been a couple since sixth grade, so Scotty knew exactly what to expect from her parents. Both of them were warm, and outgoing, and generous. Too generous, Scotty sometimes thought.

They smother you with kindness. That's how he sometimes described them.

Scotty felt smothered by this lavish party, with the enormous, seemingly endless buffet table, the overstocked bar, the five-piece band out on the terrace, the young waiters parading around in their black tuxedos, carrying silver trays of salmon and caviar hors d'oeuvres.

After all, it was a little too early to celebrate.

Scotty and Lora had received preliminary acceptance at Princeton, but nothing official yet. And Scotty might not be able to go anyway. He was still waiting to hear about his scholarship.

Scotty and Lora had urged the DeMarcos to wait a while before having the party. For one thing, it was only November. They still had the rest of their senior year at Glenview High to finish.

But, Mr. DeMarco, in typical fashion, had insisted on throwing this huge, expensive party. "Don't worry about it," he had said, his youthful face beaming happily, one big arm around each of them, crushing them both in an affectionate hug. "We'll throw another party after the school year. Or maybe *two* parties — one for each of you!"

Scotty and Lora finally gave up trying to discourage him. "What's the point?" Lora asked, as they were sitting in the front seat of her father's BMW, parked up by Rainer Point, overlooking the town. "Daddy will always be Daddy."

"But it's so bogus!" Scotty exclaimed unhappily.

"I mean, throwing a party for us for no reason."

"I wish you wouldn't say 'bogus' all the time," Lora said, squeezing his hand affectionately. "I mean, we're going to Princeton, you know — not Ohio State."

They both laughed.

"You're a stuck-up snob," Scotty said.

"And you love it," she replied and kissed him for a long time.

Scotty did love it, he had to admit. He liked everything about Lora. He liked how her wavy, blonde hair caught the sunlight, how soft it felt in his hands. He liked staring into her wide, green eyes. He liked the way people said she looked like a model, like a young Christie Brinkley.

He liked walking down the hall at school with her, holding hands. "You know we're a cliché," he'd tell her. "I mean, the football quarterback and the Homecoming Queen? Get real!"

"I don't feel like a cliché," she'd reply in her serious way. "I just feel like me."

He had to admit he didn't at all mind that they were a cliché. Being with Lora always made him feel good. And he was proud of being the starting quarterback of the Tigers. He'd been voted all-state last year in his junior year. That was pretty good.

Scotty liked the fact that everyone thought of him and Lora as a couple. And he liked the fact that other kids were jealous of them. And of him. He didn't think about it a lot, but when he did, he admitted to himself that having this long, steady relationship with one girl was maybe the most admirable thing about him.

Other kids, even his best friends, even Bender, his very best friend, seemed sort of aimless to him. Immature.

Scotty like being responsible. Maybe it was because his father had been so irresponsible. Running off without a word, leaving Mrs. Singleton to bring up Scotty and his younger brother Denny.

How could he *do* that to us? Scotty often asked himself.

He never came up with a satisfactory answer.

Lora's parents seemed to have such a close, stable relationship. Maybe that was why Scotty liked them so much.

He realized he liked being with the DeMarcos as much as with his own family. When he didn't feel smothered by their wealth, by their enthusiasm, by their generosity.

Now he found himself looking around the large, brightly lit rec room, crowded with kids from school, relatives of both families, and a lot of people he'd never seen before, and *definitely* feeling smothered.

"We never should have agreed to this," he whispered, leaning against Lora.

"We had no choice, remember?" she whispered back, as her father rambled on with one of his endless, meandering toasts.

"But it's so embarrassing," Scotty moaned, staring across the room at his friend Bender, who was leaning against one of the sliding glass doors, staring back at Scotty with his eyes crossed and his tongue hanging out of his mouth.

"Don't think of it as a going to Princeton party. Think of it as a going-away party for me," Lora said, playfully stepping down hard on his foot until he winced in pain, her eyes straight ahead as if concentrating on her father's toast.

Scotty was tempted to pour his Coke down the front of her green velvet party dress, but managed to hold himself back.

He had almost forgotten that Lora and her parents were going away. Off to London and Paris for a week. Mr. DeMarco had some sort of architectural business to take care of in London, so why not turn it into a spur-of-the-moment family vacation?

He glanced at his mother, in her flowing fuchsia-and-electric-blue dress, which was just a little too snug on her plump body, her platinum hair piled high on her head, standing in front of Mr. DeMarco, glass in hand, listening so intently.

For a brief moment, Scotty felt real envy. He wanted to be in the DeMarco family. He wanted to go on unplanned trips to Europe, too.

Oh, well, some day soon, I *will* be a member of the family, he thought, glancing affectionately at Lora.

". . . I'm real proud of these kids . . ." Mr.

DeMarco was saying at the front of the room.

And then Mrs. DeMarco looked away from her husband and gasped.

Mr. DeMarco stopped abruptly in mid-sentence. All eyes turned to where his wife was staring — to the buffet table, where Fluffernutter, Lora's little white cat, had leaped up and was enthusiastically sampling a good helping of the salmon mousse.

"Oh, Fluffernutter!" Lora cried, letting go of Scotty's hand and rushing toward the buffet table.

One of the tuxedoed waiters got there first and lifted the still-chewing cat off the table, setting it gently down on the linoleum floor.

"I think that was a sign that I've been talking too long," Mr. DeMarco said, grinning. He held up his glass one more time. "To Scotty and Lora," he announced, looking for Lora. He couldn't see her because she was down on the floor scolding her cat.

There was a clinking of glasses, and conversations resumed around the room. Scotty breathed a loud sigh of relief, took a long gulp of Coke from his glass, and started over to thank Lora's dad for the toast, even though he hadn't really heard much of it.

"Hey, man," Bender caught his arm. "Watch out for those caviar thingies. I tried one, but it tasted real fishy."

"I'll be careful," Scotty said dryly.

Bender was tall and lanky, the tallest one in the room even though he was only seventeen, and still growing. He should've played basketball, Scotty thought. He never could figure out why his friend wanted to be an offensive tackle.

"What kind of a party is this without any pizza?" Bender complained, only half serious.

"It wasn't *my* idea, man," Scotty said, sighing. "You want to go out for a pizza? I'll go with you."

"Yeah. Sure," Bender said sarcastically, glancing down at Lora who was still on the floor playing with Fluffernutter, unaware that she was getting white cat hair all over her green velvet dress. "You ready for Friday night?"

Scotty nodded. What with all the excitement over being accepted at Princeton and the party, he hadn't had much time to think about the game. "Lincoln isn't that good," he said.

"They're five-and-oh!" Bender exclaimed, pushing his heavy, black-plastic Buddy Holly eyeglasses up on his narrow nose. "They beat Westerville 35 to zip, and we could only tie Westerville."

"They got lucky, man," Scotty said, grinning. "They're bogus. Totally bogus. We can take 'em."

He saw Mr. DeMarco coming toward him, so he slapped Bender's hand in a low five and started to push his way through the crowd to meet him.

Mr. DeMarco, chewing a fried chicken finger, beamed at Scotty, raking back his thick, brown hair with one hand. He's so proud of his hair, Scotty thought. He's always telling everyone how he's forty-five and still has every hair he ever had.

"Hey, thanks for the toast," Scotty said, trying to sound enthusiastic.

Mr. DeMarco brushed chicken crumbs from his wide red tie. "I think I went on a bit too long, but I just couldn't help it." He flung an arm around Scotty's shoulder, nearly knocking Scotty over. "I'm just so proud of you two!"

"Thanks," Scotty said uncomfortably.

"You know, I have a little bet on the game Friday night," he said confidentially, his arm still around Scotty's shoulders, guiding him toward the hallway that led to the rest of the house.

"You're betting on Lincoln?" Scotty joked.

Mr. DeMarco stopped for a moment, then laughed. "No way," he said. "You're going to be all-state again this year, Scotty. And you're going to take the Tigers to the state championship. I know it."

"Well . . . I don't know," Scotty said, feeling his face grow hot. "We've got some tough games. And with Jergens hurt . . ."

"You just have to throw more," Mr. DeMarco said. It was one of his steady themes. Scotty was too generous, he was always saying. Scotty should forget about sharing the glory. He should throw the ball more. The team should ride on Scotty's arm.

"I don't think Coach Hawkins would agree," Scotty always replied.

"Who *cares* about Hawkins?" was Mr. DeMarco's answer. "He's a chemistry teacher. What does *he* know about football?"

Scotty never won this argument. He seldom won any argument against Lora's father. Mr. DeMarco was too powerful and too insistent. He never gave up until he got his way.

"Listen, Scotty, I meant everything I said in that toast," he said, turning serious, his face close to Scotty's. "Keep making me proud, son. I know you will. I know you and Lora both will. Keep making me proud. You know, when you graduate from Princeton in four years, there'll be a place waiting for you in my firm."

Scotty's mouth dropped open in surprise. "Really?"

It was quite a generous offer. Mr. DeMarco's architectural design firm was the biggest in the state and was rapidly getting a national reputation.

Scotty planned to go into architecture at Princeton. His dream was to build amazing skyscrapers, to change skylines. Now it looked as if his dream would most certainly come true.

"Thank you, Mr. DeMarco. That's just awesome," he exclaimed. "I really don't know what to say."

Mr. DeMarco was looking past Scotty, back into the room. The glass doors had been opened. Outside, the band had started to play, and people were drifting out onto the large, flagstone terrace to dance. "I can't believe what a beautiful evening we got," he said to Scotty. "Imagine? Sixty-five degrees in November? It's like spring out there. Luck just seems to rain down on you and Lora."

"I guess so," Scotty said, still thinking about Mr. DeMarco's amazing offer. He said good-bye to him and headed excitedly over to Lora, who was talking animatedly, circled by friends from school.

It took Scotty a while to separate her from the group. Then he led her out onto the terrace, which was lit by pale pink light from paper lanterns strung around the sides.

"If all the leaves weren't down, I'd think it was summer," Lora said, taking a deep breath of the fresh, cool air. "What were you and my dad talking about?"

Scotty couldn't hold in the news a second longer. He told Lora about her father's job offer.

"That's so exciting!" Lora cried. She kissed him enthusiastically.

Walking with his arm around her shoulder, he led her across the crowded terrace. The swimming pool was drained and covered with its winter canvas tarp. He led her past it, past the small pool house and into the large, sloping backyard, away from the lights and the music. They stepped over the wet grass, walking around the carefully trimmed evergreens and shrubs.

"I shouldn't have complained," he said softly. "It's turned out to be a great party. Totally awesome."

"I think Fluffernutter stole the show," Lora said, snuggling against him.

"Fluffernutter stole the salmon," he corrected her. "I should've brought *my* pet. That would liven up the party."

"Your snake?" She made a disgusted face. "Yuck."

He pretended to be hurt, as he always did when she insulted his snake. "I think Ernie is cute," he teased.

Lora started to say something — but only managed a choked gasp as a dark figure, arms raised to attack, leaped out at them from behind a tall bush.

Chapter 2

Scotty threw his arms up as the dark figure lunged at him, wrapping him in a tight bear hug.

"Denny!" Scotty yelped. "Are you *nuts*?!"

"You scared me to death!" Lora cried, holding her hand up to her thudding heart.

Scotty's seven-year-old brother let go of Scotty, tossed his head back, and laughed. "Gotcha!"

"You got us, all right," Scotty agreed, still feeling the effects of the shock. He reached forward and picked Denny up off the ground.

"Hey — put me down!" Denny protested, still laughing.

But Scotty held his brother up over his head like a pair of weights and began to twirl him easily.

"Put me down! I'll puke on you!" Denny

screamed. "I had a big dinner, Scotty! I'll puke on you!"

Scotty quickly returned his brother to the ground.

"Hey — you're strong," Denny admitted grudgingly.

"You're a featherweight," Scotty said, straightening his necktie and sports jacket.

It was true. Scotty and Denny didn't look at all like brothers. Denny was short and slender. Scotty was tall, broad-chested, with a thick football player's neck, muscular arms, and big hands. Denny had curly black hair that he wanted kept cut very short because he didn't like it to be curly; small, dark eyes; and delicate features. Scotty had straight, light brown hair that he kept short on top but down to his collar in the back, big blue eyes, and a large nose that looked as if it had been broken even though it hadn't. Denny always looked serious. Scotty seldom did.

"What were you doing behind that bush?" Lora demanded, holding Denny in place by pressing both hands against his shoulders.

"Hiding," he said.

"Hiding? Why?" Lora asked, not letting him go, even though he was trying desperately to squirm away.

"To scare somebody. It's a party, right?"

Lora laughed. Denny scampered back out of her grasp.

"Denny knows how to party," Scotty exclaimed,

putting his arm around Lora's shoulder. She shivered. There was a chill in the air. "It's a party, so you scare someone."

"What *else* is there to do, stupid?" Denny asked, sneering.

"You don't have to call names," Scotty said, frowning.

"Well, you're stupid," Denny repeated. He said the word a few more times. It was his favorite word. He said it all day long.

"Why don't you go inside and play in the sour cream dip?" Lora suggested.

"You're stupid, too," Denny told her. He turned and ran back toward the terrace. "I'm going to tell Mom you two were kissing and stuff!" he yelled before disappearing into the crowd.

"He's real cute," Scotty said sarcastically.

"He *is* kind of cute," Lora said, nestling her head against his shoulder. He smelled her hair. It smelled of coconut.

"He's a shrimp," Scotty muttered. "He'll never make the team."

Mentioning the team made him think of the game against Lincoln the following Friday night. "I can't believe you're missing Homecoming," he said, not meaning to whine.

"I know. But what can I do?" She shrugged. "I'll be thinking of you."

"In Paris," he said, rolling his eyes.

"You can beat Lincoln without me, Scotty."

"No. You're my good-luck charm," he said, only half kidding.

"That's what I am?" she cried, pretending to be offended. "I'm a good-luck charm? That's why you keep me around?"

He nodded, teasing her. He liked it when her green eyes lit up, and her face got all fiery. "That's all," he said. Then he quickly turned serious again. "You're missing the dance and everything."

"Oh, come on, Scotty," she cried, giving him a hard, playful shove. "You don't care about the Homecoming dance, do you? You *really* wanted to stand up in front of all those gawking creeps — I mean, all of our classmates — and be crowned Homecoming King and Queen?"

He turned his glance toward the house. The band was taking a break, but people stayed on the terrace, standing in small groups, talking and laughing.

"I know it's all bogus," he began.

"Yes. It's totally ridiculous," she interrupted.

"But it's kind of an honor," he continued seriously. "And it *is* our last Homecoming dance. I mean, we'll be graduating and everything. I mean . . ." His voice drifted off. He felt embarrassed. Everything he was saying sounded so nerdy.

She looked up at him, holding onto his arm, leaning against him, but didn't say anything.

"Well, you know how everyone expects us to be the perfect couple," he said. "I'll have to answer a million questions. 'Where's Lora?' 'Why aren't you going to the dance?' 'Did you and Lora have a fight?' " He shook his head. "It's going to be totally bogus."

"Hey, I just had a funny idea," Lora said, a sly grin forming on her face, her emerald eyes catching the light from the half moon in the clear sky above them.

"Huh?"

"I think it would be really funny if you got a date to the dance."

He stared at her, his face filled with confusion. "What? What do you mean?"

She chuckled. "You know. Ask somebody else to the dance. It would be great. You'd show up with some other girl, and everyone would totally freak!"

He studied her face, trying to decide if she was serious or not. "You're kidding — right?"

"Of *course* I'm kidding," she replied. "But it *would* freak everyone out, wouldn't it?"

"You have a weird brain," he said. He wrapped his arms around her waist and kissed her.

The party ended a little after midnight. Scotty's mother had taken Denny home a few hours earlier. Now, suddenly feeling very tired, Scotty said good night and thanked Mr. and Mrs. DeMarco.

Lora, yawning loudly, walked him to the front door. "Don't look so sad," she said. "I'll only be gone a week. I'll send you a postcard from the Eiffel Tower. And I'll think of you all the time. I promise." She gave him a long, sweet kiss.

"See you in a week," he said glumly. He started out the door.

"Be good," she called after him. "Stay out of trouble."

Trouble? Scotty thought, heading to his car. What a strange thing to say.

How could *I* ever get into trouble?

Chapter 3

Scotty stormed into the locker room and heaved his helmet across the room. It hit a locker with a loud *clang* and bounced onto the floor.

"Come on, man," Bender urged, slapping Scotty's shoulder pad. "We'll get 'em next half. It's not so bad."

"It's nine to nothing," Scotty growled, kicking his helmet hard as it rolled up to him on the cement floor.

"Hey, we'll catch 'em," Barker, a running back, yelled, sitting down on the bench across from Scotty. "I almost broke one, you know. If I hadn't slipped . . ."

Scotty looked toward the doorway as his teammates entered, most of them downcast and silent.

I'm letting them down, he thought, picking up his helmet, inspecting the scratch he had made by heaving it into the locker.

I'm letting them down.

"We've been down before," Bender said, untying

his cleats so he could tie them again. "It's no big deal."

"I know I'm going to break one," Barker said, after guzzling about a quart of Gatorade. "Just give me the ball over right tackle. Their whole right side is slow, man. I can get around 'em."

"I should have gotten rid of the ball," Scotty said quietly to Bender. "I never should've let 'em get me in the end zone."

"It was my fault," Bender said. "I let that guy through. He just rolled over me like a tank. He must weigh three hundred pounds. And he's only a sophomore."

Scotty grabbed a paper cup of Gatorade and downed it. Then he took a towel and wiped the perspiration off his face. From out in the stadium, he could hear the band going through its Homecoming routine. What was that song they were playing? "Zip-a-Dee-Doo-Dah"?

"I just lost my concentration," he said glumly, scratching his head. "I should've grounded the ball, just heaved it or something. Instead I stood there like a jerk and ate it."

He reached into his locker and pulled out his black-and-silver Raiders cap.

I'm letting them all down, he thought. On Homecoming.

At least, Lora isn't here to watch me blow it.

Maybe that's the problem, he thought. Lora isn't here to watch. At the party last weekend, he was only kidding about her being his good-luck charm.

But it was obvious he performed better when he knew she was there, watching him, cheering him on.

Up at the front, across from the showers, Coach Hawkins slammed a locker with his fist, his usual way of getting their attention when they were losing at halftime. "You can beat these guys," he said, his high-pitched voice echoing off the low ceiling. "You just have to execute. It all comes down to who executes best."

"You wear that Raiders cap in the shower?" Bender asked, grabbing it off Scotty's head and examining it.

Scotty grabbed it back. "It's sort of a good-luck cap. Lora gave it to me."

Maybe that's your problem," Bender said, finishing with his cleats, leaning forward to grin right in Scotty's face. "You're thinking about the dance."

"I'm not going to the dance," Scotty said, his eyes on the coach, who was diagramming a complicated defensive formation on the small chalkboard.

"Huh? Say what?"

"You heard me," Scotty said edgily. "Lora is in Paris, remember?"

"I don't believe it!" Bender exclaimed, grabbing a plastic water bottle, tilting it over his head, and letting a stream of water run down his face. "The quarterback and the head cheerleader won't be at Homecoming?"

"You can go in my place," Scotty said dryly. He tapped his hands nervously against the bench. He hated halftime. It was always his most nervous time of the game. "You got a date, Bender?"

"Yeah," Bender nodded, drying his face with a towel.

"With who?"

"I don't remember. I called so many girls. I don't remember which one said yes." He laughed.

Scotty forced a laugh, but he was thinking about the game. And about Lora.

My good-luck charm, he thought.

"Hey — did you hear me?" Coach Hawkins cried, glaring at Scotty.

Scotty looked up, startled. "Yeah, I heard you," he lied.

"Well, let's see you do it," Hawkins squeaked. "You guys can beat Lincoln in your sleep."

"We just can't beat 'em when we're awake!" Bender whispered.

"Let's get out there," Hawkins yelled, heading for the door. "Win one for the Gipper!"

He said it every week. No one really knew why.

"Go Tigers!" someone yelled.

"Go Tigers!" several voices repeated.

I've got to get up for this, Scotty thought. I'm not going to be a loser on Homecoming. No way!

He jumped to his feet and stood up on the bench so the rest of the team could see him. "Let's kick their butts!" he shouted, gesturing with his helmet high over his head. "Let's kick their butts! Go Tigers!"

His cheers got them all shouting enthusiastically.

That's more like it, he thought.

Pulling on his helmet, he jogged out of the locker room, and led his team onto the field. His heart began to pound as he stepped under the bright, white lights, the cheers from the bleachers rising over the drums of the departing marching band.

He ran down the line of players, slapping everyone a high five, a tradition he had started. The quarterback has to be a leader, he told himself.

Now I'm going to show them I'm a leader.

Whoops of victory pierced the silence of the locker room as the Tigers swept in after the game, laughing, cheering, shoving each other, butting heads, a noisy, sweaty celebration that Coach Hawkins couldn't stop if he wanted to.

"We shut 'em out! We shut 'em out!" Bender was screaming, swatting his towel wildly at anyone who passed.

Well, we *did* shut them out in the second half, Scotty thought, joining the celebration, chanting along with his teammates. The final score was 14–9. But, secretly, Scotty felt disappointed. The defense had been responsible for both Tiger touchdowns, scoring the last one on a fumble recovery in the final two minutes.

Of course, the stadium erupted into total bedlam. And Scotty was thrilled that they were going to win. But happy as he was, Scotty wished that he had had a little more to do with the Tigers' victory.

Actually, he had played his worst game of the season. He had only completed four or five passes in the second half, all of them for short yardage. He hadn't been able to move the team well at all. And after he messed up a handoff in the beginning of the fourth quarter, Coach Hawkins had actually taken him out for one series of downs, something he hadn't done all season.

I'm glad Lora wasn't here to see this game, he thought, as he joined the raucous cheers, slapped hands, laughed and shouted with his teammates, and pretended he was as happy as they were.

The only way Coach Hawkins was able to stop the locker-room victory party was by blowing his whistle until his round face grew red as a balloon, and then reminding them that they all had to appear at the traditional Homecoming bonfire behind the stadium in less than ten minutes.

After a quick shower, Scotty got into his street clothes, pulled on his down jacket and his Raiders cap, and started to the door, intending to hurry home and skip the bonfire.

"Hey — Singleton!"

It was Bender, pulling a green-and-white Glenview sweatshirt over a T-shirt as he chased after Scotty. "Wait up. I'll walk to the bonfire with you."

"Is that what you're wearing to the dance?" Scotty teased. "Couldn't you have at least found a *clean* sweatshirt?"

"Hey, it's almost clean." Bender grinned. And

then he added, "At least, I'm *going* to the dance."

"You really are bogus, man," Scotty said, shaking his head. "You really know how to kick a guy when he's down."

"How can you be down?" Bender asked, pushing open the door. A rush of cold air greeted them, feeling even colder because they had just stepped out of a steamy shower. "We won the game, right? Even though you stunk up the joint." Bender laughed to show he was teasing.

"Hey, watch it," Scotty said edgily.

"Friends have got to be honest with one another, right?" Bender asked.

"Wrong," Scotty said.

"Oh. Then I take it back. You were awesome tonight," Bender said, grinning.

Scotty punched him hard on the shoulder. Then the two of them began to jog around the parking lot to the back of the stadium.

"Hey, we're just in time," Bender said.

Mr. Velasquez, the principal, was holding a long, flaming torch, about to light the bonfire. A crowd of two or three hundred Glenview students, parents, and people from the neighborhood huddled in sweaters, down jackets, and winter coats, looking exaggeratedly bright and colorful under the high stadium lights.

Scotty followed Bender up to the front. Pieces of lumber, old two-by-fours, fireplace logs, sticks, rags, old cushions, newspapers, and assorted flammable items had been piled into a mountain nearly two stories tall.

Across the way, Scotty saw three Glenview policemen eyeing the proceedings warily, shifting nervously, their eyes on Mr. Velasquez's torch. The Homecoming bonfire wasn't the police department's favorite event, Scotty knew. One year, Scotty's freshman year, the celebration had gotten out of hand, and a house had been set aflame.

"Cut the lights!" Velasquez yelled. A few seconds later, the high stadium lights obediently faded out, surrounding everyone in darkness except for the orange-yellow light of the wavering torch.

A strong gust of wind blew past, bending the torch flame, pushing it downward. The crowd grew silent, drew closer. Scotty pulled down his Raiders cap, then shoved his hands into his jeans pockets.

Light the fire already, he thought. It's getting cold out here!

Velasquez, with his usual dramatic flare, raised the torch high over his head, then lowered the flame to the pile of wood. The flames took hold slowly at first. Sticks crackled. A small yellow flame began to spread.

Before long, the entire mountain burst into flame, the orange-yellow light licking up toward the black, starless sky. It's really awesome, Scotty thought, looking around the circle of cheering faces. Everyone looks so orange and warm.

He took a deep breath. It smelled so good. A

branch crackled and broke, making a group of kids jump back. The flames leaped higher and higher. The fire had become a pulsating, yellow mountain, warm and alive.

"Who brought the marshmallows?" someone shouted.

It got a pretty big laugh.

"Look out — here comes Smokey the Bear!" someone else shouted.

This remark got only groans.

Scotty stepped a little closer, allowing the darting, bright flames to warm him. Velasquez tossed the torch into the fire, then raised his hands over his head, trying to get everyone's attention.

"We had a victory here tonight!" Velasquez shouted in his booming, deep voice. "Let's let the team know we appreciate them. Let's really hear it for the Fighting Tigers!"

This was the excuse the crowd was waiting for to go wild. A deafening cheer rose up, kids slapped hands, and hats and gloves were tossed into the fire. A shoving match started between a group of guys very near the fire, and the three policemen moved quickly to break it up.

The crowd started to chant, "Tigers! Tigers! Tigers!" And when the team paraded in a single line in front of the fire, the wild cheers and celebrating started all over again. Scotty got the biggest cheer of all. He grinned and waved at everyone, holding his hands over his head in a double victory sign.

What a night! Scotty thought happily. He wished

Lora were there. It would've been so much more fun with her.

And then suddenly the crowd was quieting down again, and Velasquez, his face bright red in the glowing firelight, was starting to talk. "We have another bonfire tradition," he shouted.

Scotty searched the crowd for Bender, but couldn't find him. Faces looked strange and distorted in the orange light. A picture of rows and rows of jack-o'-lanterns popped into his mind.

What was Velasquez going on about?

". . . when we crown the Homecoming King and Queen," the principal's voice boomed over the crackling and spitting of the fire.

What? Scotty wondered. What is he saying?

"And so I'd like to call our Homecoming King and Queen up here right now!" Velasquez shouted enthusiastically. "Scotty and Lora — get up here where everyone can see you!"

"Oh, no," Scotty groaned out loud. "Didn't anyone tell him?" He could feel his heart sink down to his feet.

"Scotty and Lora! Let's give it up for them!" Velasquez shouted.

Didn't anyone tell him Lora isn't here? Scotty thought. What am I going to do? This is so embarrassing.

As the crowd cheered, he realized he had no choice. Slowly, hands shoved in his pockets, keeping his eyes on the ground, he made his way toward Velasquez.

Oh, please, let me die right here, he thought. Before the jokes start. Before everyone has a good time laughing at me.

"Lora? Where are you?" Velasquez called when the cheers died down.

"She stood him up!" some guy screamed.

The crowd roared with laughter.

Scotty felt his face grow hot.

"She had another date!" another joker added.

Another roar of laughter. At Scotty's expense.

"Where's Lora?" Velasquez asked Scotty.

"She's in the parking lot with Bender!" someone shouted.

The crowd thought this was hilarious.

Scotty glared angrily into the fire. He had never been so embarrassed in his life, but he didn't want to let these clowns know they were getting to him.

"Lora isn't here," he told Velasquez, leaning close so the principal could hear him over the crowd. "She's away with her family."

"Oh. Right," Velasquez said, slapping his forehead. "Someone told me that this afternoon." He turned away from Scotty to address the crowd. "Lora is away with her parents. What a shame! But at least we can crown the Homecoming King!"

Scotty gritted his teeth and let himself be crowned with the stupid crown. He felt like a total dweeb.

Finally, after a few cheers by the cheerleaders, the bonfire ceremony was over. People started to wander off in groups, still laughing and cheering.

Scotty tore off the crown and tossed it into the fire. Then, ignoring calls from a couple of friends, he put his head down and started to run at full speed toward the student parking lot. His face still felt hot from the fire. The rush of air was cold and refreshing.

"Singleton — you going to the dance?" someone called.

"Hey — where's Lora?" someone else yelled.

He ignored them and kept running. A car squealed out of the parking lot, burning rubber as it roared off down Fairwood Street. "Good game, Scotty!" a guy yelled from a car as Scotty ran past. He acknowledged the compliment with a quick wave, but kept running.

His car, the old Pontiac his mom had bought secondhand, came into view at the very end of the lot. Scotty slowed to a walk and reached into his jacket pocket for the car keys.

He was struggling to unlock the front door when he saw something down low against the fence.

It was a girl.

What was she doing down there? Was she okay?

Scotty stepped back from his car and walked over to her. As he came closer, he saw that she was on her knees, leaning over a bicycle, which was lying on its side.

She was wearing a thin, pale green windbreaker. Her back was turned to him. In the white light suspended over the parking lot, he could see that she had long, red hair, which flowed down to her waist.

Hearing him approach, she turned her head and gave him a shy smile. "Hi," she said breathily.

Chapter 4

"Flat tire?" Scotty asked.

"Yeah." She made a face.

"That's really bogus," he said, shaking his head.

She's very pretty, he thought. Her long, red hair falling loose behind her was really wild and sexy. And she had a high forehead, and big, brown eyes, and full, red lips.

He thought she looked very dramatic. Like an actress.

I've seen her around school, he thought. But he couldn't remember her name.

"It's a pretty cold night for a bike," he said.

"You want to buy me a car?" she cracked. Then she laughed to soften the remark. She had a light, breathy laugh, like her voice.

She climbed to her feet. He was surprised by how short she was. Her head didn't come up to his shoulders. She looked frail and light in the thin windbreaker, which flapped in the wind. "I think it's a puncture," she said, and kicked at the tire. "I'll have to walk it home."

"How about a lift?" Scotty said, pointing to his car. "We can toss the bike in my trunk."

She looked so light and fragile, as if a strong wind might blow her away.

"Thanks," she said, her big, brown eyes examining him. "I'm Shannon Smith."

Right, he thought. Shannon Smith. He remembered her now. She had only been at Glenview a year or so. He'd seen her sitting in the lunchroom by herself. She didn't seem to have many friends. He remembered her wild red hair.

"I'm Scotty Singleton," he said.

"I know." She looked down at her bike. "Everyone knows *you*," she added, her voice a whisper.

He raked his hand back through his short hair. He suddenly felt awkward, nervous. "So? Want a lift?"

Another car squealed out of the parking lot, the kids inside yelling and singing, the radio blaring. He looked around. The lot was empty now, except for him and Shannon.

"Thanks," she said. "I'm pretty cold." She bent over to pick up the bike. He helped her carry it over to his trunk. Then he popped the trunk and shoved it in.

She lowered her dark eyes, smiled at him, a teasing smile, and slid into the passenger seat. He climbed in behind the wheel and started the engine.

"Aren't you going to the dance?" she asked, toying with a strand of her hair, tangling it and untangling it around her fingers.

"No," Scotty said uncomfortably. He rubbed his cold hands together, waiting for the car to warm up.

"I don't have a date, either," she said softly, playing with her hair. She reached over and touched the back of his hand. "Thanks for rescuing me." Her hand was surprisingly warm. He could still feel the warmth of it after she pulled it away.

He backed up, then headed out of the narrow lot. Up at the school, he could see couples heading in to the dance. He looked for Bender, curious to see who Bender's date was, but didn't see him.

I'm sure I'll hear all about it tomorrow, he thought.

He glanced over at Shannon as he pulled into the street. He liked the way she nibbled at her bottom lip. She glanced back at him, shyly.

"You were good tonight," she said softly.

"You mean at the game?" He shook his head. "I was bogus. Totally bogus."

"No, you weren't," she protested, letting go of her hair, dropping her hand to her lap. She scratched the knee of her jeans with slender fingers. "We won, didn't we?"

"No thanks to me," he said moodily, turning onto Park Street.

"Are you always real modest?" she asked, touching the back of his hand again.

Her touch sent a shock of electricity up his arm. "Where do you live?" he asked.

"At Sharpes Corners," she said, looking out the

window. "You know, in the Old Village."

"Yeah, sure," he said. He didn't go to the Old Village much. None of his friends lived there. The houses were old and small and close together. He remembered hearing on TV about a big effort to restore the Old Village to its former glory, or something.

"Do you like football?" he asked, glancing away from the road to look at her. She was playing with her hair again, winding it around one hand. He realized he was very attracted to her.

"Not much," she replied and then laughed at her answer. "But I like going to the games. My brothers all like football. I guess that's why I don't like it."

"How many brothers do you have?" he asked, slowing for the light at Harbor Crossing.

"Three," she said, making a face. "Three big louts."

"Let me guess," he said. "You don't like your brothers?"

"We don't have much in common," she said, sliding down in the seat, raising her knees to the dashboard. "They're all older than me. They're all big. Really big. The oldest one, Kurt, was a pro wrestler. A pro. Do you believe it?"

"Wow," Scotty said. "Remind me to stay on your good side!"

He had meant it as a joke, but he saw her face turn serious. "I will," she said softly.

They drove in silence for a while. She's so pretty,

Scotty thought. Why doesn't she have a date tonight?

"You want to stop and get a hamburger or something?" he asked. The words popped out. He hadn't really thought about it. As he said it, it felt as if someone else were talking.

I haven't been out with another girl in . . . *how many* years? he asked himself.

Never, he realized.

He'd been with Lora since sixth grade.

Well, I'm not really *out* with Shannon, he told himself. This isn't a date or anything. I'm just helping her get home. So what's wrong with stopping for a hamburger on the way?

"I'd love to," she said breathily, her voice so soft he could barely hear her.

"Great," he said. "I'm always starving after a game." He turned the car around and started to drive to Henry's, the hamburger restaurant near school where everyone hung out. He had gone a couple of blocks when he decided that wasn't a good idea.

There'll probably be a lot of kids I know there, he thought. And they'll see me with Shannon. And they'll start making jokes. Or they'll start making up stories about me. Or word will get back to Lora that I had a date with another girl.

Why look for trouble?

"Know any good places in the Old Village?" he asked.

She nibbled at her bottom lip, her expression thoughtful. "Well, there's a Burger Basket on Ridge just before the railroad tracks."

"Sounds perfect," he said. "Let's go there."

"Okay," she said softly.

Did she sound a little disappointed, or was he just imagining it?

A few minutes later, he found the Burger Basket and pulled into the lot. There were only two other cars in the lot, he noticed with relief.

This looks like a pretty rough neighborhood, he thought, looking around at the low, dark buildings and empty lots across from the hamburger restaurant.

As they walked in through the glass doors, Shannon took his hand. Her hand felt so warm, so light, so fragile. She smiled up at him, a playful smile. Her hair smelled sweet, like cinnamon and oranges.

He guided her to a booth in back, away from the windows.

Hey, I'm not doing anything wrong, Scotty thought.

So why do I feel so strange?

Chapter 5

He liked the way she kept touching his hand as she talked. She was always gesturing with her small hands, tugging at her hair, reaching across the table to touch his arm or his hand, as if she had known him for years.

And he liked the way her red hair fell, tangled and wild. Lora was always fussing with her hair. It had to be perfect, not a hair out of place. But Shannon didn't seem to care. She tossed her hair back over her shoulder as she talked, or twirled a strand around her fingers, or tugged at it, smiling, as she leaned forward to listen to him.

She smiled at him with those dark, pouty lips. Her smile was knowing, almost smug, not at all an innocent little girl's smile.

The restaurant was empty except for a pair of silent old men hunched over cups of coffee, and four tough-looking teenagers Scotty had never seen before in a booth next to the window.

He felt comfortable knowing that no one from

school would see him here. And he felt excited sitting here with Shannon, a kind of excitement he had never felt in his life. The excitement of doing something wrong.

Or of *thinking* about doing something wrong.

Of course, he kept reassuring himself, there's nothing wrong with having a hamburger with someone and driving her home. It's not like Lora and I are *married*, he thought, scolding himself for feeling guilty.

"You're a senior, right?" Shannon asked, wiping hamburger juice off her chin with a paper napkin.

"Yeah. You, too?"

She nodded. "What are you doing after graduation?"

"Oh, I'm going to Princeton," he said casually. "Where are you going?"

She looked down. "Probably look for a job, I guess."

He could feel his face redden. She must really think I'm a rich jerk, he thought. Why did I assume she was going to college?

"I'm . . . uh . . . hoping to get a scholarship," he added quickly. "My mom can't really afford it unless I get a scholarship."

"Where's your dad?" she asked.

Scotty was a little startled by the question. He responded with a broad shrug, as if to say, "Who knows?"

For some reason, this struck Shannon as funny.

Her laugh was high and fragile, like the tinkling of a glass wind chime.

They talked for an hour after their hamburgers were finished. Scotty was usually exhausted after a football game, but being with her was keeping him wide awake.

They didn't have much in common. She hated school, hated Glenview, seemed generally unhappy with her life but didn't have any plan for changing it. Unlike Scotty and Lora and their friends, she didn't seem to have any ambition, any goals, any dream.

When he asked her what she'd really like to do with her life, she had to think about it. Finally, tugging at her hair, she said, "I don't know. Be a rock star maybe. Maybe be like Madonna."

As he drove her home, she slid low in the seat, her knees on the dashboard. She turned on the radio and cranked up the volume until the entire car throbbed and vibrated, and sang along in her whispery voice, ignoring Scotty entirely except to point the directions to her house.

The house was a little box, so small Scotty nearly drove right past it. It was entirely dark. He drove up the dirt driveway, his headlights rolling over a rusted pickup truck, tireless, up on cinder blocks in the middle of the narrow front yard. The house was white clapboard but looked as if it hadn't been painted for a long time.

Scotty clicked off the blaring radio.

"Home sweet home," Shannon said, sighing.

How do her three big wrestler brothers fit into that tiny house? Scotty wondered.

He jumped out, ran around the car through the twin white headlight beams, and pulled open the car door. She reached up her hands, and he pulled her to her feet on the soft dirt drive.

To his surprise, she didn't let go of his hands. Squeezing them tightly in her warm hands, she leaned forward, raised herself on tiptoe, and pressed her mouth against his.

Her lips were wet and burning hot.

Her soft hair brushed against his face.

She leaned forward, pressing against him. He started to back away, but realized she didn't want the kiss to end. Giving in to it, he put his arms around her.

She kissed harder, harder.

Hungrily.

Finally she let go. Backed away. Smiled up at him. That sexy, knowing smile.

Wow, he thought.

"Thanks for the lift," she said, breathing hard.

"Uh . . . no problem." He couldn't think of anything else to say. "Hey — almost forgot your bike."

He could still feel the heat of her mouth on his, could still feel the brush of her hair against his face. Feeling crazy and exhausted and excited and confused all at once, he walked quickly to the trunk, opened it, and pulled out the bike.

"You can just leave it here. One of my brothers

will fix it for me in the morning," she said, pulling the light plastic windbreaker around her.

He set it down beside the drive.

"Shannon — are you busy tomorrow night?"

"What?"

He walked back toward her. "Do you want to go to a movie or something?"

She smiled. The half moon in the dark, starless sky above them sparkled in her eyes.

I don't believe I just asked her out, he thought. What am I *doing*?

"Yes. Okay. Neat," she said.

"I'll come by about seven."

What am I *doing*?

She turned and ran quickly to the dark house without looking back. He climbed into the car, closed the door, and looked for her. But she had disappeared. Probably already inside.

The car bumped over the dirt driveway as he backed out to the street.

One date is no big deal, Scotty thought.

Lora is off in Paris and London having the time of her life. Why shouldn't I have a little fun, too?

Besides, Lora will never know. . . .

Chapter 6

Saturday was gray but not as blustery. It felt to Scotty more like a day in late September than November. He had slept in, then had a long, leisurely breakfast. When Bender came over to help rake leaves as they had arranged, Scotty was still in his pajamas.

"You sick or something?" Bender asked, walking in through the back door without knocking, as usual.

He startled Scotty from his thoughts about Shannon.

"You sure look serious this morning," Bender said, grabbing a piece of cold bacon off Scotty's plate and stuffing it into his mouth.

"Oh. I was just thinking about . . . the game," Scotty said, thinking quickly.

"Great game," Bender said, wandering around the kitchen on his long, lanky legs, looking for more food to scavenge.

"Yeah," Scotty agreed, trying to clear the fog from his head. "I'll get dressed. Be right back, man."

"Sure. I'll just make myself a sandwich or something," Bender called after him.

He eats as much as a herd of elephants, Scotty thought in his room, pulling on jeans and a sweatshirt. But he's the skinniest, lightest tackle on the team.

A few minutes later, they were raking the front yard, attacking the large, dead leaves with enthusiasm. "Hey, you guys," Mrs. Singleton called, poking her head out of an upstairs window. "What are you doing?" She had a pink bath towel wrapped around her head.

"What are we doing?" Scotty shouted up to her. "What does it *look* like we're doing? We're raking the leaves!"

"Well, why are you raking in one direction and Bender raking in the other?" she demanded. "You're making two separate piles!"

Scotty and Bender looked at each other. "That's just the way we rake," Scotty replied.

"The earth is round, Mrs. Singleton," Bender added. "Scotty and I are bound to meet sometime!"

"Very funny!" she called sarcastically, and slammed the window shut.

"No sense of humor," Bender muttered, leaning on the rake, then pretending to fall off it. He toppled sideways to the ground. Bender loved falling down. He thought it was hilarious. And he was very good at it.

"How was the dance?" Scotty asked, thinking about Shannon as he started to rake again.

I can't believe I asked her out, he thought. Am I really going to go through with it?

Of course.

He realized he hadn't heard Bender's reply.

"Hey, everyone was asking about you and Lora," Bender said. He was raking with the wrong side of the rake. Anything for a laugh.

"Stop goofing. We'll never get finished," Scotty said, laughing.

"So what did *you* do after the game?" Bender asked.

"Oh, I just went home and . . . watched a video," Scotty told him, avoiding his glance.

"Yeah? What'd you see?"

"Uh . . . I don't remember, man. It was just some dumb movie Denny rented."

I'm such a bad liar, Scotty thought. I can never think fast enough when I want to tell a lie, and I'll bet my face is bright red.

Bender, raking in long, slow sweeps, didn't seem to notice. "So what are you doing tonight? Want to come over and shoot some pool or something?"

"I can't," Scotty said quickly. Too quickly.

Bender looked over at him. "How come? Hot date?"

"Yeah, sure," Scotty said sarcastically, still avoiding Bender's eyes.

Bender laughed at the idea. "Lora would murder you," he said.

"I . . . uh . . . have to study tonight," Scotty lied.

One lie after another, he thought, feeling guilty.

"You? Study?" Bender exclaimed, and fell backwards into the leaf pile he had made. "I thought you got your perfect grades without cracking a book." He sat up. Flat, brown leaves clung to his hair. "Besides, man, they already took you at Princeton. Why knock yourself out?"

"I can't just veg out all the rest of this year," Scotty replied. "Then people would think I was *you!*" He laughed at his own joke and tossed the rake to the ground. "This is boring," he said, helping Bender to his feet. "Let's go check out Ernie."

"You still have that snake?" Bender asked, loping along behind Scotty, around the side of the house to the backyard.

"Yeah. I built this neat cage for him," Scotty said. "On the side of the garage. I put a heater in it and everything, and Ernie gets plenty of sun and fresh air. Mom wouldn't let me keep him in the house since he got so big. She's scared of him."

"Scared of snakes? How weird!" Bender exclaimed.

Scotty gave him a playful shove. Bender pretended to go flying into the side of the garage.

They stopped in front of the large mesh-and-glass cage Scotty had built. "Hey, you've practically got a whole tree in there," Bender said, peering in from the top.

"Well, Ernie's a tree snake," Scotty explained. "I wanted him to feel at home."

The bright green snake was coiled up in the V formed by two branches, its head hidden from view.

"That's the most amazing color," Bender said. "That green is almost neon. I'd like to have a shirt that color."

"I thought *all* your shirts were that color," Scotty joked.

"Just the dress-up ones," Bender said. "So, how about it, Scottso — change your mind. Come over tonight. You can study next year."

"No, really, I can't," Scotty insisted. "I've . . . just got a lot of work to do."

Going out with Shannon has *got* to be wrong, he thought. And here I am, lying to my best buddy.

But so what?

So I'll be *bad* for just one night.

"Hey, Scotty!" His mother yelled from the back door. "Scotty — you back there?"

He stepped away from the cage. "Yeah, Mom!"

"Mail just came," she shouted. "Come look. You got a postcard from Lora!"

Scotty pulled his Raiders cap low over his forehead as he and Shannon walked out of the movie theater. "How'd you like it?" he asked, his hand on her back, guiding her toward the car.

He had taken her to the old Westside theater in the next town, deliberately staying as far away as possible from the tenplex at the mall, or anywhere else he might be recognized.

"It was pretty cute," she said thoughtfully. "But I didn't get some of the humor, I don't think. It was very dry."

He had watched her during the movie and hadn't been able to tell if she was enjoying it at all. For the most part, she sat through it, expressionless, nibbling on her lower lip. Near the end of the movie, she had taken his hand between hers and held it tightly, staring straight ahead at the screen.

He couldn't help stealing glances at her. She was wearing a tight wool sweater and a very short green leather skirt over sheer tights.

I can't believe I'm sitting here with her, he thought.

He was so nervous and excited, he could barely follow the movie.

"I thought John Candy was a riot," he said, trying to keep the conversation going. So far, it hadn't been as easy to talk to her as the night before.

"John Candy. Is he the fat one?" she asked, lowering herself into the car.

Of *course* he's the fat one, Scotty thought as he walked around the car and slid into the driver's seat. Who *else* would he be?

He was starting to think that asking Shannon out was a big mistake when, without warning, she leaned across the gearshift and kissed him.

She smelled so sweet, like oranges. Her hair brushed lightly against his face, tickling his cheeks, sending a chill down his neck.

She leaned back into her seat, smiling at him, licking her lips.

He took a deep breath. "Would you like to go up to Rainer Point?" he asked softly, suddenly feeling nervous. Everyone knew that Rainer Point was a big make-out spot. How would Shannon react to that idea?

Shannon laughed and shook her head no.

Scotty felt embarrassed. Too fast, he thought. I moved too fast. That wasn't too cool of me. I'm such a jerk! And now she thinks I'm a jerk, too!

But then she touched the back of his hand and said, "Let's go to my house instead."

He looked over to see a very playful smile on her face. "What?"

"Let's go to my house," she whispered. "We'll be all alone. My brothers are away, and my parents are at an all-night party."

"Really?" he gulped, his voice cracking.

She nodded her head, her long hair covering her face. "Really," she said, pulling the tangles of red hair away.

He turned the car around and headed toward her house. The night was clear and cold. There were a lot of cars on the road, people out looking for fun on Saturday night. An accident at Penn Crossing had the traffic at a standstill.

They sat in awkward silence. She smiled at him. He tried to think of something to talk about. But they'd already gone over last night's football game again, and they'd already discussed the movie, and school, and the weather.

He was grateful when Shannon reached over and turned on the radio. Again, she turned it up until the car felt about to explode, and sang along, so softly he could see her lips moving but couldn't hear her sing.

We don't have much in common, he realized. This will have to be our only date.

But she really is a babe!

When he reached her house on Sharpes Corners, he pulled up the dirt drive and cut the headlights and the engine. The house was completely dark, as the night before.

As soon as they got inside, she slammed the front door. Then, staring boldly, almost challengingly into his eyes, she pulled off his Raiders cap and tossed it across the dark room.

Then she started covering his face with kisses.

Wow! he thought. This is *awesome*!

"You're *my* baby now," she whispered, holding his head with both hands as she kissed him.

"You're *my* baby now."

Chapter 7

Scotty was awakened the next morning by the phone ringing. He stirred, shook his head as if trying to shake away his sleepiness, and pulled himself up to a sitting position.

Downstairs, he could hear the thunder of Denny's sneakers against the living room floor as he ran to answer the phone. "I'll get it!" Denny screamed.

Scotty yawned and stretched. His head felt like a lead weight. When had he finally rolled back home? It must have been after one in the morning.

And what time was it now? He tried to focus on the digital clock beside his bed, but it was a blur.

"Scotty — phone for you!" Denny shouted from the foot of the stairs, loud enough to wake the dead. "It's a girl!"

"Huh?" Scotty said aloud, scratching his head. Could it be Lora?

No. Her plane doesn't arrive until this evening.

He lumbered over to his desk, tossed a dirty T-shirt out of the way, and picked up the phone. "Hello?" His voice sounded low and husky.

The voice on the other end woke him up immediately.

"Good morning, baby," Shannon chirped.

"Huh? Shannon?" His throat felt dry. He realized his heart was pounding.

"I had such a good time last night," she said softly.

"What time is it?" Scotty asked.

Why is she calling me? he wondered. What does she want?

"It's early, but I just wanted to talk to you," Shannon replied in a little girl's voice. "Did you dream about me?"

"Listen, Shannon — " he started. He could hear his mom padding down the hall, coming toward his room.

"Are you coming over to see me today, baby?" Shannon asked in a tiny voice.

"No, listen. Shannon, I — "

Mrs. Singleton poked her head into the room. Her platinum hair was piled high on her head, tied with a purple ribbon, but she was still in her bathrobe. "Who is it, dear?" she asked, her expression disapproving.

"I'll have to call you later about that," Scotty said quickly into the phone. "Talk to you later, okay?" He hung up the receiver. "Just a girl from school," he told his mother, trying to sound nonchalant. "She had a question about the psych homework."

"So early?" Mrs. Singleton asked, turning her disapproving gaze on the bedtable clock.

Scotty could read it now. It was 8:08. Sunday morning.

"I guess she was getting an early start on it," Scotty said. "I probably should, too."

He hated lying. Whenever he did it, he had the feeling lights lit up on his face, blinking on and off, "Lie! Lie! Lie!"

"When did you get in last night, Scotty?" she asked, tightening the belt on the loose-fitting robe.

"Not too late." Another lie.

"Well, I'm just going down to start breakfast. You want pancakes this morning?"

"No. Something light," Scotty said, making a face.

He stood leaning on the desk, listening to her slippers thud down the stairs. He heard her ask Denny what he was doing up so early. Denny already had the TV in the living room going. Scotty could hear the loud boings and crashes of some kind of cartoon show.

I've got to tell Shannon not to call, he decided.

I've got to make it really clear to her that it's over between us. I mean, we just had the one date. It was just a one-time thing.

When he had said good night to her, standing in the dark, narrow hallway of her tiny house, he tried to let her know that he wouldn't be seeing her again.

"I'll call you sometime." That's what he had told her. "I'll call you sometime."

The meaning of that is pretty clear, he told himself.

Shannon had smiled back at him in the dark, but she had to know what he was telling her.

It was over, over, over.

After all, Lora would be home tonight. He realized he couldn't wait to see her. An entire week was a long time without seeing Lora.

Much too long.

He showered and pulled on a pair of gray sweatpants and a matching sweatshirt. Maybe Bender and I can go to the playground and play a little roundball, he thought. Shoot some hoops. Or maybe a long bike ride. He felt like getting some exercise.

He was down in the kitchen, finishing his cornflakes, sitting at the breakfast counter with Denny and his mother, when the phone rang again.

Scotty started toward the wall phone beside the refrigerator, but Denny got there first. "Who is it?" he asked into the receiver. Denny never bothered to say hello. He always picked up the phone and asked, "Who is it?"

He held the phone out to Scotty. "It's for you," he said. Then he grinned. "The same girl!"

Scotty caught the surprised expression on his mother's face as he hurried over and took the phone from his little brother. "Hello?"

"Hi, baby," Shannon said in her whispery voice.

"Whatcha doin'? You didn't call me back."

"Uh . . . listen . . . uh . . ." Scotty looked back at his mother and Denny. They were both staring at him. "I'm going to take this call upstairs, okay?" he said. "It's homework stuff." He handed the receiver to Denny. "Hang up when I get upstairs, okay?"

Grinning, Denny took the receiver and held it up to his ear. "I can hear her breathing," he said.

"Just hold it for a second," Scotty snapped. He hurried out of the kitchen, through the front hall, and up the stairs to his room, thinking hard about how to get Shannon to stop calling him.

"What does she think she's doing?" he muttered to himself aloud.

As he picked up the phone in his room, he was breathing hard from taking the stairs three at a time. "Hi, Shannon. Listen — "

He heard giggling, realized Denny was still on the kitchen phone.

"Denny?"

"Yeah?"

"Get off the phone. Hang up — now."

Silence.

Scotty waited for the click, the signal that Denny had hung up.

"Denny?"

"Yeah?"

"Get off the phone!"

Denny giggled, made a rude noise with his lips, then finally hung up.

"Who was that?" Shannon asked.

"My dumb kid brother," Scotty said. "He's really bogus."

"He sounds really cute," she said. "I can't wait to meet him."

Meet him? thought Scotty. Why would she ever meet Denny?

"When are you coming over, baby?" she asked. "I'm kinda lonely."

"I can't come over, Shannon," he said. He decided to be really straight with her.

"What?"

"Listen, I'm, like, really busy. You know, with school and everything. And I've got stuff to do around here for my mom. And a lot of studying to do."

"Didn't you have a good time last night?" she asked, suddenly sounding hurt.

"Of course, I did," he told her. "I had a great time, Shannon. Really. But . . . but you shouldn't call. I'm very busy now." He took a deep breath. "And I'm not going to be able to go out with you again."

She giggled. "Aw, you're teasing me. Right?"

"No, really. I'm not," he said. "I have to go now. Good-bye, okay? I'll see you in school next week."

He hung up before she could reply.

The receiver was all wet from his hand perspiring. He stood there for a moment, leaning on the desk, waiting for his heart to resume its normal pace, staring at the phone, half expecting it to ring again.

But it remained silent.

Feeling a little better, he headed downstairs to finish his breakfast. Denny had returned to the cartoons on TV. His mother was unloading the dishwasher. "I thought I'd go over to Bender's. Maybe play some basketball or something," he told her.

She turned around and stared at him, surprised. "Did you forget?"

"Huh? Forget what?" He picked up a piece of cold toast and chewed it.

"About Denny's school fair? Remember? You promised to help out?"

"What?" Scotty cried. "I did? When did I promise? In my sleep?"

Her expression turned stern. "Come on, Scotty. You promised me. I'm the class mother, remember. How will it look if you don't show?"

"But, Mom — "

"It isn't anything difficult. Just coat-check duty. Come on, Scotty. You promised."

He hated it when his mother whined like that. But it was starting to come back to him. He had been feeling guilty because he'd promised to take Denny out bike riding, but then Lora had come over, and he'd gone off with her instead. And so he'd promised he'd go and help out at Denny's school fair.

"Okay. I'll check coats," he said glumly.

What a boring way to spend a Sunday.

His mother smiled. "Good. It should help the time pass for you. When the fair is over, Lora should be almost home. That's exciting, isn't it?"

"Yeah," he said quietly. He couldn't let on to his mother how pleased he really was that Lora would be back.

"I'm going to play video games at the fair," Denny said, entering the room to get a box of juice from the refrigerator.

"You have video games at home," Scotty said.

"So?" Denny hurried back to his cartoons.

A few hours later, Scotty was in the noisy, crowded front hall of Denny's school, checking coats as parents and kids streamed in for the annual fair. Luckily, it was a clear, dry day, so the coats weren't wet or snow-covered. Across the hall, Mrs. Singleton and two other women were selling tickets from large ticket rolls.

"Where's Lora?" a voice asked.

Scotty, weighed down with two long, down overcoats, turned to see Mrs. Farberson, a friend of his mother's, smiling at him.

"She's in Paris," Scotty said. "With her parents. But she's coming home tonight."

"I don't mean to embarrass you," the large, red-faced woman said, handing Scotty her fur-collared coat, "but you and Lora just make the most wonderful couple."

"Thanks," Scotty said awkwardly.

"I *am* embarrassing you. I'm sorry," Mrs. Farberson said, taking the coat-check ticket from him. "But you're just so cute together."

Scotty smiled, an uncomfortable smile. "Thanks," he said again.

Please go away, he thought.

He hated it when people said that he and Lora were "cute." This wasn't the first time he had heard it. But he wished it were the last.

"I know your mother is so proud of you," she gushed. She turned. "Oh — there's your mother over there. I must go say hello. 'Bye, Scotty. Say hi to Lora for me."

He watched her make her way through the crowd, then went to hang up her coat.

The rest of the afternoon was uneventful. Only three other people asked him where Lora was, two of them, friends of the DeMarcos, commenting on what a wonderful couple they were.

Scotty realized he should have been used to the compliments. He and Lora had been together since sixth grade, after all. But even though he really was nuts about Lora, it never failed to embarrass him when people made a fuss about what a terrific couple they were.

It's *our* business — not theirs, he thought.

That evening, he, Denny, and his mother had just finished dinner, fried chicken and french fries from a take-out place down the street. He was about to go upstairs to do some homework, when the phone rang.

"I'll bet that's Lora," Mrs. Singleton said, glancing at the kitchen clock. "It's early, but I'll bet she's calling you from the airport."

Scotty hurried over to the kitchen wallphone and eagerly grabbed up the receiver. "Hello?"

"Hi, baby. Aren't you coming over tonight?" Shannon half talked, half whispered, more of a plea than a question.

Scotty looked back at his mother, who was staring at him expectantly.

"I'm sorry," he said coldly into the receiver. "We already subscribe to *TV Guide*." He hung up the receiver.

His mother was still staring at him, a thoughtful expression on her face.

"I don't believe those sales people," Scotty complained, shaking his head. "They're so bogus! Can you imagine — calling at dinnertime on Sunday night!"

Why was his mother staring at him like that?

Did she suspect something? Or was he just being paranoid?

He was halfway back to the table when the phone rang again.

Chapter 8

Scotty hesitated, staring at the phone on the kitchen wall. It rang again.

"Aren't you going to answer it?" his mother asked impatiently.

"Yeah. I guess." He walked over to it, let it ring a third time, then, with a heavy feeling of dread, picked it up. "Hello?"

"Hi, it's me."

It was Lora.

"Lora? Where are you? At home?" he asked feeling happy — and relieved.

"Yes. I'm home. Totally wrecked. The plane was delayed for over an hour."

"How was it?" Mrs. Singleton called from across the room. "Did she have a good time?"

Scotty repeated the question. "I had a *great* time!" Lora exclaimed. "Paris is so beautiful. Like a movie set. Not like a real city at all. I just couldn't believe it, couldn't see enough. One day, yesterday I think, I'm too tired to think clearly, we were at

Montmartre, looking down from way up high, and it started to snow. This gentle, light snow. It was the most beautiful thing I've ever seen. I don't think I'll ever forget that moment."

"Wow!" Scotty said. "Sounds neat!"

"Get down," Lora said.

"What?"

"Oh. Sorry. I was talking to Fluffernutter. *Get down, you dumb cat.* She won't get out of my lap. Scotty, I think Fluffernutter missed me more than you did!"

Scotty forced a laugh. "That's impossible," he said.

"You missed me?" she asked.

"Of course I did," he said. "It was really bogus without you around. It just felt so weird."

He couldn't help it. As he said those words, Shannon forced her way into his mind. He thought of Saturday night in Shannon's steamy, dark living room.

"I'm happy to be back, too. I thought about you all the time," Lora said.

Scotty felt so guilty, his words caught in his throat.

"Scotty — ?"

"Uh . . . listen, Lora, let's spend all of next weekend together, okay? Just having fun. Only the two of us." He heard the clatter of dishes behind him. His mother was clearing the dinner dishes, noisily loading the dishwasher.

"Scotty, have you forgotten? The Junior Chamber of Commerce thing? You know, the Autumn Ball, or whatever they call it?"

"Let's skip it," he urged. He really felt like being with her and no one else. He had to make it up to her for what he had done, for sneaking out with another girl, a girl he had no real interest in.

"We can't skip it, Scotty," Lora said, sighing. "We're being crowned Teens of the Year, remember?"

"So?" he asked, realizing he was sounding just like Denny.

"So? So they're giving us each five hundred dollars," she said.

"Oh. Right. Well," he said, changing his tone, "I'm really looking forward to that!"

She laughed. "Maybe we can sneak out early," she said playfully. "Maybe we'll take the money and run."

"I like the way your mind works," he said.

"Fluffernutter, get down!" she shouted. "Scotty, I'd better get off the phone. I'm so tired. I think I'm still on Paris time. I don't know *what* time it is."

"Okay. See you tomorrow in school," he said, not wanting to hang up.

"Yeah. See you tomorrow," she said softly, and then added, "I missed you."

"Me, too," he said and hung up feeling very guilty.

"Did they have a good time?" Mrs. Singleton

asked, struggling to close the dishwasher. The handle always stuck.

Scotty hurried over to help her. "Yeah. She said it was great. It snowed one day."

"In Paris? That must have been beautiful," she said dreamily. "I've always wanted to see Paris in the snow."

Scotty's mother had never been to Europe. With the two boys to bring up, there was never enough money for such an extravagant trip.

"Well, I'm glad they made it back okay," she said, giving the counter a final wipe with the dish towel.

Scotty suddenly had the urge to get out of the house, to get into the car, to drive somewhere fast, to drive anywhere, to just get away. "I'm going out for a short while," he told his mother, avoiding her glance.

"You going to Lora's?"

"No. She's too tired. I'm just going for a ride, maybe stop at Bender's," he said, heading to the front closet for his jacket.

"On a Sunday night? Don't you have homework?"

"I'll be back in a few minutes," he said impatiently.

"Do what you want." She disappeared up the stairs.

Scotty pulled on his jacket and searched the shelf for his Raiders cap. Rummaging through the scarves and gloves and woolen ski caps, he couldn't find it.

My cap. Where could it be?

And then he realized. He had left it at Shannon's.

Yes. She had tossed it across the room, and he had never retrieved it.

Maybe I should drive over there and get it, he thought, stepping out the door into a blustery, cold night. It *is* my favorite cap, after all.

I'll just knock on the door. Stay on the front stoop. Ask for my cap.

No way, he told himself.

No way I'm going back to Shannon's. I'm never going back there. Never.

It was a promise he was making to himself, a solemn promise, to him — and to Lora.

Never.

She can keep the hat.

He climbed into the old Pontiac and drove aimlessly around town for nearly an hour. Houses and shops whirred by in the darkness as a light fog settled in. Scotty paid no attention to where he was or where he was going. He felt like driving, just driving.

He didn't think about anything. The darkness, the cold air, the wisps of soft, gray fog all calmed him. By the time he returned home and pulled the car into the garage, he was feeling very relaxed.

The next morning, he arrived at school early, a little past seven-thirty, and found Shannon waiting for him at his locker.

Chapter 9

Scotty stopped short, several yards away. "Shannon?" His voice echoed in the empty corridor.

A warm smile spread across her face. She didn't wait for him to come closer. She ran up to him and jumped up to give him a playful kiss on the cheek.

"Surprised?"

"Yeah," he said, taking a step back. He pulled off his backpack and let it slide to the floor.

She was wearing a bright red turtleneck sweater that clashed with her red hair, and tight black denims. Stepping forward quickly, she tilted her head up for another kiss.

"Whoa. Stop," he said sharply.

"It's okay, baby," she replied softly. "It's nice and early. There's no one around."

"Shannon — what are you *doing* here?" Scotty demanded.

"I wanted to see you," she said, tossing her long hair back over one shoulder. "You're my baby now."

"No, I'm not," he said angrily. He picked up the

backpack and slammed it against the wall. "Stop saying that."

Her dark eyes narrowed. "You liked it Saturday night," she said. She looked about to cry.

She's a good actress, he thought.

It made him even angrier.

"Saturday night was great," he told her. "But it was just one date, okay? It was great. But that's it. We can't go out. Okay? We can't."

"But, baby — "

"Shannon — please!" He looked behind him. A few kids were wandering into the building. Lockers were being opened. Voices echoed down the long corridor. "I'm going with someone," he told her. "Someone I'm very serious about. She's very important to me and — "

"Hey, man — how's it going?"

A hand grabbed Scotty's shoulder from behind.

Scotty wheeled around to see Bender grinning down at him. "Where were you yesterday afternoon?" Bender asked. "I called your house and — "

Bender stopped because he noticed Shannon. "Oh," he said, seeing the forlorn expression on Shannon's face and realizing that he had interrupted a conversation. "Sorry, man. I didn't know . . ."

Bender's face filled with embarrassment. Waving his big hand at Scotty, he started to back down the hall.

"No, Bender — wait!" Scotty said. "Wait up!" He picked up his bookbag.

"I've got to get to homeroom," Bender shouted, still looking embarrassed, and disappeared around the corner.

Shannon stepped in front of Scotty, blocking his way. The hall was crowded now. Scotty looked toward the doors, expecting to see Lora come walking in.

"You're not being nice to me, baby," Shannon said, putting a hand gently on the front of Scotty's jacket.

"Shannon, give me a break — "

"I was so nice to you," she said softly, ignoring his anger, not moving her hand from his chest. "But you're not being nice to me." A tear formed in the corner of each eye.

The bell rang.

She lifted her hand off the front of his jacket. The single tears were rolling down her pale cheeks. She turned quickly and ran.

He stared after her, watching her run through the crowded hall, her hair flowing wildly behind her. A few seconds later, she turned the corner and disappeared from view.

Maybe I finally got through to her, he thought. Maybe she finally gets the picture.

Feeling a lot better, he unlocked his locker and got ready to start the school day.

"Shouldn't I get my coat?" Lora asked.

"No. It isn't that cold out. Really," Scotty urged. "You'll see."

She followed him out the door and onto the lawn behind the school. They were both carrying brown paper lunchbags and cartons of milk. It was Scotty's idea to eat their lunch outdoors, not only for the fresh air but for the privacy.

"I feel like you've been gone a lot longer than a week," he said, sitting down under a large maple tree, bare and wintry-looking. He patted the leafy ground beside him. Lora sat down.

"You're just saying that to be sweet," she said, affectionately pressing her forehead against his cheek.

"Yeah, you're right," he said, and laughed, casually putting an arm around her shoulders.

It was so easy being with Lora, he realized. So comfortable. So *right*.

"What have you got?" Lora asked, removing his arm so she could open her lunch.

"Ham and cheese, I think. Every day it's ham and cheese. So boring."

"Well, who packs your lunch?" she asked.

"I do!"

They both laughed.

"It's not too cold out here. You were right," she said, unwrapping her tuna fish sandwich. Half the tuna fish fell out onto her lap.

"Smooth move," Scotty said.

"The food was a little better in Paris," Lora said, picking up a clump of tuna with her hand and popping it into her mouth. "The bread. The bread was the most spectacular thing. I could just live on the bread. It was so good!"

"Better than Wonder Bread?" Scotty joked.

"Hey, Scotty?" Lora's tone suddenly changed.

"Yeah?" he asked, with a mouth full of sandwich.

"Who's that girl?"

"What?"

Lora pointed.

Scotty looked up to see Shannon standing on the walk a few yards away. Her light windbreaker was open, and she had her hands on her hips as she stared intently at Scotty and Lora.

"Why is she looking at us like that?" Lora asked.

"I don't know," Scotty told her. "I've never seen her before."

Chapter 10

Scotty walked home after school, thinking about Shannon. The sky had turned gray and threatening. Gusting winds tossed waves of dead, brown leaves at his feet, but he stepped through them without noticing.

Shannon, what am I going to do about you? he thought.

How can I get through to you?

It had been so embarrassing at lunch. Shannon had stood there like a statue, staring angrily at Scotty and Lora for the longest time. What did she think I would do? Scotty asked himself. Go running over to her and invite her to join us?

Why can't she take a hint?

I've been straight with her. I've told her exactly how I feel. What more can I do?

He turned the corner onto his block and saw Shannon sitting on his front steps.

Oh, man.

Now what?

She hadn't seen him yet. She was sitting with her head down, her knees tucked between her hands. His first impulse was to turn and run in the other direction.

But that wouldn't do any good, he realized. She'd be sitting there when his mother got home with Denny. And how would he ever explain Shannon to his mother?

No. He had to face her. He had to make her understand that she had to leave him alone.

He took a deep breath and, with long, determined strides, walked over the leaf-strewn lawn to the front stoop. "Hi, Shannon," he said wearily, letting his expression show how unhappy he was to see her.

"You have to break up with her," Shannon said, raising her head slowly. Her eyes were red-rimmed, as if she'd been crying. Her hair was more tangled than usual, one twisted strand falling down over an eye.

"What? Are you crazy?"

She didn't react to him at all, didn't even look at him. "You have to break up with her," she repeated in a low, steady voice.

"Shannon, there's no way I'm breaking up with Lora," Scotty said, standing over her, shifting his weight uncomfortably. He pulled off his backpack and heaved it onto the walk. "No way."

"But you're *my* baby now." She tugged at the strand of hair, but didn't push it away from her face.

"No. I'm not," Scotty said firmly. "I'm not! Hear me? I'm *not!*" He held himself back. He could feel his anger taking over, feel it turn to rage. He felt himself going out of control.

Why didn't she listen to him? Why was she doing this to him?

He wanted to hit something. He wanted to hit *her*.

He closed his fists, then opened them again.

Get control, get control, get control, he repeated to himself.

"I'm not good enough for you?" she asked forlornly, looking up at him, staring into his eyes with her big, brown, sad eyes. "Is that it?"

"No, that's not it," he said coldly. "We had one date. Now it's over. I already told you." He looked down the street, afraid he might see the Pontiac heading home with Denny and his mother.

"You're hurting my feelings," Shannon wailed, tears running down her puffy cheeks. "You're hurting my feelings, Scotty. I'm getting very upset."

"Don't be upset," he said, feeling very helpless, nervously watching the street. "It was just *one* date, Shannon. Be fair — okay?"

"My brothers won't like this," she said, wiping her wet cheeks with her hand.

"What?"

"My brothers," she said, sniffling. "They don't like it when people aren't nice to me."

She's threatening me, Scotty thought angrily. I

don't believe this. She's threatening me with her three monster brothers.

"I'm trying to be nice to you," he said. "I'm trying to be honest. Okay? I think you should forget about me. I think — "

He stopped. He saw his mom's car turn the corner, Denny beside her in the front seat.

"Listen, Shannon — you've got to go — *now.*" He grabbed her arms and pulled her to her feet.

"Let go of me!" she cried, struggling away from him.

"My mom is almost here," he said frantically. "You've got to go."

"But I want to meet Mom," she insisted, following Scotty's gaze to the street. "I think it's time I met Mom, don't you?"

"No!" The car was half a block away. "Listen, Shannon — go now and I'll call you tonight," he offered, tugging at the sleeve of her windbreaker.

"Huh? Really?" Her whole face brightened.

"Yeah. I'll call you. After dinner. We'll have a long talk," he said. "Just go. Now. Please!"

"Okay, baby. Call me tonight," she said, smiling for the first time. She started toward the driveway, but he grabbed her and pulled her the other way, to the side of the house.

"Go that way. Call you tonight. Promise," he said.

She ran off, stopping once to look back at him uncertainly, then disappeared through the hedges to the street just as his mom's car pulled up the driveway.

"AAAAAAGH!" Scotty screamed, letting out only a little of his anger and frustration.

What am I going to *do*?

Furiously, he picked up his bookbag and heaved it toward the front door. He hadn't meant to throw it as hard as he did. It crashed into the storm door, shattering the glass.

"No!" he screamed. "Oh, no!"

He could hear the car doors slam around back, could hear Denny's high-pitched voice repeating, "I'm hungry! I'm hungry!"

Scotty started trudging up the driveway to join them when something caught his eye. A shadow. A large one. Moving quickly from the side of the house, along the hedges toward the street.

"Hey — " Scotty called out.

He saw a man, a very large man, wearing a long raincoat, appear between the hedges, then quickly duck out of view.

"Hey — " Scotty called again, at first not believing his eyes. He stood frozen on the driveway, more surprised than frightened, staring at the hedges that were now still.

Someone was here, Scotty thought.

Someone was watching Shannon and me.

And then he realized. It must have been one of Shannon's brothers. "My brothers are enormous," she had told him, and this guy, even seen from behind, seen in a split second, was certainly enormous, his raincoat billowing behind him as he ran.

"My brothers don't like it when people aren't nice to me," Shannon had said. It was definitely meant as a threat. And one of the three hulks was standing there the whole time, standing in the shadows at the side of the house, watching, listening.

Maybe the whole family is crazy, Scotty thought, chilled by the thought.

What am I going to do?

Trying to conceal his troubled feelings, he hurried around to the back where his mother was struggling with the back door, several shopping bags in her hands. "Scotty," she called out, "are you just getting home?"

"Yeah," he lied. He was getting used to lying.

"I'm hungry," Denny whined.

"I know, I know," Mrs. Singleton groaned.

"The front door is broken," Scotty said. "The glass on the storm door, it's shattered."

"What?" His mother's mouth dropped open. "How?"

Scotty shrugged. "I don't know. I saw it as I came up the drive. Looks like somebody threw something at it."

"Well, maybe we'll just remove it or put the screen back up," she said, frowning. "A new storm door is not in my budget." She brightened and held up the shopping bags. "Especially after the money I spent on this."

"What's that?" Scotty asked.

"I'm hungry," Denny shouted.

She pushed open the door, and they went inside. "It's the new outfit I bought for Saturday. You know. For the Junior Chamber of Commerce."

"You bought a special dress for that?" Scotty asked. He started to open the refrigerator, but Denny got there first, darting between his legs to win the race.

"Of course," his mother said, smiling as she held up the silky chartreuse dress to show him. "It's a special day, isn't it? I had to buy the perfect dress in honor of the perfect couple. I'm just so proud of you and Lora. Everyone is."

"I'm not," Denny said. "I'm hungry."

In his room after dinner, Scotty tried to concentrate on his government studies text. But he couldn't read an entire paragraph without thinking about Shannon. And about her brother, spying on them.

Slamming the book shut in exasperation, he reached for the phone. I'm going to call Shannon, he decided, and tell her once and for all that I don't want to go out with her again, that I don't want her to ever call me again.

But then he pulled his hand back. No. I've already told her. A hundred times. I promised to call her tonight. But I'm not going to. And when she sees that I'm not calling, she'll realize that I'm serious.

And then her enormous brother will beat me to a pulp, he thought.

He stared at the phone. No. No way. I'm not going to call her.

He opened the textbook again and shuffled through to find his place. He still hadn't found it when the phone rang.

He felt his heart skip a beat. He jumped to his feet.

It rang a second time. A third.

He didn't want to pick it up, but no one downstairs seemed to be answering it. "Hello?" he said softly, timidly.

"Where were you, man?" a familiar voice asked without any greeting.

"Bender?"

"Yeah, it's me. Where were you?"

Scotty was so relieved to hear Bender's voice, he could barely hear what his friend was saying. "What do you mean?"

"Where were you? Why weren't you at practice?" Bender asked impatiently.

"Oh, no!" Scotty slapped his forehead. He had been so obsessed with Shannon that he'd forgotten all about his after-school football practice.

"Coach Hawkins was really steamed," Bender said. "He gave Berman extra time. Had him passing all afternoon."

Berman was the second-string quarterback. He wasn't bad. Scotty knew if he slipped up, Berman would take his place in an instant.

"Tell me Berman wasn't any good," Scotty pleaded.

"He wasn't bad," Bender said. "He's really got an arm. He can heave the ball a mile. I think Hawkins was impressed."

"You're a real pal," Scotty said sarcastically. "I *asked* you to tell me he wasn't any good!"

"So where were you?" Bender asked.

"I was . . . busy," Scotty said, struggling unsuccessfully to think of a good excuse. "I had to do some things . . . for my mom."

There was a long silence at the other end. Scotty knew that Bender wasn't buying his story.

"You've been acting kind of weird lately," Bender said finally. "Who was that girl you were talking to?"

"Girl?"

"Yeah. You know. Real little. With the wild, red hair."

"Oh. I don't know her name. She has a locker next to mine, that's all," Scotty told him.

I'm lying to everyone now, he thought.

He had a sudden strong urge to tell Bender everything, but held back. Bender would just make a joke, Scotty thought. Or he might tell someone else. I've got to handle this on my own.

He knew he couldn't take a chance. What if word somehow got back to Lora?

"You sure everything's okay?" Bender asked.

"Yeah. Fine," Scotty said. "See you tomorrow, man."

He hung up and reached for the textbook. "How

am I ever going to read this?" he asked himself aloud.

The phone rang again.

Bender almost always called back with something he'd forgotten. Scotty picked up the receiver. "Hello?"

"Baby, you didn't call." Shannon's whispery voice reverberated in his ear. He could feel his neck muscles tighten.

His entire body tensed. He couldn't hold back his anger any longer. "I didn't call you — and I'm *never* going to call you!" he screamed.

He could hear a sharp intake of breath followed by a low whimper on the other end. He didn't care if he hurt her now. He was too angry to care.

"I don't *want* to call you, Shannon!" he cried. "I don't want to *see* you! We're not going out. Not ever. Hear? I don't want to go out with you."

He took a breath. His heart was pounding. His mouth was dry. There was no sound at all on the other end of the line.

"Leave me alone," he continued. "I mean it. Leave me alone, Shannon. Don't call me again." He slammed the receiver down without waiting for any kind of reply.

"There," he said aloud and reached for his textbook. "That's done."

Chapter 11

Scotty felt good the next morning, having slept well, a peaceful, dreamless sleep. Lora called while he was eating breakfast. He was happy to hear her voice.

"I've been thinking about your birthday," she said.

"Huh?" He swallowed a mouthful of Frosted Flakes. "My birthday is two weeks away."

"So? How shall we celebrate?" she asked. "Should we have a party or something?"

"A party? No. I — " He realized he wasn't awake enough to discuss this. "Can we talk about this later?"

Lora always did this to him. She couldn't bear to be thinking about something alone. If she had something on her mind, she had to call no matter what time it was and make him think about it, too.

"Want to meet after school?" she asked.

"No. I've got football practice," he said. A heavy feeling of dread sank through his body. He knew he was going to be chewed out by Coach Hawkins this afternoon for missing practice. "How about lunch?"

"Okay," she agreed. "The usual place. And think about your birthday, okay?"

"Okay," he said, and hung up. He gulped down the last spoonful of the sweet cereal, tilted the bowl to his mouth to drink the milk, then started to look for Denny. "Denny — where are you? We're going to be late."

Denny came limping into the room, one sneaker on, one off. "I've got a knot in my shoe," he whined, handing the shoe to Scotty.

How does he do it? Scotty wondered, shaking his head. How does he get a knot in his shoe *every* morning?

Scotty dropped Denny off at the elementary school, then continued on to the high school a block away. When he turned the corner and started down the corridor to his locker, he was relieved to see that Shannon wasn't waiting for him there.

He smiled, feeling better, feeling the sense of dread begin to lift. He locked up his coat, then, carrying the books he'd need that morning, talked with friends until the bell for homeroom rang. Shannon was nowhere to be seen.

After fourth period, he met Lora at their usual meeting place outside the lunchroom. "You got a haircut!" he exclaimed, immediately noticing her new, short hairdo.

"Do you like it?" she asked, patting it in exaggerated fashion like a primping movie star. "I wanted to look nice for Saturday."

"Are we really going to show up for that thing Saturday?" he asked, rolling his eyes.

"No. You're going to turn down the five hundred dollars," she replied dryly. "What do you need money for?"

"Okay, okay. We're doing it," he said. "But it's going to be so bogus."

"It's only a few hours of your life, Scotty," Lora said, pulling him into the lunchroom. "What could be so terrible?"

As they ate their sandwiches, Scotty kept alert, looking for Shannon. But she never appeared.

He didn't see her all day. Driving home after football practice, he wondered if she'd be waiting for him on the front stoop.

The afternoon was warm for November, but gray clouds were rolling in, bringing a chill to the air. The bare trees seemed to shiver along the sides of the street as he turned onto his block and then pulled up the drive.

He glanced at the front stoop, then moved his eyes around the front yard.

No Shannon. She wasn't there.

"All right!" he shouted happily inside the car.

He jumped out of the car and stretched. He suddenly felt very light, as if a heavy weight had been lifted from him.

Finally.

I finally made her understand.

Carrying his backpack by the straps, he started to the back door. But he stopped on the walk, suddenly remembering Ernie, his snake, and lowered the backpack to the ground.

I'd better check on Ernie, he thought. I forgot all about him yesterday.

Walking quickly, he headed to the side of the garage. Two fat, gray squirrels scampered along the fence at the back of the yard, kicking up the dead leaves as they ran.

When the cage came into view, Scotty stopped.

And gaped.

The screened cage top was off, lying on the ground beside the cage.

Had Ernie escaped?

Scotty started to run. How had the top come off? It was too heavy to be blown off by the wind. Someone had to have *taken* it off.

But — wait. The snake hadn't escaped. It was still in the cage.

Yes. As Scotty came up to it, he could see Ernie on the glass cage floor.

"Ernie, what's — ?" Scotty started to say. But his mouth dropped open in horror, and he never finished his greeting.

The snake, he saw, had been cut in two.

Chapter 12

"You have to break up with her, baby."

Shannon called him right after dinner. He was upstairs, pacing back and forth in his room, unable to get the picture of his pet snake out of his mind. Ernie had been sliced cleanly across the middle, cut into two almost-perfect halves.

Scotty was standing right next to the phone when it rang. Startled, he uttered a short cry, then picked up the receiver before the first ring had ended. "Hello?"

"You have to break up with her, baby."

Shannon didn't even bother to say hello. Her voice was as whispery as ever, but there was a hard, determined tone to it, an edge Scotty had never heard before.

"Shannon — did you kill my snake?" he asked angrily, balling his free hand into a tight fist.

"You have to break up with her. You *have* to."

"Did you? Did you kill my snake? Answer me!"

"You have to break up with her, Scotty."

Scotty made the fist tighter and tighter until his hand ached with pain. Slowly, he relaxed his hand. His voice trembled from anger as he spoke. "Stop repeating that and answer my question."

"You've hurt me, baby," she said, her little-girl voice returning. "Please don't make me hurt you more."

"More? What do you mean by *more*, Shannon?" he screamed. "You're admitting it? You're admitting that you did it?"

"Come over tonight, and we'll talk about it," she whispered.

"What? Are you serious — ?"

"Come over," she repeated playfully. "There's no one here but me. I'm very lonely, baby."

"Shannon — I — I'm going to call the police," he said, surprising himself. He didn't know if he was serious or not. He hadn't really thought about it. The words just popped out.

"The police?" her voice grew even tinier. Then, to his surprise, she giggled. "My brothers wouldn't like that."

"I don't care about your brothers," he declared. "I've decided. I'm calling the police."

There was a pause. Then she said softly, "No, you're not. Because then Lora would find out. Wouldn't she? And her parents. I'd have to tell everyone then, wouldn't I? Everyone would know about you and me, baby."

"Now, wait — " He didn't know what to say next. Shannon was right, of course. There was no way he could go to the police. If Lora found out, she'd break up with him. He'd lose her. He'd lose . . . everything.

Besides, he had no way of proving that Shannon killed the snake. The police would laugh at him, wouldn't listen to him at all.

"Come over, baby," she urged. "Stop being so silly."

"I'm never coming over," he said slowly, speaking each word clearly and distinctly. "Hear me? I'm never coming over. And if you call me, or threaten me, or do something else to me — *anything* — I'll call the police, Shannon. I really will."

He hung up the phone and realized he was trembling all over.

A loud knock on the bedroom door made him jump.

The door swung open, and Denny came skipping in, a big grin on his face. "What do you want?" Scotty snapped, not meaning to sound so harsh, trying to calm down, not wanting Denny to see how upset he was.

"Can I ask you a favor?" Denny asked, fiddling with the homework papers on Scotty's desk.

"Yeah. I guess."

"It's a pretty big favor," Denny said.

"That's okay. Go ahead and ask."

"It's kind of a *really* big favor," Denny said reluctantly.

"Denny — " Scotty snapped angrily.

"Could I borrow Ernie?" Denny asked. "We're

having a science show-and-tell, and I told everyone I was bringing a snake."

"No. Sorry," Scotty said quickly. He pictured the snake, lying so still and straight, cut into two halves, its insides pouring out onto the glass cage floor.

"Why not?" Denny asked angrily, shoving Scotty's papers across the desk.

"Ernie escaped," Scotty said, thinking quickly. "I . . . uh . . . didn't get a chance to tell you."

"He escaped?" Denny stared up at him, his face filled with surprise.

"Yeah. The lid came off somehow. It was off when I came home, and Ernie was gone."

Actually, Scotty had lifted the two snake halves into a plastic trash bag and buried the trash bag in the dirt behind the garage.

"You mean, Ernie is out in the backyard somewhere?" Denny asked, looking upset.

"I don't think so," Scotty told him, putting a reassuring hand on his shoulder. "I searched all over for him. I think he probably went to the woods. Snakes like it in the woods."

Denny wanted to talk about it more, but Scotty had homework to do and guided him out of the room. That night, Scotty couldn't get to sleep. The picture of his pet, sliced so neatly, so coldly, so cruelly, wouldn't fade from his mind.

It was already dark when football practice ended the next afternoon. The sky was inky black with eerie gray streaks of clouds, ghostly images floating low overhead. The air was cold and damp.

"It could snow for the Madison game Friday night," Scotty said, zipping his down jacket up to the top, ducking his head into the collar for protection against the damp wind.

Bender pulled his Hard Rock Cafe cap low on his forehead as he loped along beside Scotty. His glasses reflected the light from a street lamp. "I guess snow would help us and hurt them," he said thoughtfully.

"How come?" Scotty asked.

Bender shrugged. "No reason. Just trying to sound as if I know something." He laughed. Scotty punched him on the shoulder.

They turned the corner onto Scotty's street. The wind seemed to blow into their faces no matter which direction they walked. Despite the cold, Bender had his down vest unzipped.

"What are you and Lora doing after the game?" Bender asked.

"I don't know," Scotty replied. "You think Hawkins will get off my case before Friday?"

"You know Hawkins," Bender said. "He thinks it's good psychology to make you mad. Thinks it gets you fired up."

"It only gets me mad," Scotty said. "I didn't play so bad today."

As they reached the corner, Bender pretended to walk right into the mailbox. He hit the mailbox hard with his whole body and fell back onto the sidewalk. Bender was always doing things like that, walking into trees, falling down. It usually cracked Scotty up, but he didn't feel like laughing today.

Scotty helped Bender up. "I hope you throw better blocks than that Friday night," he said.

He looked up and saw Shannon standing on the sidewalk in front of them. The streetlight above cast her in an eerie green glow. She was wearing the same plastic windbreaker. Her jeans were tucked into knee-high black boots. In the pale light, she looked frail and tiny, old-fashioned-looking with her long hair flowing freely behind her shoulders, like a Victorian painting of an angel.

"Hi, Scotty," she said softly, smiling with pleasure at the shock on his face.

"Shannon, I warned you — " Scotty said, looking at Bender, who was staring wide-eyed at Shannon, nervously readjusting his cap.

"Why didn't you come to see me last night?" Shannon asked, still smiling, stepping closer.

Scotty didn't reply. He could feel his muscles tense. He was too angry to be embarrassed, but he wished Bender weren't there.

"Hi," Bender said to Shannon. "I'm Scotty's good-looking friend. David Bender. But you can call me Bender like everyone else."

Shannon didn't look at Bender, didn't acknowledge that he was there. "You hurt my feelings, baby," she said to Scotty in her little-girl voice. "Why didn't you come over?"

Scotty's face was frozen in anger. He refused to

reply, hoping his silence would force her to retreat, to disappear.

"Hey — if you two want to be alone . . ." Bender said, casting a meaningful look at Scotty.

"No," Scotty replied quickly. "Let's go, man. I don't know this girl."

"She seems to know you — *baby*!" Bender cracked. He smiled at Shannon, who continued to ignore him.

"Why won't you be nice to me, Scotty?" Shannon asked, her tiny voice barely carrying over the wind. "I was very nice to you. Remember?"

"Wow!" Bender exclaimed.

"Let's go, man," Scotty said, avoiding Shannon's stare.

He started to walk past her, but she stepped into his path, blocking his way. "Don't go, Scotty."

Still ignoring her, he pulled to the right, walking fast. "Let's go, Bender," he insisted.

But Shannon grabbed his arm with both hands, as if making a high, shoulder tackle. "Wait, baby."

"Hey — let go!" Scotty protested.

Shannon slid her hands down the sleeve of Scotty's jacket and squeezed his hand between hers. Scotty saw Bender behind them, staring in disbelief. He tried to pull his hand away from her, but her grip was surprisingly strong.

"Don't go, baby," she pleaded, tears running down her cheeks.

"Come on, Shannon — let go of me!" Scotty cried.

"You two want to Indian wrestle?" Bender suggested. "How about two out of three? I'm betting on *her*!"

"Let go. I don't want to hold hands!" Scotty yelled, surprised by how strong this frail-looking little girl was.

"Don't go. Please — stay with me!" Tears were streaming down her face. "Don't make me hurt you, Scotty. I don't want to hurt you."

As she said this, she grabbed two of his fingers with one hand, the other two fingers with her other hand.

"Hey — !" Scotty cried, struggling to free himself.

But she was so strong, so surprisingly strong.

And then, her face distorted with fury, Shannon pulled down hard, yanking the fingers in two different directions.

At first, Scotty didn't feel anything.

He heard the loud *crack*.

It was loud enough for all three of them to hear it.

He screamed as the pain coursed up his arm, then shot through his entire body. Everything went red, then white. He dropped to his knees. He had never felt such pain. His entire right side throbbed. Gasping for breath, he held his arm close to his body, as if trying to protect it, to squeeze away the pain.

When Scotty focused again, he saw Bender, looking pale, his mouth open, gulping air, his eyes wide behind the black-framed glasses, gaping at Shannon with shock and disbelief.

Shannon had stepped back under the eerie green light of the street lamp. She seemed to be shocked by what she had done. Wet tears slid down her cheeks. She tugged at the sides of her hair with both hands.

"Shannon — my hand — " Scotty managed to cry out in a terrified voice he didn't recognize. He held the injured hand up by the wrist with his left hand.

"I'm so sorry, baby," she cried, shaking her head. "I'm so, so sorry." Then she turned and ran, her windbreaker flapping noisily behind her.

"My hand — " Scotty called after her. He turned his gaze on Bender. "It's — it's broken!"

Chapter 13

Behind him in the bleachers, Glenview fans cheered
and shouted. Scotty leaned forward on the bench
to get a better view. On the first play from scrimmage, Berman went back to pass. He looked left,
then right.

Too long. You're taking too long, Scotty thought.
You're going to eat the ball.

He was right. Berman was swarmed by three
gold-and-green-uniformed Madison players. He hit
the ground hard, sacked, and they piled on top of
him.

The crowd in the bleachers groaned and then
grew quiet.

Scotty turned downfield to see the cheerleaders.
They were facing the crowd, clapping in rhythm,
shouting a "Go, Tigers" cheer. Lora stood in the
center, leaping high in her short, green-and-white-
skirted cheerleader uniform. She looks great,
Scotty thought.

Shifting the heavy cast on his hand, he turned back to the game in time to see a handoff to Barker, stopped at the line of scrimmage. Third down. The Madison players seemed really fired-up. A cheer went up from the Madison supporters on the other side of the field.

Scotty groaned as the next play began, and Berman fumbled the snap from center. Luckily a Glenview player fell on the ball. But now it was fourth down. The Tigers had to punt.

I should be in there, Scotty thought, pounding his knee with the heavy, white cast over his hand. He looked down at the cast, feeling his anger starting to rise.

But he realized he was more angry at himself than at Shannon. I let everyone down, he thought. I let Coach Hawkins down. I let the team down.

He looked past the bench toward the cheerleaders. Lora had turned around to watch the punt. Her short hair glowed golden under the bright white stadium lights. She turned and looked back at him, her smile momentarily fading. Their eyes met. He waved at her with the cast. She turned back to the field.

I let Lora down, too, Scotty thought glumly. And her parents. And everyone else who believes in me.

The punt was short. The Glenview supporters in the bleachers behind the team bench groaned. Madison would be starting out on the Glenview forty-five.

"Dee-fense! Dee-fense!" the cheerleaders were chanting.

After Shannon broke Scotty's hand, Bender had taken him to the emergency room at Glenview General. On the way, Scotty had to explain a little bit about Shannon, after first making Bender swear to total secrecy.

"She's been after me for weeks," he lied, feeling bad, feeling guilty about all the lying he'd had to do. But what choice did he have? "She calls me, and comes to my house, and follows me everywhere," he told Bender. "She wants me to go out with her, but of course I won't. She's crazy. Just plain crazy."

"You've got to call the police," Bender urged.

"No, I can't," Scotty said, resting his head on the seat in Bender's car, grimacing as his hand throbbed with pain. "The police won't do anything."

"But she broke your hand, man!" Bender exclaimed, nearly driving through a stoplight. "That's assault, isn't it?"

"She'd just say it was an accident," Scotty said softly, afraid to tell Bender the real reason he didn't want to call the police. Afraid to tell Bender any of the real story.

"Well, at least you can call her parents," Bender suggested, turning into the hospital driveway. "Let them know what their daughter is doing. Tell them she's got to be put on a leash or something."

"Yeah. That's a good idea," Scotty had said thoughtfully.

Bender was right, he realized. He *could* call Shannon's parents and tell them that Shannon was driving him crazy. Or maybe even talk to one of her brothers.

The whole family couldn't be as weird as she is — could they?

He told everyone, including his mother, that he had slammed his hand in a car door. Lora had been terribly sympathetic. She called him a clumsy clod, but she said it in a nice way. Coach Hawkins hadn't been as nice.

That night, trying to get to sleep, Scotty kept hearing the crack his fingers made as Shannon pulled them in different directions. The pain had subsided, but his hand itched constantly, and of course, he couldn't scratch it.

The next morning, he tried calling her house at lunchtime, hoping to catch someone home while Shannon was in school. He had carefully rehearsed what he was going to say, repeating it endlessly in his mind. He was going to tell them that he was a friend of Shannon's and that as a friend, he was calling to say that she needed help, that he was very worried about her. He was going to tell them that she had been calling him constantly, following him around, and threatening violence.

It was the truth, after all.

If they weren't sympathetic, he was going to threaten to call the police. He hoped he wouldn't have to do that. He wanted to stop Shannon. But he didn't want to get her so upset that she'd do something drastic, like call Lora.

Despite his endless rehearsal of what he was going to say, his heart was pounding as he punched in her phone number. The phone rang and rang, but no one answered.

He tried again right after school. Again, no one was home.

That night, he dialed her house again, hoping that one of her parents or brothers would answer. But he immediately recognized Shannon's breathy "Hello?" and slammed down the phone.

Her "hello" had sounded so eager, so hopeful, that for a moment Scotty had felt sorry for her. But then he glanced at his hand in the big, white cast and rememberd that the football season was over for him, as were his chances of being named all-state, and he felt only anger.

He tried calling three more times during the week. But Shannon had answered each time, and each time he had immediately hung up. Finally he gave up the idea, and his carefully rehearsed speech faded from his mind.

Now, here he was on Friday night, sitting on the team bench in his street clothes, balancing his heavy cast on his lap, feeling terribly guilty and terribly sorry for himself at the same time, watching the Tigers lose to a team he knew he could have beaten.

The final score was 21–3.

As the team trudged to the locker room, Scotty

stayed on the bench, slumping low, feeling chilled by the night air, staring across the now-empty field as people made their way out of the stadium.

"Hey, man, we missed you," Bender said, standing over Scotty, his helmet in his hand, his hair matted down on his head, sweat covering his forehead despite the cold night air.

"Yeah, well . . ." Scotty stared across the field uncomfortably.

"Only one more game," Bender said, breathing hard. "That girl still bothering you?"

"No," Scotty told him, still avoiding his glance. "I haven't seen her all week."

"Hey — that's great!" Bender said. "That's terrific."

"You haven't told anyone about her?" Scotty asked nervously.

"No. No way," Bender replied, looking hurt that Scotty would ask that question. "You meeting Lora?"

"Yeah. She's getting changed. Then we're going to go get something to eat. Want to come?"

"No. Thanks. I'm going to hang out with some of the guys on the team. Later, okay? I've got to get changed." He jogged off toward the locker room.

Scotty stayed on the bench for a while, staring at the shiny green turf, thinking about Shannon and about Lora. He was startled when the stadium lights went out, casting everything in darkness.

Standing up, he turned to see Lora watching him from the cinder track at the edge of the field. "Hi," she called, waving. She had changed into maroon corduroys. Her shearling coat was open, revealing a white, crew-neck sweater. "What on earth are you doing?"

"Nothing much," he said, hurrying over to her. "Just waiting for you."

"You were sitting there feeling sorry for yourself," she said, taking his arm and giving him a quick kiss on the cheek. Her nose and lips felt hot against his cold face. "Admit it."

"Maybe a little," he confessed, smiling guiltily.

"Well, I have some news that should cheer you up," she said, holding tightly onto his arm as they walked to the parking lot.

"The Junior Chamber of Commerce disbanded, and we don't have to go to that stupid thing tomorrow?" he joked.

She slapped his arm, accidentally hitting the top of the cast. "Oh. Sorry. No. My news is that Daddy has decided to take on an intern for the summer at his firm, and you're it."

"Huh?"

"You heard me, Scotty. You can work as an intern there this summer, and he'll even pay you. Not a lot, but it'll give you some spending money for when we're at Princeton in the fall."

"Wow! That's great!" Scotty exclaimed, brightening.

"Am I cheering you up?" she asked, clinging to him, pulling the shearling coat together with her free hand.

"Yeah. You're doing a great job," Scotty said sincerely.

"Well, here's more," she said, grinning at him. "Daddy says you can come up to the Cape with us in August and stay for two whole weeks."

Scotty stopped and turned to her. "Really?" He hadn't looked forward to August. He knew Lora would spend the whole month up at the Cape with her family, and he wouldn't get to see her. "That's awesome!" he declared.

"Stick with me, kid," she said playfully. "I'll show you a good time."

"August is a long way away," he complained. "It's only November."

"Hey — I'm trying to cheer you up," she said, laughing. "Give me a break."

"Please — don't say *break*," he groaned, holding up his cast.

She gave him a playful shove. He reached for her, but then stopped short as the parking lot came into view.

There, leaning casually against the hood of his Pontiac, was Shannon. She was wearing the same outfit as the last time he'd seen her — jeans tucked into high black boots, the plastic windbreaker, which she always seemed to wear no matter how cold it was.

Did she see him?

No. Not yet. She was looking toward the other stadium exit.

Looking past her, trying to decide what to do, Scotty's eyes bulged in surprise. Someone else was standing a few cars down, hiding in shadows, keeping low behind a black Jeep.

It was the large man Scotty had seen running along the hedges from his yard. Shannon's enormous brother!

A wave of fear shot through him. Why had Shannon brought her brother? Why was he hiding in the shadows a few cars away from Shannon?

She had already broken his hand. Wasn't that enough? Now, what did she and her huge brother have planned for him?

"Uh . . . can we take your car?" Scotty asked Lora, trying to make his voice sound normal.

Lora looked at him, confused. "Huh? Why?"

"Uh . . . mine doesn't have much gas," he lied.

"Well, okay. I'm parked on the street," she said, still clinging to his arm. "Your muscles are all tight," she said, squeezing his bicep through his jacket. "How come you're so tense?"

"You just excite me," he cracked, leading her quickly in the other direction, away from the parking lot.

"Hey — what's the rush?" Lora protested.

"I'm hungry," he lied. "Let's go get some burgers."

Did Shannon see me? he wondered. What is she doing there? Is she going to wait there all night?

He turned back to see.

"Oh!" He gaped in horror as he saw the flames shoot out from the front seat of his car.

Still standing a little in front of the car, Shannon stared at him, hands on her hips, just stood and stared, as still as a statue, bathed in the yellow glow of the fire.

Chapter 14

"I have to tell you something, Shannon, and you have to listen to me," Scotty said, softly, seriously.

She tugged at a strand of her hair, but didn't reply.

They were sitting on the sofa in her living room, its cushions worn and sagging. The only light came from a dim bulb in the back hallway.

She edged closer to him, her face covered in shadow. He could smell the sweet, flowery perfume she was wearing.

"Will you listen to me?" he asked softly. "I have the feeling that you do not listen to me, Shannon."

She leaned forward, bent her head, and brushed her hair against his cheek. It sent a shiver of excitement through him.

"Shannon — ?" He really wanted to talk to her, to communicate with her. He had to set things straight, once and for all.

She pressed her head against his shoulder, a tender gesture.

"Shannon — ?"

"You hurt me, Scotty," she whispered.

He leaned away, tried to get some room between them. "That's what I want to talk to you about," he said.

The ceiling creaked. What was that sound? Footsteps? Was someone walking around upstairs?

"You hurt me," she repeated. She raised her head and stared at him, her dark eyes burning into his. "And when I get hurt, I hurt back," she told him, still whispering.

"That's what I wanted to talk to you about," he said, edging away, trying to back away from the warmth of her, the fragrance of her perfume. "You see, I can't see you. Ever again."

She stared at him, her face expressionless, beautiful in the dim light.

"I know we had something really special," Scotty said. "But you have to understand that it's over. I really can't see you."

She remained silent. The only sounds now were the creaking of the ceiling, her soft, rhythmic breathing, the insistent pounding of his heart.

"Do you understand?" he asked, raising his voice for the first time.

"Let me see your hand," she said, reaching for him.

He pulled his arm away. "You broke my hand, Shannon. Why do you want to see it?"

"Let me see the other hand, baby. I want to tell your future."

"No," he insisted. "I'm *telling* you the future. I cannot see you again."

Her lips puckered into a childish pout.

"Do you understand? Do you finally understand?" Scotty demanded.

"I'm very hurt," she said, still pouting. "You have hurt me a lot, Scotty. And my brothers don't like it when I'm hurt."

As she said this, the floorboards creaked and groaned. The room filled with dark figures, moving quickly through the shadows, large figures, lumbering noisily.

A light went on overhead. Three enormous men stood in front of the couch, glaring at Scotty. Even though they were indoors, all three were wearing long trench coats with wide lapels. All three had round, red faces, topped with short-cropped white-blond hair.

"My brothers don't like people who hurt me, Scotty," Shannon said in her whispery voice, speaking tonelessly, without any expression at all.

"Now, wait — " Scotty started, suddenly terrified. He looked up at the three identical brothers looming menacingly over him, so big, so muscular, their faces locked on him, seething in silent anger.

"Get him," one of the brothers said, raising his arms as if to perform a stranglehold.

"Get him," the others grunted.

Scotty uttered a low cry and shrank back on the sofa as the three enormous men circled the couch, then closed in on him.

Chapter 15

The phone was ringing.

He stirred, pushed himself up, and squinting against the morning light, looked for Shannon's brothers.

The phone rang again.

"It was a dream," he said aloud, his throat still clogged with sleep.

Of *course* it was a dream. An ugly, frightening dream. But just a dream.

He picked up the phone and cleared his throat. "Hello?"

The dream lingered in his mind. He expected to hear Shannon at the other end.

"Hi, did I wake you?"

"Lora?" He was relieved to hear her voice. He glanced at the clock. Ten-twenty.

"Who were you expecting?" she asked teasingly. "Your mystery girl?"

Her joke sent a shock wave down the back of his neck.

Did she know something? Did she mean something by that?

Of course not.

Don't go completely mental, Scotty, he scolded himself.

"I guess I slept late," he said uncertainly. "What's happening?"

"That was so horrible with the car last night, I just wondered how you were," she said.

"I'm okay, I guess. Mom took it pretty well," he told her, remembering the night before with a shudder. It all came back to him in a series of ugly pictures flashing before his eyes: the flames licking up from the car, Shannon seeming to disappear into thin air along with her mysterious brother, Scotty running to the car, the fire trucks, the hoses, the crowd of onlookers.

"Did the firemen figure out what caused the fire?" Lora asked.

"Yeah. They think it was a match," Scotty told her. "They think someone came out from the game, lit up a cigarette, and tossed the match into my front seat. It was so bogus of me to leave the window open."

Of course, Scotty knew that wasn't how his car was set on fire. He knew that Shannon had done it. He could still see her standing there staring at him and Lora as the flames grew higher and higher behind her.

I've got to talk to Shannon, he thought. I've got to make her see that this all has to stop.

He glanced down at his broken hand. It itched like crazy. He banged the cast against the wall, but it didn't help.

This all has to stop. It *has* to!

"Mom's making her famous Belgian waffles for breakfast," Lora said.

"Is *that* what smells so good?" he joked, sniffing loudly into the receiver.

"Why don't you hurry up and get dressed and come over for breakfast?" Lora suggested.

"Well, no I — "

"Don't say no," she interrupted. "Say yes."

"But I'm going to see you in a few hours at this stupid Junior Chamber of Commerce thing."

"Oh, I see," she replied sharply. "And seeing me twice in one day would be too much for you, huh?"

"Okay. I'll be there in fifteen minutes," he quickly agreed. "Don't eat all the waffles before I get there."

"Me?!" she cried with exaggerated indignation. "You pig! I'm not the one who swallows the waffles whole! I wouldn't touch your stupid waffles!"

"Don't yell," he said softly.

"Why not?" she screamed.

"Because I have a broken hand."

She laughed. "You're weird, Singleton. Hurry over, okay? I want to show you the dress I'm wearing this afternoon. Wait till you see it. It's a riot.

It looks like something my grandmother would wear."

"Can't wait," he said sarcastically. He faked a loud yawn.

"Hey — be a good sport about this afternoon," she said.

"Huh?"

"Be a good boy at the Autumn Ball and maybe I'll buy you a balloon."

"See you," he said, and hung up.

When he came downstairs, his mother was on the phone with the insurance company about the car. "Be home in a few hours," he whispered. She looked up, concentrating on her conversation, and gave him a quick wave. "But I need a car right away. Can you get me a replacement?" she was saying.

Feeling guilty, Scotty headed out the front door and began walking to Lora's house, only four blocks away. It was a clear, crisp day. The sky was bright blue and cloudless.

Much too nice a day to be cooped up with the Junior Chamber of Commerce, he thought unhappily.

The Belgian waffles cheered him up a little. Mrs. DeMarco kept pouring more batter on the waffle iron, bringing replacements to the table so fast Scotty could barely keep up. Finally, feeling stuffed, he begged her to stop. "I won't fit into my jacket this afternoon!" he told her.

"Speaking of that hideous jacket," said Lora, getting up from the table, "come see my dress." She grabbed his hand and pulled him to her room.

"Hey, what's wrong with my jacket?" he asked, pretending to be offended. They'd had this conversation before.

"It looks just like a horse blanket I saw at the riding stable last week," Lora told him.

"Yeah, but what's *wrong* with it?" he joked.

They both laughed. She closed the door to her room, threw her arms around his neck, and kissed him. "You always make me happy," she said.

Normally he'd feel happy, too. But this morning, every nice thing Lora said just made him feel guilty.

She pulled the dress out of the closet. He agreed that it was weird-looking. It was a blue sheath dress made of some sort of shiny material. "I'm going to look like a grownup," she said, holding it up in front of her. "And you're going to look like a horse!"

"Lay off my jacket," he grumbled, making a sour face.

She whinnied at him, doing a pretty fair imitation of a horse.

"Give me a break, Lora!" he cried.

She whinnied again, laughing. He started to chase her around the room. Laughing, they stumbled out into the hall.

"It's still early," she said, taking his hand. "We don't have to be there till two. Come out in the backyard for a while."

She led him out through the sliding glass doors. They crossed the terrace, stopped to look at the covered swimming pool, then started walking slowly, arm in arm, down the wide, sloping lawn.

"Daddy's real excited that you're going to intern at his place this summer," she said, taking a deep breath of the fresh, sweet-smelling air.

"Not as excited as I am," Scotty told her.

"I think it's real cute how he's kind of adopted you," Lora said chirpily. "I think he always wanted a son. Instead he got me."

"You're all right," Scotty said, grinning.

"Thanks a bunch," she said sarcasatically, giving him a playful shove.

She stopped suddenly. "What's that?"

Scotty followed her stare. There was a small, dark object lying in the grass near the wooden fence.

"That's odd," Lora said. "Let's see what it is."

As they stepped closer, walking quickly over the wet grass, the object came into view. It was a black cap, lying upside down.

"Hey — isn't that the Raiders cap you always wear?" Lora asked.

Scotty gasped.

"How did your cap get back here?" Lora asked him, puzzled.

"I don't know," he said, overwhelmed by a sudden feeling of dread.

He held back while she ran to get the cap.

"Lora? Wait!" he called.

But he was too late.

She bent over to pick up the cap, looked inside it, then, raising her hands to her face, started to scream.

Chapter 16

"What is it?" Scotty cried, running over to her, his heart pounding.

"It — it's Fluffernutter!" she wailed.

Scotty put an arm around Lora's heaving shoulders and stared into the cap. The white cat was dead, its blue eyes already sunken back in a gruesome, glassy stare. Its body had been bent and stuffed tightly into the baseball cap.

"Who did this?" Lora wailed, tears pouring down her cheeks. "Who did this?"

Scotty stood gaping at her. Lora had always seemed to be in complete control. He had never seen her cry before.

"Fluffernutter!" she cried. She picked up the baseball cap and cradled it against her chest. "Poor Fluffernutter."

Shannon did this, Scotty realized.

I left the cap at her house. She never returned it.

Until now.

She'll do *anything*, he realized. *Anything*. She doesn't care what she kills or who she hurts.

He stared at the cast on his hand. First Shannon took out her jealousy on me. And now she has taken it out on Lora.

What am I going to do? What *can* I do?

I've go to stop Shannon. But how?

"Who did this?" Lora demanded, staring at him now, still cradling the dead cat in her arms. "Who?"

"I don't know," Scotty said softly, his arm around her tenderly. "I just can't imagine. . . ."

How long can I keep lying to Lora? he asked himself.

How many more horrors is Shannon going to commit before I'm forced to tell Lora the truth?

"Who did this? Who did this?" Lora repeated, holding the cat tightly, closing her eyes. Then she opened them and stared at Scotty, her expression hardening. "How did Fluffernutter get in your cap? How did your cap get in my backyard?"

"I don't know," Scotty lied. "I haven't seen the cap for days. I lost it over a week ago."

"You lost it?"

"Yeah. I've been looking and looking for it," he said. "I think maybe I must've left it at your house sometime."

"Poor Fluffernutter," Lora said, wet tears covering her eyes again. "I just don't understand this." She stared hard at Scotty, as if expecting him to have an answer.

He gently took the cap with its twisted corpse out

of her hands and set it back down on the ground.

I've got to tell her the truth, he decided.

I've got to stop lying. I just can't take this anymore.

I'll tell her about Shannon. Lora will be hurt and upset, but she'll forgive me. And once she knows the truth, we can both go to the police. We can stop Shannon once and for all.

Scotty took a deep breath. "Lora — I have to tell you — "

But before he could say another word, a large, dark figure stepped up from behind and grabbed Scotty by the shoulder.

Chapter 17

Scotty spun around in terror.

"Mr. DeMarco!" he cried.

Lora's father grinned at him, squeezing his shoulder. "Sorry if I startled you. How is my favorite couple today?" He was wearing a smartly tailored, black wool suit, already dressed for the afternoon affair.

"Daddy — Fluffernutter is dead!" Lora wailed, pointing down to the cap on the ground. "Somebody killed her!"

Mr. DeMarco's broad smile shrank to an openmouthed look of shock, and his normally ruddy face paled. He let go of Scotty's shoulder as he saw the contents of the cap.

He didn't say anything. His mouth froze in an O of surprise and puzzlement. He leaned his head down to examine the cat, then looked up at Scotty. "Isn't that your cap?"

Scotty felt his face grow red. "Yes," he muttered. "It's been lost for days,"

"How strange," Mr. DeMarco said, tucking his necktie back under his suit jacket with a trembling hand. "How strange."

It isn't strange at all, Scotty thought guiltily.

I could explain it to you in less than a minute.

But the desire to explain, to tell the truth, had left him. He knew he couldn't face both Lora and Mr. DeMarco together. They would be so disappointed in him. So hurt by his betrayal.

Things would never be the same again, Scotty realized.

Silently, he walked back to the house with them. The walk took only a few minutes, but it seemed like an eternity.

The Junior Chamber of Commerce Autumn Ball was held in the ballroom of the Sheraton. The room was vast, with rows of crystal chandeliers suspended from the high ceilings over the dozens of round, white tableclothed banquet tables spread over the room. There were tall flower arrangements as a centerpiece on every table. A large parquet dance floor stood to the right of the tables. In the front of the room, beyond the table of honor, stood a low stage where the dinner-jacketed orchestra sat.

Scotty immediately saw that he and Lora were just about the only young people in the room. They arrived a little after two to find the place already crowded, the orchestra already playing some lilting elevator music, waiters passing through the room with silver trays of hors d'oeuvres, a long line at the punch bowl.

Scotty's mother had her platinum hair piled high on her head and moussed until it stood as stiff as a sculpture. She wore her new chartreuse cocktail dress, the brightest dress in the room. But Scotty didn't mind. He was used to his mother's flamboyant style. Actually, he realized, the clothes she wore and her platinum hair were the only flamboyant things about her.

Mr. and Mrs. DeMarco were somewhat somberly dressed, especially in comparison with Mrs. Singleton. Mr. DeMarco wore his black wool suit with a dark, narrow tie. Mrs. DeMarco had chosen a tailored gray suit, the color just a shade darker than her graying hair, with a high-collared white blouse, offset by a dark blue silk scarf worn loosely as a tie around her neck.

Lora actually looked sensational in the blue sheath dress she had made fun of that morning. It had seemed dowdy and old-fashioned when she held it up in her room. But on her, Scotty thought, it became a very sexy party dress.

But of course, none of them were in a party mood this afternoon.

Mr. DeMarco had buried Fluffernutter by the fence in the backyard. Scotty's Raiders cap had been thrown into the trash.

They had all come to the hotel together in Mr. DeMarco's BMW. Mr. DeMarco had tried to cheer everyone up by telling funny stories he had heard at work. But, still thinking about the murdered cat in the backyard, they were a pretty grim crowd.

Now they entered the ballroom with forced smiles. The adults hurried to greet friends, shaking hands, kissing cheeks. Scotty and Lora got in line for some punch, both of them feeling tense and uncomfortable.

Scotty had dreaded this afternoon for weeks. He knew it would be boring and difficult, keeping a smile plastered to his face for hours as people, mostly friends of the DeMarcos, congratulated Lora and him, slapped him on the back, and told them what a good-looking couple they made and how proud everyone was of them.

But after what had happened, it was even harder than Scotty had imagined to keep it together. He didn't feel like smiling at these people, like making small talk about the warm winter they'd had so far, about school, and about the Tigers and what a shame it was that Scotty had broken his hand and couldn't finish the season.

Knowing how his hand had been broken, knowing how Lora's poor cat had been killed — knowing that he himself was largely responsible for the terrible things that were happening — was driving Scotty over the edge.

He felt like tearing off his stupid, plaid sports

jacket and the necktie that was choking him and tossing them in the trash. Then he'd run out the door and keep running.

Away from Lora. Away from the DeMarcos, even though they'd been so nice, so giving. Away from his mother. Away from Glenview. Away from everyone he knew.

Away from . . . Shannon.

He'd run and run and never stop.

"What are you thinking about?" Lora asked, filling a cup of the dark purple punch for him and handing him the glass cup, some of the liquid spilling over the sides.

"I'm thinking about how great you look in that dress," he lied. He spilled a little of the punch back into the gigantic crystal punch bowl.

She forced a smile. "And I'm thinking how that jacket *still* looks like a horse blanket!"

He laughed, pleased to see her smile again. They headed toward a corner, away from the dance floor crowded with people talking and laughing, where they could drink the awful, sweet punch in quiet.

But there was no escape today.

"Kids! Kids!" cried an excited woman's voice, and Mrs. Benedict, the president of the Junior Chamber of Commerce and organizer of this event, came hurrying over. She was a tall woman, as thin as a rail, dressed in a straight, black skirt that emphasized her slimness. She wore four or five huge, sparkling rings on her fingers and had at least six strands of gold and emerald beads around her neck, which clattered noisily as she came running up to them.

"Oh, we're all so excited!" she gushed, beaming at them both. "You two look wonderful."

Lora thanked her. Scotty nodded, nervously straightening his light brown hair with one hand.

"We're going to have lunch. Then I'm going to present your awards to you," Mrs. Benedict said. "And the check, of course," she added, and laughed a high-pitched laugh.

"Thank you," Lora said. Scotty repeated her words, shifting his weight uncomfortably, staring down at his empty punch cup.

"We're all so proud of both of you," Mrs. Benedict said. "You're both just so exceptional. And I understand you're both going to Princeton next fall. How wonderful!" She stopped. And blinked. "I'm embarrassing you, aren't I," she said in a subdued voice.

"No, not at all," Lora said quickly.

"Everyone's being so nice to us," Scotty added.

"I didn't mean to make you uncomfortable," Mrs. Benedict said. "I know this must be hard for you. My son Tim — you know Tim — well, he refused to come today. He's home playing Nintendo or goofing off. I'm sure you'd rather be doing that, too. It's just so refreshing to meet two truly *nice* young people these days."

"Thanks," Lora and Scotty said. They both shook hands with Mrs. Benedict, and she walked away, her necklaces clinking.

"She's not so bad," Lora said, watching her stop to greet some late arrivals.

"Her son's a total nerd," Scotty said, snickering.

"I don't think anyone wearing that sports jacket should call anyone else a total nerd," Lora cracked, "And what about that tie? Is that a clip-on?"

Scotty made an unhappy face, but he was secretly pleased that Lora was making jokes again. "Save my place against the wall here, okay?" he asked, handing her his empty punch cup.

"Where are you going? Are you ducking out?" she asked suspiciously.

"No," he told her. "I'm going to the bathroom. We can't be together *every* second, you know."

She stuck her tongue out at him. He rolled his eyes and started off across the room.

"Hey — what happened to your hand?" a middle-aged man in a red blazer asked as Scotty passed.

"Hunting accident," Scotty replied. He didn't know why he said that. The words just came to him. He decided he was starting to feel a little better, too.

He was making his way past the rows of tables when a young man he recognized as a cousin of the DeMarcos came hurrying up to him, a concerned look on his face. "Hey, Scotty!" he called.

Scotty tried to remember his name. "You're Paul, right?"

"Right," the young man said, not smiling. "I think you should go out front."

"Huh?" Scotty wasn't sure he heard him correctly.

"I think you're needed out front," Paul repeated, his forehead wrinkled with concern. "There's someone out there. A girl."

Scotty had a heavy, sinking feeling. "A girl? Out front? Why do they need me?"

"Well . . ." Paul reached a hand over his shoulder and rubbed the back of his neck. "Sorry. Stiff neck. I woke up with it."

"What about this girl?" Scotty demanded.

"She doesn't have an invitation, so they're not letting her in. But she says she's your date." Paul looked meaningfully across the room at Lora, who was still talking to her father.

"My date? That's totally bogus," Scotty said. "They should just send her away. I don't know who it could be." He lowered his voice confidentially to Paul. "Why would anyone want to crash *this* party?" He laughed.

Paul didn't seem to catch his humor. "Well, the lunch is going to be really fabulous," he replied, studying Scotty's face. "You'd better go out front. The hotel people are waiting for you, Scotty."

"Okay," Scotty said, realizing he had no choice. He could feel all of his muscles tense as he turned and walked to the ballroom doorway. He could hear his mother calling him from somewhere near the stage, but he just kept walking, taking long, steady strides.

What am I going to do? he thought, trying to fight down the panic he felt.

What am I going to say to Shannon? How can I get rid of her before anyone sees her?

A gong rang behind him in the ballroom. He heard chairs being scraped across the floor. Lunch was being served. He had felt hungry a few moments before, but now his stomach was tied in a knot.

He stepped out into the hallway. Two uniformed hotel workers, serious-looking young men with slicked-back black hair and hard expressions, were standing beside a wooden desk that had been set up to check off guests on the list as they arrived.

And there was Shannon. Standing between them, her arms crossed over her chest.

Scotty stopped at the doorway and stared at her.

What did she think she was doing? How did she have the nerve to come here?

Her hair had been carefully brushed for once, he saw, and tied back with a red hair ribbon. She was wearing a bright red dress, very tight, cut low in the front, very short, ending only halfway down her thighs.

She unfolded her arms to gesture at the two hotel guards, and Scotty saw that she was wearing short, red gloves that matched her dress.

Is that her idea of dressing up? Scotty thought. He was no fashion expert, but he knew that Shannon didn't look right for *this* place!

She looked so . . . tacky. Why had he ever thought

she was neat-looking? What had he seen in her?

He cleared his throat nervously and started toward her.

She saw him while he was still halfway across the lobby and called to him. "Scotty — here I am!"

"Shannon — what are you doing here?" he asked coldly, stepping up to the desk. One of the guards kept Shannon back, holding her by the arm.

"Tell them who I am, baby. They don't believe me," she said in her little-girl voice, making her eyes real big.

"She doesn't have an invitation, sir," the guard said, letting go of Shannon's arm. "Is she with you?"

"I'm your date, right, Scotty?" Shannon asked before Scotty could reply to the guard.

Scotty stared at her. "Shannon, I can't believe you're doing this," he said, his heart pounding but his voice low and steady.

"Tell them, Scotty," she said, smiling at him, ignoring his words. Her lips were covered with bright red lipstick. Some of it had smeared onto her front teeth.

"Why, Shannon?" Scotty asked, more of a plea than a question. "Why are you here?" He glanced back to the ballroom entrance, hoping no one was coming to look for him.

"I'm your date, baby," she insisted in her tiniest voice. "Tell them." Her voice remained tiny, but her eyes narrowed and her expression grew hard.

She pulled away from the guards and latched her arm around his.

"Sir, is she with you or not?" the guard asked impatiently.

"Tell them, baby," she said, pulling him toward the ballroom doors, her face hard, determined. "I'm your date. I'm coming in. I want to meet everybody."

Chapter 18

"No," Scotty cried, trying to disentangle himself from her. "You can't!"

"I'm going in with you, Scotty." She clung to his arm, holding him tightly, staring up at him, her dark-lipsticked mouth set in a stubborn pout.

My life will be ruined, he thought, feeling himself overcome with panic. If I walk into the ballroom with her, if Lora sees me with her, if everyone sees her — my life will be ruined.

That's what Shannon wants. She wants to ruin my life.

"No!" he cried again, and pulled himself free of her grasp.

"Miss — " one of the hotel guards called, stepping around the desk, an alarmed look on his face.

"Stop, Miss," the other one called, looking suspiciously at Scotty.

"I'm your date. I'm going in there!" Shannon screamed. Her dark eyes flared angrily. Then she spun away from him and started to run across the lobby toward the ballroom, moving awkwardly in her red high-heeled pumps.

"Stop her!" Scotty pleaded.

She's going to humiliate me, he thought. She's going to humiliate me in front of everyone I care about.

He hesitated only a second. Then, seeing that the two guards were frozen in indecision, he took off after her.

She turned her head back as she ran and saw him coming. "I'm going in!" she yelled.

"No!" He leaped after her, and, ignoring the cast on his hand, made a diving tackle.

"Let go!" she shrieked.

His arm circled her waist. The force of his dive sent them both sprawling to the lobby carpet.

"Aaaiii!" he screamed in pain as she landed on his cast.

Heads turned. A woman across the lobby gasped. The two guards were moving fast toward Scotty.

"Let go! Let go! Let go!" Ignoring the pain shooting up his arm, he pulled himself up and forced her down onto her back. She swung her fists up at him. But he had her securely pinned on the floor.

Crying out, she reached up and pulled his necktie hard, choking him. As he struggled to loosen the tie with one good hand, she pulled herself out from under him, shoved him hard, and rolled on top of him.

This can't be happening, Scotty thought, looking up to see a horrified crowd around them. The two guards were bent over them, trying to pull Shannon off him.

"I'm going in!" she shouted, as the guard lifted her up by the arms. "I'm going in!" Her hair had come loose from the ribbon and was flying wildly about her face.

"What's going on here?" an important-looking man in a dark blue suit cried, breaking through the circle of onlookers.

"I'm going in," Shannon insisted, as the two guards struggled to pull her to the front exit.

Somewhat dazed, Scotty climbed to his feet. He touched his cheek. It felt wet. Looking at his hand, he realized his face was bleeding. Shannon must have scratched him as they scuffled.

Trying to catch his breath, he glanced toward the ballroom. Luckily no one had come out to witness the embarrassing scene. He looked around the crowd in the lobby and didn't recognize anyone.

"Are you okay?" the man in the dark suit asked.

"Yeah. I think so," Scotty said, holding his cheek. The hand under the cast throbbed with pain.

Shannon was being pulled, struggling and screaming, out of the lobby. People gasped and moved quickly out of the way as the two guards, one on each side, tried to remover her.

I've got to get back inside, Scotty thought, feeling a little relieved. Lora must be wondering where I am.

First, I've got to find a men's room and wash off this blood.

Then he gasped as he saw Shannon kick one of the guards hard in the knee. The guard cried out in pain and dropped to the floor.

With a burst of speed, Shannon broke away from the other startled guard, and came running back toward Scotty, heading to the ballroom.

"I'm your date, Scotty!" she yelled, staring at him, her eyes wild and frantic as she passed him, running awkwardly in the bulky high heels. "I'm your date! You can't keep me out!"

"Shannon — stop!" he yelled. He grabbed her again with his one good hand, and held on tight.

"Young man, I — I cannot allow this," the man in the blue suit sputtered. "You and your girlfriend must leave at once."

"But I'm going in," Shannon insisted.

"Shannon — please," Scotty begged, holding on desperately to her arm.

Suddenly, she stopped struggling. She looked up at him with her little-girl face and brushed his bleeding cheek tenderly with her gloved hand. "Tell them I'm your date, Scotty."

"Young man, I must insist — " the important-looking man, obviously the hotel manager, said.

An idea flashed into Scotty's mind, an idea born of panic, of desperation.

"Shannon — if I take you out next weekend, will you go home now?" he asked, not loosening his grip on her arm.

"You're hurting me," she cried, staring into his eyes.

Reluctantly he let go of her arm. "How about it, Shannon? Please? I'll take you out Saturday night. I promise."

"Really?" she asked in her tiny voice. "Just you and me?"

"Yes. Just you and me," he said quickly, seeing that she was considering it. "You go home now, and I promise I'll take you out next weekend."

"You promise?"

"I promise."

"Hope to die?" she asked.

Something about the way she said that gave him a chill. "I promise," he repeated, still breathing heavily, his chest heaving, his heart pounding. "Please, Shannon. Go home, okay? And Saturday night will be our night."

She stared up at him for a long moment, pulling loose strands of hair away from her face, "Okay," she said finally.

He breathed a loud sigh of relief, then bent down and picked up her red hair ribbon from the floor. "Good," he said softly, handing it to her.

He looked back toward the ballroom. No one had come out. He could hear voices and the clink of dishes and glasses. They must be halfway through lunch, he thought.

"Walk me to the door?" Shannon asked, pulling the red ribbon back and forth through her hand.

"Okay," Scotty quickly agreed.

Anything to get her out of here!

What am I going to tell Lora?

He felt his cheek. The bleeding seemed to have slowed. Some dark, dried blood flaked off on his fingers.

"I didn't mean to hurt you, baby," Shannon said softly.

"It's okay," he replied, leading her quickly to the door. People were staring at them from all over the huge lobby.

"You'll come to my house Saturday night?"

He pushed open the glass door and guided her out of the building. "Promise," he said.

The sky was overcast with dark clouds hovering low. It looked as if it might snow. The sudden cold made the cut on his face sting.

She looked up at him one more time as if trying to read in his face whether or not he was telling the truth. Then, without saying another word, she turned and began running along the walk that led past the hotel parking lot, her clunky red shoes clicking over the pavement.

What have I done? he thought. And then: What am I going to do?

He watched her as she passed the parking lot, running so awkwardly, not looking back. And then he saw the figure step out from behind a parked car in the main drive.

It was Shannon's brother. Scotty recognized him immediately even though he had never clearly seen his face. He recognized him from his enormous size and from his long raincoat.

The man was moving quickly toward Scotty,

pointing at him, calling to him even though he was too far away for Scotty to make out the words.

Does her brother follow her everywhere? Scotty wondered. What does he want?

Scotty had no intention of waiting to find out. He spun around, pulled open the door, and nearly knocking over an elderly couple who were trying to exit, bounded back into the hotel.

He won't follow me into the ballroom, Scotty decided. Taking long, quick strides, he headed across the lobby and down the hall toward the ballroom in back.

He was nearly there when he remembered that his face was cut. Looking down, he saw that his shirt had come untucked during his wrestling match with Shannon, the white flaps hanging down over his pants. A button had been torn off his sports jacket. His tie hung loose and crooked.

What should he do now?

Behind him, he saw Shannon's brother lumber into the lobby, looking in all directions, obviously searching for Scotty.

The ballroom offered safety. But Scotty knew he couldn't go back in there looking the way he did. He had to get himself cleaned up a bit first.

Praying that the hulking figure hadn't spotted him, Scotty ducked into the men's room, pulling the door closed behind him. He looked for a door lock, but there was none.

Moving to the mirrors over the row of sinks, he examined himself. The cut wasn't as bad as he had feared. It was just a scratch, actually. He picked up some paper towels from beside the sink, wet them, and dabbed the dried blood away.

Unfortunately, he had bled onto his shirt collar. He tried dabbing at the stain with the wet paper towel, but it only smeared the blood, making a larger stain.

He combed his hair, surprised that his hands were still trembling. Then he tucked in his shirt and retied his tie.

I don't look too bad, he thought.

Maybe I can go back in and pretend nothing happened.

And then, in the mirror, he saw the men's room door open and Shannon's brother step in.

Chapter 19

Gaping into the mirror, Scotty hesitated for only a second.

As the big man moved through the narrow corridor that led to the sinks, Scotty darted to the stalls. He leaped into the nearest one and pulled the stall door closed, latching it silently.

Did he see me?

Does he know I'm in here?

His heart pounding, Scotty climbed up onto the toilet, hunched on the seat, keeping his feet off the floor so they couldn't be seen in the space beneath the stall door.

His chest felt tight. He had a strong urge to cough. His fright was making it hard to breathe.

Hunched on top of the toilet seat, he held his breath, forced himself not to cough . . . and listened.

The heavy footsteps against the marble floor grew louder. Closer.

Peering down beneath the stall door, Scotty could see the man's shadow on the floor. He was standing right in front of the stall.

He knows I'm here, Scotty thought, still holding

his breath even though it felt as if his lungs were about to burst. He knows.

He's standing there, waiting for me.

He's not going to make a move until I come out.

The shadow on the white tile floor shifted. Scotty could hear the man's shoes scrape as he moved.

Is he coming to get me? Scotty wondered, frozen in fear.

Is he going to force open the stall door, grab me, and pull me out?

The shadow on the floor seemed to freeze in place. Then, as Scotty stared down from his uncomfortable perch, it slid out of sight.

The shoes scraped heavily, moving away.

Scotty still didn't breathe, listening to the shoes move against the tile. When he heard the restroom door squeak open and then close, he exhaled loudly, but still didn't move.

He listened carefully.

Silence.

Struggling to catch his breath, he climbed down off the toilet seat. He unlatched the door, pulled it open, and stepped out.

Shannon's brother was waiting for him at the first sink. "Tricked you," he said, smiling. He had short blond hair, a round, red face with small gray eyes over a pudgy pug nose.

He took a step toward Scotty and pointed with two fingers. "I want to talk to you." He had a reedy, high-pitched voice, a voice much too small for a man of his size.

"I've got to g-go," Scotty managed to stammer. With a determined burst of speed, he ran toward Shannon's brother, then dodged away from him and scampered through the narrow corridor to the exit.

"Wait — " the brother cried, lurching toward Scotty.

But Scotty already had the restroom door open. He ran through it and across the lobby, past the two uniformed guards at the desk outside the ballroom door and into the ballroom.

Dessert was being served from pastry carts. Coffee was being poured from silver coffeepots. The room was quiet except for a few low murmurs.

Why isn't anyone talking? Scotty wondered, his eyes surveying the room. He quickly understood why. Mrs. Benedict was standing in the center of the main table, about to speak.

Forcing a smile to his face, hoping he looked at least a little normal, Scotty made his way through the tables to the front, being careful not to look at anyone. He didn't stop until he reached the table. Then he found his seat and slid in silently beside Lora.

She turned immediately and stared at him questioningly. "Scotty, where've you been?" she whispered. "You missed lunch."

"We're so proud of both of them," Mrs. Benedict was saying into the microphone standing just a few feet away, holding a stack of notecards in front of her. "Before I call them up to award them their prizes, let me tell you a little about these two young people and their accomplishments."

Lora continued to stare at him, searching his face. Suddenly, her eyes widened in surprise. "Scotty — you've been bleeding. What did you do to your face?" she whispered.

"I tripped," he whispered. "In the men's room. I fell onto the sink."

Her expression remained one of bewilderment. He wasn't sure whether she believed him or not.

"As you can see, both of them are citizens of the community as well as students," Mrs. Benedict was saying. She looked over at Scotty and Lora and blinked hard when she saw that they weren't paying attention to her speech.

"You're sweating like a pig," Lora whispered loudly. "Scotty, are you okay?"

I'll *never* be okay, Scotty thought glumly.

Never.

Not as long as Shannon is around.

She's never going to leave me alone. She's never going to quit.

All of my plans, all of my hopes — my whole life — it's all ruined.

"I'm going to to call Scotty and Lora up now, so let's give them a warm round of applause," Mrs. Benedict said.

Chapter 20

Scotty called Lora Wednesday night. He had carefully rehearsed what he was going to say, but he was very nervous, uncertain of how she would react.

The phone rang once, and he dropped the receiver. Doing everything with one hand was really difficult, he had discovered. The big cast had been removed on Tuesday, replaced by one that was smaller but just as clunky.

He fumbled around on the floor of his room for the receiver. When he managed to return it to his ear, Lora was already on the other end. "Hello? Hello?"

"Hi, it's me," he said.

"Scotty, have you been avoiding me?" she asked.

"Huh? What are you talking about?"

Did she suspect something about Shannon?

"I haven't seen you since Saturday afternoon," Lora said.

"Yeah. I know," he said. "I've been studying and stuff."

"You've been kind of weird lately," she said. "I mean, weirder than usual."

"Is that a compliment?" he joked.

"Is anything the matter?" she asked.

What a question!

"No," he said. "Not really." There was an awkward silence, and then he began his prepared speech. "Lora, would it be okay if we don't go out Saturday night?"

"What?" The question seemed to take her by surprise.

"You see, my cousin is sick up in Meritville, and I thought I'd drive up and see him Saturday night."

"I thought you didn't have a car," she said suspiciously.

"Mom got a loaner from the insurance company. A Ford Taurus. It's actually much better than our car," he said.

"But can you drive with one hand?" she asked.

She suspects something, he thought. That's why she's asking so many questions.

"Yeah. No problem," he said. "I know we usually go out on Saturdays, but Eddie has always been a real pal and — "

"Scotty, I think you're confused," she said, suddenly sounding very cross.

"What?"

This wasn't going right, he realized. She was supposed to be sympathetic. She was supposed to tell him it was perfectly all right for him to go visit his sick cousin.

"How could you forget your own birthday?" she cried.

"Huh?"

"You can't visit your cousin on Saturday night, Scotty. That's the night we're celebrating your birthday, remember? I've made big plans. I'm picking you up at your house at nine and taking you someplace very special." She paused and then added sharply, "Doesn't *any* of this ring a bell?"

"Oh. Yeah," he said.

How could he have forgotten his own birthday? Lora had made such a fuss about how she was going to plan something really neat.

Oh, well, he thought, sighing. Lora isn't picking me up till nine. That'll give me time to get over to Shannon's early. I'll talk with Shannon, tell her I can't ever see her again, get everything straight with her once and for all, and be back at my house by nine.

"I feel like a total dork," he told Lora. "I — I just wasn't thinking clearly. Forget everything I said. I'll go visit my cousin on Sunday."

"That's better," she said. But she still sounded very suspicious.

"Uh . . . Lora?"

He had this sudden urge to tell her how sorry he was. He wanted to tell her that he hadn't meant to mess everything up. He wanted to tell her that Shannon didn't mean anything to him, that he didn't even like Shannon, that she was a mistake, a horrible mistake that he had regretted from the first night he had met her.

He felt like telling Lora everything, just letting it all spill out. Not to cleanse himself. Not to make himself feel better. But just to let Lora know that he didn't like having to lie to her, that he didn't like what Shannon had forced him to become.

"Yes?" Lora asked, a little impatiently.

"I just want you to know I care about you," he said. His throat tightened. He couldn't say more.

"Me, too," she said quickly.

"No matter what happens," he added.

"What?" she cried. "What do you mean? Scotty?"

"I'll call you," he said and gently hung up the phone.

Chapter 21

Saturday was gray and cold. A sharp wind blew down from the north, toppling garbage cans, sweeping the fallen dead leaves over the front yard like a crackling, brown river. The sun never appeared, and by late afternoon it was as dark as midnight.

Scotty didn't notice the wind or the cold as he climbed into the white Taurus a little after six o'clock to drive to Shannon's house. Thinking about her, about all she had done, about all she *could* do to ruin his life, he had felt edgy all day. But now, as he backed down the drive and headed toward the Old Village, his nervousness gave way to anger.

He had had only one date with Shannon. He had made no promises to her. He hadn't misled her in any way. What right did she have to keep pestering him, to follow him, to call him constantly, to try to invade his life?

She had no right. No right at all.

His mind whirled as he repeated over and over the things he planned to say to her. All of his attempts to get through to her, to make her stop, to get rid of her, had failed.

But not tonight, he told himself. Not tonight.

Tonight would be different. Tonight he would *make* her understand. Tonight he would make her *promise* to leave him alone.

And if she didn't agree?

He would talk to her parents. Or her brothers. He would tell them how unbalanced Shannon was. How dangerous.

Dangerous.

Well, Scotty thought, I can be dangerous, too.

I can get tough if I have to.

Distracted by his angry thoughts, he sped through a stop sign. The squeal of another car's brakes alerted him to what he had done, but he didn't look back.

I'm going to make this short, he told himself, glancing down at the digital clock on the dashboard. Six-twenty.

He knew he had to be back home by nine, when Lora planned to pick him up.

No problem, he thought.

As he drove into Shannon's neighborhood, the houses passing by in the darkness were smaller and closer together. A burst of wind shook the car. He gripped the wheel tighter with his left hand, his other hand resting uselessly on his lap.

Halfway down the block, he squealed to a stop. He had driven right past Shannon's house. Cursing to himself, he threw the car into reverse and backed up along the curb. He parked at the bottom of her dirt driveway. Then he cut the engine and climbed out, slamming the door behind him.

The house was dark except for a dim yellow light glowing behind the lowered window shade in the front window. Scotty jogged up the drive, ducking his head against the strong wind.

Why did I ever come here? he thought.

Why did I ever get involved with her?

He couldn't decide if he was more angry at Shannon or at himself. His temples throbbed as he climbed the two steps of her front stoop. He felt strange, out of control, angry, and nervous — and a little frightened.

Taking a deep breath, he raised his hand to knock on the front door, and it was pulled open.

Shannon stood in the pale yellow light. She was dressed all in white, in a short, straight skirt and a white turtleneck sweatertop. Her red hair shone in the light, falling softly down in front of her shoulders.

She smiled at him, her dark eyes lighting up.

She looks like a little angel, Scotty thought.

What a joke.

"Hi, baby. You're late," she said softly.

Stepping into the small front room, he didn't return her smile. "Hi," he said, keeping his expression hard.

"Let me hang up your coat," she said, reaching up to help pull off his down jacket.

"No. I'm not staying long," he said sharply, looking around at the threadbare furniture, the peeling wallpaper, the bare floorboards. "Are your parents home? Or your brothers?"

She gave him a devilish look. "No, baby. Don't worry. No one's home. We're all alone." She took his jacket and hung it up in the front closet.

She smelled sweet and flowery. He realized she was wearing a lot of perfume.

"Please don't call me baby," he said sharply.

When she turned around, she had a slightly mocking expression on her face. "Why not, baby?" she asked in her whispery voice.

"Because I'm *not* your baby!" he shouted.

She put her hand gently on his shoulder. "I made you a special dinner. Because this is such a special night."

He stared at her, surprised. "You cooked dinner?"

"Yes. Just for the two of us. Look." She pointed to a small table in the adjoining room. It had been set for two. A single candle glimmered in the center. "Surprised?"

"Shannon, I'm sorry. I'm not going to stay," Scotty said. He struggled to remember what he had planned to say, what he had rehearsed over and over in his mind all week. But he was drawing a blank.

"Come sit down, Scotty," she said, taking his hand.

He pulled his hand away. "Didn't you hear me?"

"How's your hand?" she asked, studying the cast. "It doesn't hurt anymore, does it?"

"Shannon — don't ignore me," he said, feeling his anger rise.

"That was such a shame, such a nasty accident," she said, pushing her lipsticked mouth into a pout.

"It wasn't an accident," he said, glaring at her. "You did it deliberately."

"I wouldn't hurt you. You're my baby," she said softly. She reached up and grabbed the back of his head with both hands. Then she pulled his head down and pressed her lips against his.

She smelled so sweet. Her lips were so soft.

"No!" he screamed.

It was hard to pull away from her, especially with just one useful hand. She grasped the back of his head, holding him tightly. It was no longer a tender hold. It was violent, desperate.

Finally he managed to duck out of her grasp. He backed away, holding his hand up as if it were a shield. "Stop it, Shannon."

"But what's the matter? Don't you *like* me anymore?" Her voice sounded tiny and hurt.

"No," he said flatly.

She stared into his eyes. "You're not being nice to me, Scotty."

"I came here to say leave me alone," he said, staring right back at her. "Leave me alone, Shannon. Don't call me. Don't follow me. Don't come to see me."

"I made such a nice dinner for us," she said.

"I want you to leave me alone. And I want you to leave my friends alone," he continued.

"I want this night to be special," she said softly.

"Aren't you listening to me?" he screamed. He could feel himself losing it, but he didn't care.

He had to make her hear him.

He *had* to!

"Listen to me, Shannon. I'm leaving now. Right now. And I'm never coming back. Do you hear me?"

"Don't leave," she said, her face expressionless now. Her smile had faded; her eyes lost their sparkle. "I don't think you should leave."

"What are you going to do? Break my *other* hand?" he cried.

"No," she said softly, "If you leave, I'll do something worse."

"Worse?" His chest was heaving. He had never felt such anger, such frustration.

"I'll tell Lora," she said.

She waited for him to react, but he just glared at her.

"I'll tell Lora everything," Shannon said, her face a pale, cold mask, revealing no emotion at all. "I'll go see her. I'll tell her that you want to be with *me* now."

"No, you won't!" he screamed. "You won't!"

In a total rage, he grabbed her narrow shoulders and began to shake her.

The next few seconds became a noisy blur.

He suddenly felt as if he weren't here in this

shabby, dimly lit living room, as if he were some-where above it, hovering over the room, watching the boy and girl struggle beneath him.

It wasn't him shaking Shannon so violently. It wasn't him roaring out his rage and frustration. It wasn't him making her head snap back like that, her long hair tossing wildly over her face, then be-hind her shoulders.

He wasn't doing it. He wasn't struggling with her, pushing her, choking her, slamming her small body against the dark wall.

"You've ruined my life! You've ruined my life!"

He wasn't crying out like that. He wasn't making her cry out.

He was above it, outside it, away from them, watching them.

And then suddenly the blur, the violent blur cleared.

And he saw everything so clearly.

Shannon was on the floor, crumpled in such a strange position, her head tilted at such a strange angle, her white skirt up over her pale thighs.

Her eyes were closed.

He could see everything so clearly.

Her eyes were closed, and she wasn't breathing.

So clear. So clear.

He had killed her.

Chapter 22

I didn't kill Shannon, he thought, staring down at her, his eyes focusing and unfocusing.

I didn't kill her.

I'm the quarterback. I was all-state last season. I should've been all-state again *this* season.

I'm too young.

I hardly knew her.

So how could I have killed her?

Lora and I are the perfect couple. Everyone is so happy for us.

So happy.

I couldn't kill Shannon.

I've already been accepted at Princeton. Of course, I haven't heard from the scholarship people yet. But it's almost a sure thing.

Lora and I will be there together.

It seems we've always been together.

We belong together. We're the perfect couple.

So I couldn't have killed Shannon.

"Get up, Shannon!" he yelled. He nudged her side with the toe of his sneaker.

"Get up! Get up — please!"

He stood over her unmoving form. He couldn't bend down. He wanted to, but he couldn't move. He could only stand there.

Maybe I'm dead, too, he thought.

No. That's crazy. Crazy.

I'm the quarterback, Scotty Singleton.

I'm the perfect couple.

There's a place waiting for me at Mr. DeMarco's agency.

So I can't be dead. And neither can Shannon.

He could see everything so clearly, every detail in the room, every thread in Shannon's white cotton sweater, every hair on her head. Her hair was splayed out on the floor. Her legs were bent beneath her.

Lora and I are the couple of the year, he thought.

He tried to remember his little brother's name. Why couldn't he think of it?

I'm not thinking clearly, he realized, staring down at her hair, so tangled and wild.

I can see very clearly. But I'm not thinking clearly.

He turned and walked over to the worn couch. He dropped down onto it, closed his eyes, and rubbed the eyelids with the fingers of his good hand.

Denny. That's his name.

Okay. That's a little better.

He sat with his eyes closed for a long time, waiting for the panic to subside.

I'm just not thinking clearly. I've got to think clearly.

What do I do now?

She can't be dead. So what do I do now?

After all, I'm the quarterback.

Coach Hawkins is really going to chew me out about this.

I'm still not thinking clearly.

Denny. His name is Denny.

That's good. That's good for a start. But what do I *do* now?

He got up and walked back to her. "Aren't you going to move?" he asked softly. "Isn't dinner going to get cold?"

Aren't *you* going to get cold?

He had to do something to clear his head. He would never think clearly if he stood staring down at her, waiting for her to move.

He would never get his scholarship.

He would never pass Go and collect two hundred dollars.

I've got to get out of here, he realized.

I've got to go somewhere and think. I'm not thinking clearly here. If I go away, I'll be able to figure everything out.

And then I'll go to Princeton. With Lora.

I'll call Lora right now. We can go to Princeton tonight.

No. He wasn't thinking clearly. Lora wasn't home.

She wasn't home.

An idea flashed into his spinning head. Even in the confusion, he knew he could figure out what to do if he got out of that house. He knew the cold air would help clear his head. Getting away from her body would help drive away his panic.

Her body?

Why did he think of her as a body now? She couldn't be dead.

He was too young.

And he was very smart. All the tests showed it.

He moved quickly to the front closet, grabbed his coat, and struggled into it, pulling it over his broken hand first, then easing his good hand through the other sleeve.

I'm not thinking clearly. I'm just not thinking clearly.

He searched the jacket pocket until he found the car keys. Then he pulled open the front door and started out.

A strong gust of wind blew him back.

I'm not thinking clearly. I've got to get away, go somewhere quiet, somewhere peaceful to think.

But I can't leave Shannon here.

She's not dead. But what if her parents come home? What if they find her lying on the floor, all twisted like that? They might *think* she's dead.

And I could get in trouble. Bad trouble.

Or what if her brothers come home? They could make a mistake, too. They could think she's dead. And then they'd come after me. Like that one huge brother of hers.

I'm not thinking clearly.

I'd better take her with me. Yes. I'll take her with me. And when I'm feeling a little better, a little calmer, a little quieter, I'll know what to do.

Picking Shannon up was hard, especially with only one good hand. Slinging her over his shoulder was even harder.

Luckily she was small and light.

Not as light as a feather, he thought. But light enough to carry out to the car.

She still felt warm as he draped her over his shoulder, holding her around the back of her legs with one arm. He made his way unsteadily to the front door, thought about getting her a coat, but decided he couldn't put her down again.

Out into the blustery wind. The front yard was dark. There was no porch light. The neighbors couldn't see him.

She started to get heavier as he carried her down the dirt drive. She was slipping off his shoulder.

Just a few more feet, he thought. The wind seemed to be blowing at him from all directions at once, making it hard to move forward, and hard to balance this heavy, sprawling weight.

He was breathing hard by the time he reached the car. Bending down, her arms dangling in front of him, he pulled open the back door. Then he bent lower until she was even with the seat, and he lurched forward, letting her go tumbling off his shoulders and onto the car seat.

She landed facedown. He waited, expecting her to pick herself up. But she didn't move.

He pushed the rest of her onto the seat, straightened her skirt, and tucked her legs in. Slamming the door shut, he leaned against the car, gasping for air, struggling to catch his breath, his shoulders aching, his broken hand throbbing all the way up the arm.

Where shall I go?

Got to think. Got to think.

Lora isn't home. The words flashed into his mind again.

Lora isn't home. She's picking me up at my house.

So he'd take Shannon to Lora's house. The back door was always unlocked. He'd hide her down in the cellar. Just for a short while. Just long enough for him to start thinking clearly again.

Having this plan made him feel a little better. He stepped away from the car and started to walk around it to the driver's side. He opened the car door, but dropped the keys onto the street.

He found them easily, then climbed behind the wheel.

"Are you still back there?" he called, struggling to slip the key into the ignition with his trembling hand.

No answer.

"Did you buckle up?" he asked.

Again no answer.

He glanced at her in the rearview mirror. She still lay facedown, her hair splayed out at odd angles all around her head.

"I know you're breathing," he called back to her. "I'm just not thinking clearly."

But that would change as soon as he dropped her off at Lora's. He'd leave her in the basement, in the cedar closet in the rec room. Then he'd go somewhere quiet and think.

The drive to Lora's was another blur. There didn't seem to be much traffic on the road. Or maybe he just didn't see the other cars.

It seemed like an instantaneous trip to him. A second later, he had pulled the Taurus up the smooth, curving drive to the back of Lora's house.

The house was dark except for the outside lights, front and back. A spotlight above the middle door on the three-car garage shone in his eyes. He climbed out of the car to get away from it.

No one is home, he realized, peering into the back windows.

Breathing a sigh of relief, he opened the rear car door. Then he bent down and started to pull Shannon out of the car. It took a long time to get her back onto his shoulders. For some reason, she seemed much heavier now. By the time he reached the back door, he was breathing noisily, and bathed in perspiration.

His entire body ached. He shifted her on his

shoulders and reached for the doorknob. She was draped over his shoulders now, like a shawl, her arms dangling down to his right, her legs to his left.

He turned the knob. And breathed a sigh of relief as the door pushed open.

Yes. Unlocked as usual.

He stepped forward, but her arms and legs caught on the sides of the door. Backing up, he turned sideways and slipped into the dark kitchen.

It was warm inside, and smelled of baked apples.

For a long moment, he stood in the doorway, inhaling the sweet smell, waiting for his eyes to adjust to the dark, balancing Shannon on his shoulders.

I'm starting to feel better already, he thought.

Just being away from her house has helped.

Now I'll take her down to the basement and go figure out what to do.

He turned carefully to the wall and clicked on the kitchen light.

Then, balancing Shannon awkwardly, he turned around.

And as he turned, Lora, Bender, the DeMarcos, his mother, and about twenty or thirty other friends jumped up from behind the kitchen counters, all shouting in unison: "SURPRISE!"

Chapter 23

"Happy birthday!" Lora cried, and then her eyes bulged and her mouth dropped open in horror as she saw the girl's body around his shoulders.

Scotty reeled back and stared into the crowd of familiar faces. Their smiles seemed to fade in slow motion as their expressions changed to horror and confusion.

Shannon slid off his shoulders and hit the linoleum floor with a soft thud. She groaned as she hit the floor and her eyes opened. "Huh?" she cried groggily.

"I knew she wasn't dead," Scotty said aloud.

The shock of seeing Lora and everyone was helping to snap his mind back to normal.

"Scotty — who is that? What's going on?" Mr. DeMarco demanded. He hurried over and knelt down beside Shannon, who was groaning loudly, lying on her back behind Scotty.

"It — it's hard to explain," Scotty said, feeling dizzy and weak.

Everything that had happened was coming back to him all at once. He was finally thinking clearly.

"I thought I killed her," he said.

There were loud gasps. Everyone started to talk at once.

Bender came over and put a hand on Scotty's shoulder. "I recognize her, man," he said quietly. "She's the one who did your hand."

"I really can't talk about it now," Scotty said, turning to watch Mr. DeMarco, who was still tending to Shannon.

"Scotty — who is she?" Lora demanded.

"I think I have to sit down," Scotty said weakly.

Her features drawn with worry and confusion, Lora took his arm and started to lead him out of the kitchen. The counter, Scotty noticed as they passed, was piled high with colorfully wrapped birthday presents.

"We didn't even have time to get the presents organized," Lora muttered. "How did you know we were here?"

"I didn't," Scotty said honestly. He decided he was going to be completely honest with her, completely honest from now on. He'd tell her everything, and pray that she'd forgive him.

She led him to the kitchen table and pulled out a chair for him. He dropped down onto it gratefully, his head spinning, the loud, excited voices echoing in his ears.

Across the room, Shannon was on her feet. Mr. DeMarco was holding her by the arm. She was tugging at her hair, pulling it behind her shoulders.

"Who is she?" Lora demanded, standing beside Scotty, staring across the room as Shannon talked to Mr. DeMarco and several others.

"She's a girl from our school," Scotty said quietly. "I met her at Homecoming, the night you were away. In Paris. I did a really bogus thing. I — I took her out while you were gone."

"You what?" Lora looked down at him in surprise.

"It's a long story," he said. "I feel really bad. I'm really sorry. But she — she's crazy, Lora. She wouldn't leave me alone. She killed Ernie, and she broke my hand. She killed your cat, too, and — "

He stopped his explanation and jumped to his feet, his eyes growing wide with fear.

Across the kitchen, Shannon had stepped away from Mr. DeMarco. As Scotty watched, she darted over to the pile of birthday presents, her eyes wild, her expression hard and determined. Without saying a word, she tore the blue and green ribbons off a pair of ski poles propped against the counter.

She grabbed a ski pole by the handle, letting its companion drop to the floor. Her eyes moved slowly around the room until they found Scotty.

"Whoa! Hold on!" Scotty heard Bender yell from somewhere across the kitchen.

Scotty stepped away from Lora and called to Shannon. "What are you doing?"

She didn't answer him. She glared at him with

pure hatred, and raised the pointed end of the ski pole toward him.

"You're not my baby anymore!" she screamed, her voice loud and raspy, unlike any sound he had ever heard from her before.

"Shannon, wait — " he cried.

But she came rushing at him, holding the ski pole like a sword.

"No!" he cried, frozen to the spot, realizing she meant to kill him.

Screaming at the top of her lungs, she lunged toward him.

He dodged, and the pointed ski pole slid a few inches past his side and rammed the wall with a loud *crack*. The handle flew out of Shannon's hand. But she quickly picked it up and came after Scotty again.

"No, Shannon — please!" He turned and ran across the kitchen. The back door was open. He heaved himself toward it, thinking only of escape.

And then stopped short.

Shannon's enormous brother stood on the other side, his face twisted in menace.

Chapter 24

Scotty backed away from the door. "She's okay! I didn't kill her!" he screamed.

Behind him, Mr. DeMarco and several others were wrestling the ski pole from Shannon's hands. She was screaming and struggling to keep it away from them.

"Your sister is okay," Scotty repeated, his trembling voice revealing his fear as the big man pushed open the door and came toward him.

"Sister?" the man asked in his high-pitched voice. He stared at Scotty questioningly and reached into his pocket.

He's got a gun! Scotty thought, stumbling backwards.

"Look out — he's going to shoot!" Scotty screamed.

But the man pulled a small leather card holder out of his pocket and flipped it open, revealing a police badge. "Lieutenant Jarmusch, juvenile division," he said, and quickly replaced the badge.

Then he bounded across the room, moving very fast for someone of his size, and grabbed Shannon by both shoulders.

She stopped screaming and struggling. She seemed to recognize him. "Uh-oh," she said quietly, rolling her eyes.

"Is everyone okay?" Jarmusch asked, holding Shannon firmly, looking around at the startled faces. "This one can be dangerous," he said.

"Uh-oh," Shannon repeated, shaking her head. "Busted again."

"You — you're not her brother?" Scotty asked, his head still spinning.

"Brother?" The big police officer laughed, a high, wheezy laugh. "She doesn't have any brothers. No family at all, as far as I can tell." His expression changed. He looked accusingly at Scotty. "I've been trying to talk to you, son."

"I — I thought you were her brother," Scotty said, embarrassed.

"Uh-oh," Shannon said and laughed scornfully at Scotty.

"This one was sent up for manslaughter," Jarmusch said, holding tightly to Shannon's shoulders. "But she only did juvenile time. You know. Like ten minutes." He snickered, shaking his head.

"She's been seeing her parole officer regularly. Has her parole officer convinced that she's got her act together. But I had a hunch she was up to no good again. So I've been doing a little surveillance work on her in my spare time. Spare time? That's a joke."

"Uh-oh," Shannon muttered. "He made a joke."

"Just chill out," Jarmusch told Shannon. "It took me till yesterday to get a legal search warrant for her house. Just as I suspected, she's been lying to us about living with her mother. She's all alone in there. No family. Nobody. I've been trying to get enough hard evidence to show that she still needs help. I don't want her to do more time. I just want her to get the treatment she needs."

Shannon puckered her lips and, looking at Scotty, made loud kissing noises.

Scotty looked away.

Jarmusch did a little more explaining, told Scotty he'd need a statement from him tomorrow, then led Shannon away. She didn't resist, looking back longingly at Scotty for a long moment, then disappearing out the back door, followed by the bulky policeman.

"I think maybe we'd better postpone this birthday party," Mr. DeMarco announced when he was gone. "I think we're all too confused to feel like celebrating."

Scotty slumped at the kitchen table as everyone filed out, retrieving their coats from the front closet. His mother stopped to put a hand on his shoulder. "Are you coming home now?"

"Soon," Scotty said. "I want to talk to Lora first."

When everyone had left, Lora, sitting across the

white Formica table from Scotty, shook her head. "You sure know how to pick 'em," she said dryly.

He looked up at her guiltily. "Don't be angry at me, okay?"

She reached across the table and squeezed his hand. "Maybe we're just trying to do things too soon, you know." Her face grew serious. "We've been acting like an old, married couple since we were twelve. Maybe it's a mistake."

"I'm the only one who made a mistake," he said softly.

"We don't have to talk about it tonight," she said, still holding his hand. A smile slowly spread across her face. "I'm just angry that that girl spoiled my birthday present for you."

"Present? What present?" he asked.

"The ski poles, of course!"

They both laughed.

"What a birthday!" Scotty exclaimed.

"Well," said Lora thoughtfully, "I'll tell you one thing. This was one surprise party that was a *surprise* — for everyone!"

They were both still smiling as she walked him out to his car to say good night.

About the Author

R.L. STINE is one of the bestselling authors of all time. His Point Thrillers include *The Boyfriend*, *The Girlfriend*, and *Hit and Run*. He lives in Manhattan.